FATHERS AND SONS

Also by Michael R. Katz

TRANSLATIONS

Alexander Herzen • *Who Is to Blame?*
Nikolai Chernyshevsky • *What Is to Be Done?*
Fyodor Dostoevsky • *Notes from Underground*, a Norton Critical Edition
Leo Tolstoy • *Tolstoy's Short Fiction*, a Norton Critical Edition
Fyodor Dostoevsky • *Devils*
Aleksandr Druzhinin • *Polinka Saks* and *The Story of Aleksei Dmitrich*

MONOGRAPHS

The Literary Ballad in Early Nineteenth-Century Russian Literature
Dreams and the Unconscious in Nineteenth-Century Russian Fiction

Ivan Turgenev

FATHERS AND SONS

A New Translation by

MICHAEL R. KATZ

W • W • NORTON & COMPANY • New York • London

First Edition

The text of this book is composed in Electra, with the display set in Bernhard
Modern. Composition by PennSet, Inc.
Manufacturing by The Courier Companies, Inc.

Library of Congress Cataloging-in-Publication Data
Turgenev, Ivan Sergeevich, 1818–1883.
[Ottsy i deti. English]
Fathers and sons / Ivan Turgenev ; translated by Michael R. Katz.
p.   cm.
I. Title.
PG3420.08E5   1994   92–40010

ISBN 0-393-03559-X

W. W. Norton & Company, Inc., 500 Fifth Avenue, New York, N.Y. 10110
W. W. Norton & Company Ltd., 10 Coptic Street, London WC1A 1PU

1   2   3   4   5   6   7   8   9   0

Translator's Introduction

On the eve of Alexander II's great reforms—including the emancipation of the serfs—in an atmosphere of uncertainty and anticipation, Turgenev began work on his fourth novel. In *Fathers and Sons* the author planned to portray a new type of hero, a "nihilist," who would faithfully represent the values of the younger, scientific generation. Set at a very specific moment in history, the novel begins on May 20, 1859, on a gentry estate in the Russian countryside.

In the period that preceded the great reforms, Russian absolutism reached its peak. The unsuccessful uprising of liberal-minded Russian officers on December 14, 1825, left an indelible impression on young Nicholas I (1825–55). He presided over an epoch in which only a few paltry attempts were made at constitutional and administrative reform. Instead, the tsar established a repressive regime, strengthening both state and security police. His minister of education instituted a policy of "Orthodoxy, Autocracy, and Nationalism" that was to serve as the firm foundation of a strengthened monarchy. A rigorous system of censorship was enforced: the philosopher Chaadaev was pursued and placed under house arrest for daring to raise awkward political questions; the members of the revolutionary Petrashevtsy circle were tried and sentenced; and literary figures, including Turgenev, were arrested. Ironically, this period also saw remarkable intellectual activity and creativity, with writers producing many of the greatest works of Russian literature.

Meanwhile, the Russian economy, burdened by the inefficient system of serfdom, steadily declined. At the same time, the tsar's relations with both noble landowners and serfs deteriorated. Revolutionary events of 1848 in Europe resulted in further repression inside Russia as Nicholas felt his own autocracy increasingly threatened. Thinking the demise of Turkey was imminent, the tsar decided to press his territorial claims in 1852. Britain and France rallied to Turkey's support, primarily to contain

Russian imperial ambitions. The Crimean War began in 1854 and ended as a ghastly fiasco for Russian foreign policy. Nicholas I died a year later during the siege of Sevastopol, and Russia went on to suffer a crushing defeat at the hands of the powers allied with Turkey. This humiliation exposed once and for all the administrative, social, and economic backwardness of the Russian autocracy and convinced even the most conservative elements that reforms could no longer be postponed.

Alexander II came to the throne in 1855 and quickly understood the significance of Russia's defeat at the hands of the West. He immediately established a number of commissions and committees to consider various plans for reform, but insisted that all precautions be taken to protect the economic interests of the nobility. On February 19, 1861, the long-awaited Edict of Emancipation was issued, freeing all Russian serfs; it declared that the peasants were to receive land, but were obliged to reimburse the nobles for it. The provisions of the edict were immensely complicated, often confusing, and sometimes contradictory. The result was bitter disappointment among the peasants, culminating in numerous disturbances, all ruthlessly suppressed.

Emancipation was followed by a series of other reforms: administrative, judicial, military, and educational. However, the actual social and economic consequences of these changes proved slight. For decades serfs remained dependent on their former masters, while age-old poverty and backwardness combined to perpetuate the survival of the old system.

Alexander also relaxed the system of strict censorship; as a result, criticism of his government increased. Russian intellectual life took a turn toward the left, and the generation of liberal reformers (including Turgenev) was replaced by a new generation of young radicals and revolutionaries.

Ivan Turgenev was born in 1818 and spent his childhood on a vast manorial estate in the province of Orel. His father was a charming aristocrat who kept his distance from young Ivan. His mother was a wealthy, embittered woman, as tyrannical in her relations with her peasants as she was with her favorite son. His was a conventional aristocratic education: governesses and tutors followed by boarding school. In 1833 he set off for Moscow University, but transferred one year later to St. Petersburg. The young student's democratic, pro-Western sympathies earned him the nickname "the American." In 1838 he departed for Europe in search of a broader education, spending three years at the University of Berlin, where he made the acquaintance of the future anarchist Mikhail Bakunin, the romantic philosopher Nikolai Stankevich, and the fiery critic Vissarion Belinsky.

Although he had a daughter by one of his serfs, Turgenev's letters and diaries indicate that he preferred intimate friendships with women of his own class. In 1843 he formed a lifelong romantic liaison with the celebrated opera star Pauline Garcia-Viardot. She was already married, but his relations with Monsieur Viardot were so cordial that a ménage à trois emerged. This curious relationship was to become the primary emotional attachment of Turgenev's life.

In 1852 Turgenev was charged with treason and spent one month in the guardhouse, after which he was confined to his estate for a year. In fact, he spent several years there, waiting for permission to leave Russia. He finally joined the Viardots in 1857 and spent the rest of his life abroad, returning to Russia only for brief sojourns. He lived in Baden-Baden until the Franco-Prussian War (1870–71), when he moved to Paris, where he remained until his death in 1883.

The official reason for Turgenev's arrest and confinement in 1852 was a controversial commemorative article he wrote on the occasion of Gogol's death. However, the author preferred to attribute his punishment to the publication of his first major literary endeavor, *A Sportsman's Sketches* (1852). This work, a collection of twenty-two stories, portrays the peasant as a human being with genuine feelings, even artistic sensibilities, while landowners are depicted as cruel, insensitive, even inhuman creatures. The impact of Turgenev's *Sketches* on Russia has often been compared to that of Harriet Beecher Stowe's *Uncle Tom's Cabin* (1851) on America. The book established Turgenev's reputation as a major figure in Russian letters.

Turgenev achieved the pinnacle of his fame and influence in the 1850s. He expanded the form of the sketch and short story into the short novel. Chronicling the development of the Russian intelligentsia in a series of works, he articulated the experiences and aspirations of his age. *Rudin* (1856), *A Nest of Gentlefolk* (1859), and *On the Eve* (1860) portrayed successive types of representative heroes and heroines, depicting both the issues and the atmosphere of those troubled times.

Each of Turgenev's novels is constructed according to a simple formulaic pattern. The action is typically "placed" on a country estate in the Russian provinces and occurs within a limited time frame. The work focuses on the impact of a forceful character from the outside on those who reside in that "place." The plot usually involves a conflict of ideas and values between the stranger and the locals, as well as a developing emotional relationship between the hero and heroine. The existence of two levels (ideological and psychological) casts in relief both the ideas and the personality of the hero.

All this is accomplished with a style that possesses both poetic and dramatic dimensions. In fact, Turgenev began his literary career by writing poetry and plays, most of which are undistinguished and derivative. But his novels have an almost lyrical aspect and frequently indulge in idyllic and elegiac reveries; on the other hand, Turgenev's plots tend toward the theatrical, as characters gather to act out short, intense scenes.

Fathers and Sons (1862) has long been considered Turgenev's best novel. It is ironic, then, that this work marked the end of Turgenev's popularity and authority in Russia. The portrait of Bazarov was attacked by both left and right: radicals regarded the hero as a caricature of themselves; conservatives felt the author was being far too generous to Bazarov. Turgenev was so discouraged by the negative reception of his work that he even considered retiring from literature altogether.

The novel is set in three specific locales: Marino, the Kirsanovs' rundown but recently reorganized "farm"; the wealthy estate of Nikolskoe, owned by the attractive widow Odintsova; and the very modest homestead of Bazarov's elderly parents. The plot is built around a series of unannounced arrivals by the hero in each of these three settings. These visits serve to illuminate the contrast between the inhabitants of each place and the hero; consequently, the hero becomes increasingly more isolated as he is shown to belong to none of these places.

All of Turgenev's novels, including *Fathers and Sons*, can be interpreted as moving accounts of the social and political development of the small but influential elite of liberal and radical Russian youth in the mid-nineteenth century. Historical, political, and ideological themes occupy a large part of the characters' discussions in *Fathers and Sons*. Nihilism is defined in a key passage, and the concept spawns a series of original pronouncements. The role of science is explored at length; positivism, materialism, Darwinism, feminism, utopian socialism, utilitarianism, as well as other Western "isms" are examined, defended, criticized, and rejected by various characters. Conflicts among classes in the social structure are highlighted: the aristocracy, the *raznochintsy* (a new group of non-noble intellectuals), and the peasants. *Fathers and Sons* contributes substantially to our understanding of nineteenth-century Russia.

But like all great art, this novel has not only a temporal dimension, but also a universal one. Turgenev writes about eternal themes of conflict and continuity between generations; of romantic love and desperate passion between men and women; of the values of marriage, children, and family; of love for nature in spite of its own placid indifference; and of human confrontation with mortality.

Turgenev was the first Russian writer to gain a following in the West and whose works were so widely translated. He had extensive contacts with Western writers and maintained a correspondence with several. He persuaded his European colleagues to take Russian literature seriously. Henry James referred to Turgenev as a "novelists' novelist" and praised his conciseness, his faithful depiction of the ordinary, and his close vision ("more ironic and more tender"). James, of course, was comparing Turgenev with "other" Russian writers. Another English reviewer made this comparison explicit:

> The present writer has no hesitation in ranking Tourguenieff as the
> greatest novelist in Russia, and almost the only one fit to take a

seat in the cabinet of European novelists of the nineteenth century. That he has been eclipsed by Dostoieffsky and Tolstoi . . . does not matter at all.[1]

Over time literary critics and historians have altered these rankings: Turgenev is now considered the least of the big three Russian novelists, especially among Western readers, even though his world view seems so familiar, his thinking, so congenial. A recent handbook of Russian literature summarizes the situation thus:

> Turgenev never approached the tragic depth of Dostoevsky or the epic range and psychological acuteness of Tolstoi. He is a great writer of surfaces—of the observed scene. In *Fathers and Sons* all his virtues—tact, intelligence, human sympathy, formal elegance —are at their peak.[2]

This new translation of *Fathers and Sons* is offered in the hope of demonstrating some, if not all, of Turgenev's many virtues—and impressive virtues they are!

MICHAEL R. KATZ
AUSTIN, TEXAS
SEPTEMBER 1993

Sources

Clarkson, Jesse. *A History of Russia*. New York: Random, 1969.

Florinsky, Michael T. *Russia: A History and an Interpretation in Two Volumes*. New York: Macmillan, 1953, 1958.

Moser, Charles A., ed. *The Cambridge History of Russian Literature*. New York: Cambridge UP, 1992.

Terras, Victor, ed. *Handbook of Russian Literature*. New Haven: Yale UP, 1985.

———. *A History of Russian Literature*. New Haven: Yale UP, 1992.

1. George Saintsbury, "Turgenev, Dostoievsky, and Tolstoy," in *Russian Literature and Modern English Fiction*, ed. Donald Davie (Chicago: U of Chicago P, 1965) 23.
2. Milton Ehre, "Turgenev," in *Handbook of Russian Literature*, ed. Victor Terras (New Haven: Yale UP, 1985) 489.

Acknowledgments

I would like to express my sincere gratitude to my former Williams colleague Bill Wagner, for checking the footnotes and answering my questions; to my research assistant at the University of Texas, Paul Ivaschenko, for his work on the manuscript; to my editor at Norton, Carol Bemis, for her invaluable assistance and friendship; and to Sally Furgeson, for her expert proofreading.

FATHERS AND SONS

Fathers and Sons[1]

Dedicated to the memory of
Vissarion Grigorevich
BELINSKY[2]

I

"Well, Peter, still no sign of them?" asked the gentleman on the twentieth of May 1859,[3] as he came out onto the low porch of a carriage inn on *** highway.[4] The man, in his early forties, wearing a dust-covered coat, checked trousers, and no hat, directed the question to his servant, a chubby young fellow with whitish down on his chin and small dull eyes.

The servant, about whom everything—the turquoise ring in his ear, styled multicolored hair, ingratiating movements, in a word, everything—proclaimed him to be a man of the new, advanced generation, glanced condescendingly down the road and replied, "No, sir, no sign of them."

"No sign?" repeated the gentleman.

"No sign," replied the servant a second time.

The gentleman sighed and sat down on the bench. Let's acquaint the reader with him while he's sitting there, feet tucked under him, gazing thoughtfully around.

His name is Nikolai Petrovich Kirsanov. He owns a fine estate, located twelve miles or so from the carriage inn,[5] with two hundred serfs, or, as he describes it, since negotiating the boundaries with his peasants and establishing a "farm,"[6] an estate with about five thousand acres of land. His father, a general who fought in 1812,[7] was a semiliterate, coarse Russian, not in the least malicious, who worked hard all his life—first in command of a brigade, then a division—and who always lived in

---

1. A literal translation of the Russian title (*Otsy i deti*) would be "Fathers and Children"; this version has been retained for reasons of tradition and euphony.
2. Vissarion Belinsky (1811–48) was the most influential literary critic of his day, a staunch Westernizer, and an enthusiastic supporter of Turgenev.
3. The novel is set before the emancipation of the serfs, which took place in February 1861.
4. Russian literary convention typically omits place names and abbreviates surnames (e.g., Princess Kh. and Princess R.).
5. An establishment where travelers could procure fresh horses and find food and lodging.
6. Kirsanov wishes to be seen as a progressive landowner who's taken steps to improve conditions for the peasants on his estate.
7. The year Napoleon initiated his disastrous military campaign against Russia.

3

the provinces, where, as a result of his rank, he came to play quite an important role. Nikolai Petrovich was born in the south of Russia, just like his older brother, Pavel, about whom more later, and was brought up at home until the age of fourteen, surrounded by underpaid tutors, free-and-easy but obsequious adjutants, and other regimental and staff people. His mother, a member of the Kolyazin family, called *Agathe* as a girl, then Agafokleya Kuzminishna Kirsanova as a general's wife, belonged to a group of "lady commandants"; she wore splendid caps and silk dresses that rustled, was the first one in church to approach the cross, spoke a great deal and in a loud voice, allowed her children to kiss her hand in the morning, and gave them her blessing at night—in a word, she lived life just as she pleased. In his role as the general's son, Nikolai Petrovich—not only was he undistinguished by bravery, but he'd even earned a reputation as something of a coward—was required, just like his brother, Pavel, to enter military service; but he managed to break his leg the very day he received news of his commission, and, after spending two months in bed, retained a slight limp for the rest of his life. His father gave up on him and allowed him to enter the civil service. He brought him to Petersburg as soon as he turned eighteen and enrolled him in the university. By the way, just about the same time, his brother became an officer in a guards regiment. The two young men shared an apartment under the distant supervision of a cousin on their mother's side, Ilya Kolyazin, an important man. Their father returned home to his division and his spouse, and only upon occasion would he send his sons large quarto sheets of gray paper covered with a sweeping clerkly scrawl. On the bottom of these sheets appeared the words "Piotr Kirsanoff, Major-General," painstakingly surrounded by flourishes. In 1835 Nikolai Petrovich left the university with a candidate's degree;[8] in the same year General Kirsanov, involuntarily retired after an unsuccessful review, arrived in Petersburg with his wife to take up residence. He was just about to move into a house near the Tauride Garden and join the English Club when he died suddenly from a stroke. Agafokleya Kuzminishna followed soon afterward: she couldn't get used to the dull life in the capital—she was consumed by the ennui of retirement. In the meantime Nikolai Petrovich, during his parents' lifetime, and to their considerable dismay, had managed to fall in love with the daughter of a certain Prepolovensky, a low-ranking civil servant and the previous owner of their apartment. She was an attractive and, as they say, progressive young woman: she used to read serious journal articles published in the section called "Science." He married her right after the period of mourning, and, forsaking the Ministry of Crown Domains[9] where his father had secured him a position, he led a blissful

8. The lowest academic rank, roughly equivalent to the bachelor's degree.
9. The branch of the tsarist government created to oversee property belonging to the Romanov family.

life with his Masha, first in a country cottage near the Forestry Institute; later in town, in a small, comfortable apartment, with a clean staircase and a chilly living room; and finally, in the country, where he settled down once and for all and where, a very short time afterward, his son, Arkady, was born. The couple lived very happily and peacefully: they were hardly ever apart, read together, played pieces for four hands at the piano, sang duets; she planted flowers and looked after the poultry; every so often he went off hunting and busied himself with estate management, while Arkady kept on growing—also happily and peacefully. Ten years passed like a dream. In 1847 Kirsanov's wife died. He hardly survived the blow and his hair turned gray in the course of a few weeks; he was hoping to go abroad to distract himself a bit . . . but then came the events of 1848.[1] He returned to the country against his will and, after a rather long period of inactivity, occupied himself with the reorganization of his estate. In 1855 he brought his son to the university; he spent three winters there with him in Petersburg, going almost nowhere and trying to make the acquaintance of Arkady's young companions. The last winter he was unable to come—and now we see him in May 1859, completely gray, stout, and somewhat stooped; he's waiting for his son, who just received his candidate's degree, as he himself had some time before.

The servant, out of a sense of propriety, or perhaps because he didn't want to remain under his master's eye, had gone to the gate and lit his pipe. Nikolai Petrovich bent his head and began staring at the decrepit porch steps; nearby, a large mottled young chicken strutted with a stately gait, treading firmly with its big yellow legs; a scruffy cat, curled up in a most affected manner against the railing, observed the chicken with hostility. The sun was scorching; a smell of warm rye bread wafted from the dark passage of the carriage inn. Our Nikolai Petrovich fell into a reverie. "My son . . . a graduate . . . Arkasha . . ." constantly ran through his head; he tried to think about something else, but the same thoughts returned. He recalled his late wife . . . "She didn't live to see it!" he whispered gloomily . . . A plump, blue-gray dove flew down onto the road and went off to drink from a puddle near the well. Nikolai Petrovich stared at it, but his ear had already caught the sound of approaching wheels . . .

"Seems they're coming, sir," announced the servant, darting in from the gate.

Nikolai Petrovich jumped up and fixed his gaze on the road. A coach appeared, drawn by a troika of posthorses harnessed three abreast; in the coach could be seen the band of a student cap and the familiar profile of a beloved face . . .

"Arkasha! Arkasha!" cried Kirsanov and ran down waving his arms

1. A series of unsuccessful revolutionary uprisings in Western Europe that led to a period of extreme reaction in Russia.

. . . A few moments later his lips were pressed against the beardless, dusty, sunburnt cheek of the young graduate.

II

"Let me shake myself off first, Papa," said Arkady in a voice a bit hoarse from the road, but still strong and youthful, as he cheerfully responded to his father's caresses. "I'm getting you all covered with dust."

"Never mind, never mind," Nikolai Petrovich replied, smiling tenderly, and twice brushed off the collar of his son's overcoat and his own jacket. "Let me have a look at you, then, let me have a look," he said stepping back; then he set off in haste toward the carriage inn, calling out, "This way, over here, bring the horses at once."

Nikolai Petrovich seemed much more excited than his son; he seemed to have become a little flustered, grown timid as it were. Arkady stopped him.

"Papa," he said, "let me introduce you to my friend Bazarov, about whom I've written so often. He's kindly agreed to pay us a visit."

Nikolai Petrovich turned around quickly and, advancing toward a tall man in a long, loose garment with tassels who had just climbed out of the coach, warmly shook his bare, ruddy hand, which hadn't been immediately extended.

"I'm very glad," he began, "and grateful you've decided to visit us; I hope that . . . may I ask your name and patronymic?"[2]

"Evgeny Vasilev," replied Bazarov in a lazy but steadfast voice; turning down the collar of his loose garment, he showed Nikolai Petrovich his entire face. Long and thin, with a broad forehead, a nose that was flat at the top but sharp at the tip, large greenish eyes, and drooping side whiskers of a sandy color, it was enlivened with a serene smile and reflected both self-confidence and intelligence.

"I hope, dear Evgeny Vasilich, you won't be bored here," continued Nikolai Petrovich.

Bazarov's thin lips moved slightly, but he made no reply and merely raised his cap. His dark blond hair, long and thick, didn't conceal the prominent bulges in his capacious skull.

"Well then, Arkady," Nikolai Petrovich began again, turning to his son, "shall we have the horses harnessed at once, or do you want to rest a little?"

"We'll rest at home, Papa; have the horses harnessed."

"At once, at once," agreed the father. "Hey, Peter, do you hear? Get a move on, lad, faster."

Peter, who in his role as enlightened servant hadn't gone up to kiss the young master's hand and had merely nodded to him from a distance, once again withdrew beyond the gate.

---

2. A middle name formed by adding a suffix to the father's first name; it is often contracted in conversation and therefore appears in various forms in the text.

"I'm here with a small carriage, but there's a troika of horses for your coach as well," said Nikolai Petrovich with some concern, while Arkady had a drink of water from an iron dipper brought by the woman in charge of the carriage inn, and Bazarov lit his pipe and walked over to the driver, who was unharnessing the horses. "But our carriage only seats two, and I don't know how your friend will . . ."

"He'll go in the coach," Arkady said, interrupting him in a low voice. "Please don't stand on ceremony with him. He's a splendid fellow, very simple—you'll see."

Nikolai Petrovich's coachman led out the horses.

"Well, get a move on, bushy beard!" Bazarov said, addressing the driver.

"Hear that, Mityukha," said another driver who was standing nearby, hands thrust into the rear slit of his sheepskin coat. "Hear what the gentleman called you? You bushy beard, you."

Mityukha merely shook his hat and pulled the reins off the sweaty shafthorse.[3]

"Let's go, let's go, lads, give them a hand," cried Nikolai Petrovich. "There'll be money for vodka!"

In a few minutes the horses were harnessed; father and son got into the carriage; Peter climbed onto the box; Bazarov jumped into the coach, buried his head in a leather cushion—and both vehicles set off.

III

"So, here you are, a graduate at last, and you've come home," said Nikolai Petrovich, touching Arkady first on the shoulder, then on the knee. "At long last!"

"How's Uncle? In good health?" asked Arkady, who, in spite of the genuine, almost childlike rapture that filled him, wanted to shift the subject of conversation as quickly as possible from high emotion to everyday matters.

"In good health. He wanted to come and meet you, but, for some reason, he changed his mind."

"Did you have to wait long?" asked Arkady.

"Almost five hours."

"Dear Papa!"

Arkady turned quickly to his father and planted a loud kiss on his cheek. Nikolai Petrovich chuckled softly. "What a splendid horse I have for you!" he said. "You'll see. And your room's been wallpapered."

"Is there a room for Bazarov?"

"We'll find one for him, too."

"Papa, please, be nice to him. I can't tell you how much I value his friendship."

"Have you known him long?"

---

3. Shafthorses run within the shafts on a Russian troika; tracehorses, outside.

"Not very."

"That explains why I didn't meet him last winter. What's he studying?"

"His main subject is natural science. But he knows everything. Next year he hopes to qualify as a doctor."

"Ah! He's a student in the medical faculty," observed Nikolai Petrovich and fell silent. "Peter," he called, extending his arm, "are those our peasants over there?"

Peter glanced in the direction his master was pointing. A few carts harnessed with unbridled horses were running swiftly along a narrow country lane. In each cart there were one or two peasants wearing unbuttoned sheepskin coats.

"Yes, sir, they are," replied Peter.

"Where're they going, to town or what?"

"To town, I suppose. The tavern," he added contemptuously and leaned slightly toward the coachman, as if in search of support. But he didn't even budge: the coachman was a man of the old school and didn't share the latest views.

"I've had a lot of trouble with the peasants this year," said Nikolai Petrovich, turning to his son. "They don't pay their quitrent.[4] What can one do?"

"Are you satisfied with your hired laborers?"

"Yes," said Nikolai Petrovich through his teeth. "But they're being provoked, that's the problem; and they still make no real effort. They spoil the harness. But they've done the ploughing well. It'll all work out in the end. Are you taking an interest in farming now?"

"There's no shade here; that's unfortunate," observed Arkady, without answering the last question.

"I've installed a large awning on the north side of the house just above the balcony," said Nikolai Petrovich. "Now we can have dinner outside."

"It'll look too much like a summer cottage . . . but that doesn't really matter. Then again, the air here's so fresh! It smells so good! You know, it seems to me the air doesn't smell as good anywhere else in the world as it does right here! And the sky's . . ."

Arkady stopped suddenly, cast a furtive glance behind him, and fell silent.

"Of course," Nikolai Petrovich observed, "you were born here, so everything must seem special to you . . ."

"Come, Papa, it really doesn't matter where a person's born."

"Still . . ."

"No, it doesn't make any difference whatsoever."

Nikolai Petrovich cast a sidelong glance at his son; the carriage traveled on for half a mile or so before their conversation resumed.

"I don't remember whether I wrote you," Nikolai Petrovich began, "your former nanny, Egorovna, passed away."

4. The system of land cultivation under which serfs farmed the landowner's estate and paid him an annual sum of money known as the quitrent (*obvok*).

"Really? Poor old thing! And is Prokofich alive and well?"

"Alive and well and hasn't changed in the least. He grumbles just as much as ever. In general, you won't find any major changes in Marino."

"Do you still have the same steward?"

"That's the one thing I have changed. I decided not to keep any of the freed serfs who used to be house servants, or, at least, not to assign them any duties carrying responsibility. [Arkady pointed to Peter.] *Il est libre, en effet*,"[5] Nikolai Petrovich said in a low voice, "but he's just a valet. Now I have a steward who's a townsman; he seems to be a sensible fellow. I pay him a salary of two hundred and fifty rubles a year. However," added Nikolai Petrovich, wiping his forehead and brow with his hand, which was always a sign of some inner embarrassment, "I just said you wouldn't find any changes in Marino . . . That's not quite true. I consider it my duty to prepare you, although . . ."

He hesitated a moment and then went on in French.

"A stern moralist would consider my candor inappropriate; but, in the first place, it's impossible to conceal, and, in the second, you know I've always maintained particular views regarding the relationship between a father and son. At my age . . . In a word, this . . . this young woman about whom you've probably heard something or other . . ."

"Fenechka?" Arkady asked casually.

Nikolai Petrovich blushed.

"Please don't say her name too loud . . . Well, yes . . . she's now living with me. I've moved her into the house . . . there were two little rooms. But it can all be changed."

"Goodness, Papa, whatever for?"

"Your friend will be staying with us . . . It's awkward . . ."

"As far as Bazarov's concerned, please don't worry about it. He's above all that."

"Well, and what about you?" Nikolai Petrovich said. "The rooms in the little wing aren't very nice—and that's a pity."

"Goodness, Papa," Arkady interrupted. "It's as if you're apologizing; you should be ashamed."

"Of course I should," replied Nikolai Petrovich, blushing even more.

"Enough of that, Papa, enough, please!" Arkady said with a tender smile. "What's there to apologize for?" he thought; a feeling of indulgent tenderness toward his gentle father, combined with a sensation of secret superiority, filled his soul. "Stop it, please," he repeated, involuntarily enjoying an awareness of his own maturity and freedom.

Nikolai Petrovich glanced at him through the fingers of his hand, with which he was continuing to wipe his forehead, and felt a pang in his heart . . . But he blamed himself for it immediately.

"Now we've reached our own fields," he said after a long silence.

"Is that our forest up ahead?" asked Arkady.

5. "As a matter of fact, he's free" (French).

"Yes. But I've sold it. It'll be chopped down this year."

"Why did you sell it?"

"I needed the money; besides, that land's to be given to the peasants."

"Who don't pay their quitrent?"

"That's their business, but they'll pay someday."

"Too bad about the forest," said Arkady and began looking around.

The area in which they were traveling couldn't be described as picturesque. Field after field stretched as far as the horizon, first gently ascending, then descending; here and there were little woodlands and winding ravines covered in sparse low-lying shrubs that called to mind their characteristic representation on ancient maps in the time of Catherine the Great.[6] They came upon little streams with cleared banks, tiny ponds with fragile dams, little villages with low peasant huts under dark roofs often missing half their thatch, small crooked threshing barns with walls of woven brushwood and gaping doorways beside abandoned threshing floors, and churches, some made of brick with the plaster falling off, others of wood with slanted crosses and overgrown cemeteries. Arkady's heart gradually sank. And, as luck would have it, the peasants they passed were all in tatters and riding pathetic nags; the roadside willows stood, bark torn and branches broken, like beggars in rags; emaciated, shaggy cows, mere bags of bones, gnawed greedily on the grass growing along ditches. They seemed to have been snatched recently from some ravenous, deadly claws—and, called into being by the pitiful sight of these enfeebled animals, there arose in the midst of this fine spring day the white specter of joyless, endless winter with its blizzards, frosts, and snows . . . "No," thought Arkady, "this land isn't very rich; it strikes one neither by its prosperity nor by its industriousness; it's impossible, impossible for it to stay like this; reforms are essential . . . but how to implement them, where to begin? . . ."

These were Arkady's thoughts . . . and while he pondered, spring was making itself felt. Everything around glittered golden green, everything—trees, bushes, and grass—waved gently and expansively, shining under the soft breath of the warm breeze; everywhere skylarks poured out their song in endless, resonant streams; lapwings called as they circled over low-lying meadows, then darted silently across tussocks of grass; rooks strutted about, appearing black and beautiful against the tender green of the low spring corn; they disappeared into the rye, which was already turning white, and only occasionally did their heads reappear amidst the smoky gray waves. Arkady gazed and gazed, his thoughts diminishing gradually and then disappearing altogether . . . He threw off his overcoat and looked at his father with such a young boy's joyous face that his father embraced him once again.

"It's not much further now," said Nikolai Petrovich. "We've only to

---

6. Empress of Russia (1729–96), who ruled from 1762 until her death. She greatly extended the boundaries of the empire and was also a great patron of the arts.

climb this little hill and then the house'll be visible. We'll get along splendidly, Arkasha; you'll help me run the estate, if you don't find it too boring. We should become much closer, get to know each other better, don't you agree?"

"Of course," said Arkady. "What a splendid day it is!"

"In honor of your arrival, my dear. Yes, spring's in full bloom. But I do agree with Pushkin—you recall the lines from *Eugene Onegin*:

> How sad your coming is to me,
> Spring, oh spring, the time of love!
> What . . .[7]

"Arkady!" Bazarov's voice rang out from the coach. "Give me a match, will you? I've nothing to light my pipe."

Nikolai Petrovich fell silent, and Arkady, who'd begun listening to him not without a certain astonishment, but not without sympathy, hastened to pull a silver matchbox from his pocket and sent it over to Bazarov with Peter.

"You want a cigar?" Bazarov shouted again.

"Sure," replied Arkady.

Peter returned to the carriage and handed him his matchbox and a fat, black cigar, which Arkady lit immediately, spreading such a strong and acrid smell of cheap tobacco around himself that Nikolai Petrovich, who'd never been a smoker, turned away, though unobtrusively so as not to offend his son.

A quarter of an hour later both carriages stopped in front of the porch of a new wooden house painted gray and covered with a red iron roof. This was Marino, also known as New Wick, or, as the peasants used to call it, Landless Farmstead.

IV

No crowd of servants came pouring onto the porch to meet the masters; only one twelve-year-old girl appeared, and after her a young fellow emerged from the house who resembled Peter; dressed in gray livery with white buttons bearing a coat of arms, he was Pavel Petrovich Kirsanov's servant. He silently opened the door of the carriage and unfastened the apron of the coach. Nikolai Petrovich, his son, and Bazarov proceeded through a dark, almost deserted hall, behind the door of which a young woman's face appeared momentarily; they entered a drawing room furnished in the latest style.

"Here we are at home," said Nikolai Petrovich, removing his cap and shaking his head. "Now the most important thing's to have supper and get some rest."

---

7. A quotation from chapter 7, stanza 2 of *Eugene Onegin*, a novel in verse (pub. 1825–31) by the most famous Russian poet, Aleksandr Pushkin (1799–1837).

"It wouldn't be a bad idea to have something to eat," observed Bazarov, stretching himself and sinking down on the sofa.

"Yes, yes, let's have supper, as soon as possible," Nikolai Petrovich said and began stamping his feet for no apparent reason. "Here comes Prokofich just in time."

A man aged sixty entered, white-haired, thin, and dark, in a brown frock coat with brass buttons and a pink scarf tied around his neck. He grinned, went up to kiss Arkady's hand, and, after bowing to the guest, withdrew to the door and stood with both hands behind his back.

"Here he is, Prokofich," began Nikolai Petrovich. "He's come back to us at long last . . . Well? What do you think of him?"

"He's looking well, sir," said the old man and grinned again, but knit his thick brows immediately. "Do you wish me to serve supper, sir?" he asked pretentiously.

"Yes, yes, please do. Perhaps you'd like to go to your room first, Evgeny Vasilich?"

"No, thank you very much, there's no reason. But have them bring my suitcase up, if you would, and this coat of mine," he added, taking off his loose-fitting garment.

"Very well. Prokofich, take his coat. [Prokofich, as if confused, picked up Bazarov's "coat" and holding it above his head, walked out on tiptoe.] And you, Arkady, do you want to go to your room for a minute?"

"Yes, to wash up," Arkady replied and headed toward the door, but at that moment a man of medium height, dressed in a dark English suit, fashionable low cravat, and patent leather shoes, entered the drawing room—Pavel Petrovich Kirsanov. He appeared to be about forty-five: his closely cropped gray hair shone with a dark luster, like new silver; his face, sallow, but without wrinkles, unusually regular and pure of line, as if carved by a light and delicate chisel, revealed traces of remarkable beauty; his bright, black almond-shaped eyes were particularly exquisite. The entire figure of Arkady's uncle, elegant and well-bred, retained a youthful gracefulness and a striving upward, away from the earth, which in most cases is lost after a man leaves his twenties behind.

From the pocket of his trousers Pavel Petrovich removed his beautiful hand with long pink fingernails—a hand that seemed even more beautiful in contrast to the snowy whiteness of his cuff fastened with one large opal—and extended it to his nephew. After completing this preliminary European-style "handshake," he then kissed him three times in the Russian manner; that is, he brushed his perfumed mustache against his nephew's cheek three times and said, "Welcome."

Nikolai Petrovich introduced him to Bazarov: Pavel Petrovich bowed his elegant figure slightly and smiled slightly, but didn't extend his hand and even put it back into his pocket.

"I thought you wouldn't come today," he began in a pleasant voice, swaying gently, shrugging his shoulders, and showing his magnificent white teeth. "Did something happen to you along the way?"

"Nothing happened," replied Arkady. "We just tarried a bit. But now we're hungry as wolves. Do make Prokofich hurry, Papa, and I'll be right back."

"Wait, I'll go with you," cried Bazarov, suddenly jumping up from the sofa. Both young men left the room.

"Who's that?" asked Pavel Petrovich.

"Arkady's friend, a very bright fellow according to him."

"Is he going to stay here with us?"

"Yes."

"That hairy creature?"

"Well, yes."

Pavel Petrovich tapped his nails on the table.

"I imagine that Arkady *s'est dégourdi*,"[8] he observed. "I'm glad he's come home."

They talked very little during supper. Bazarov especially said almost nothing at all, but ate a great deal. Nikolai Petrovich related various episodes from his life as a farmer, as he put it, and talked about impending government measures, committees, deputies, the need to introduce machinery, and so on. Pavel Petrovich paced slowly back and forth in the dining room (he never ate supper) and occasionally sipped a goblet filled with red wine and even less frequently uttered some remark, or rather exclamation, such as "Ah! Aha! Hmm!" Arkady related some Petersburg news, but felt a certain awkwardness that usually overtakes a young man who's just ceased being a child and who's returned to the place where others are used to seeing and regarding him as such. He dragged out his speech for no reason, avoided using the word "Papa," and once even replaced it with "Father," pronounced, it's true, between his teeth; with excessive carelessness he poured much more wine into his glass than he really wanted and then drank it all. Prokofich didn't take his eyes off him and merely chewed his lips. After supper everyone immediately went their separate ways.

"Your uncle's a bit of an eccentric," Bazarov said to Arkady, sitting down next to his bed in his dressing gown and smoking a short pipe. "Such dandyism in the country, just think! And his fingernails, what fingernails, they could be put on display!"

"But you don't know," Arkady replied, "what a social lion he was in his own day. Sometime I'll have to tell you his story. He was quite a handsome man and used to turn women's heads."

"So that's it! Does it for old time's sake. Pity there's no one out here to charm. I kept looking at him: he has such astonishing collars, as if

8. "Has grown smarter" (French).

made of stone, and his chin's so exquisitely shaved. Arkady Nikolaich, don't you think it's a bit absurd?"

"Perhaps, but he's really a fine person."

"An archaic phenomenon! But your father's a splendid fellow. He wastes his time reading poetry and hardly understands estate management, but he's a good sort."

"My father's pure gold."

"Did you see how shy he is?"

Arkady nodded his head, as if he himself weren't shy.

"It's quite astonishing," Bazarov continued, "these aging romantics! They'll expand their nervous systems to the breaking point . . . then, all equilibrium will be destroyed. Anyway, good night! There's an English washstand in my room and the door doesn't lock. Nevertheless, one must encourage it all—English washstands, that's real progress!"

Bazarov left and Arkady was overcome by a joyous feeling. It's very pleasant to fall asleep in one's own house, in a familiar bed, under a blanket made by loving hands, perhaps his nanny's, those affectionate, kind, untiring hands. Arkady remembered Egorovna, sighed, and wished her eternal peace . . . He didn't pray for himself.

Both he and Bazarov soon fell fast asleep, but other people in the house were unable to sleep for some time. His son's return had excited Nikolai Petrovich. He lay down in bed, but didn't blow the candle out and, resting his head on his arm, thought long and hard. His brother sat up in his study long past midnight in a broad Hambs[9] armchair before the fireplace in which some embers were glowing dimly. Pavel Petrovich hadn't gotten undressed; he'd only exchanged his patent leather shoes for some red Chinese slippers without heels. In his hands he held the latest issue of *Galignani*,[1] but he wasn't reading; he stared fixedly into the fire where a bluish flame flickered, first dying down, then flaring up . . . God knows where his thoughts wandered, but it wasn't only to the past; the expression on his face was intense and gloomy, which doesn't happen when a man's absorbed only in recollections. And in the little back room sitting on a large trunk, wearing a light blue sleeveless jacket, a white kerchief thrown over her dark hair, was a young woman, Fenechka; she was either listening or dozing or looking through the open door, behind which a child's cot could be seen and the even breathing of a sleeping child could be heard.

V

The next morning Bazarov woke up before everyone else and left the house. "Hey!" he thought, glancing around, "this place isn't much to look at." When Nikolai Petrovich divided the estate with his peasants,

9. A French furniture maker (1765–1831) who lived in Petersburg.
1. A liberal newspaper, *Galignani's Messenger*, published in English in Paris.

he'd been obliged to build his new manor house on a plot consisting of some ten acres of completely flat and barren land. He constructed the house and outbuildings, laid out a garden, and dug a pond and two wells; but the young trees hadn't taken, too little water collected in the pond, and that in the wells had a brackish taste. Only one small arbor of lilacs and acacias did fairly well; they sometimes had tea or ate dinner out there. In a few minutes Bazarov had covered all the paths in the garden, looked over the cattle sheds and stables, and come upon two local lads whose acquaintance he made at once; he set off with them to a small marsh, about a mile from the manor house, to search for frogs.

"What do you need frogs for, sir?" one of the boys asked.

"I'll tell you what for," Bazarov replied; he had a special flair for inspiring trust in members of the lower class, although he never indulged them and always treated them in an offhanded manner. "I'll cut the frogs open and look inside to see what's going on; since you and I are just like frogs, except that we walk on two legs, I'll find out what's going on inside us as well."

"What do you want to know that for?"

"So I don't make any mistakes if you get sick and I have to make you better."

"Are you a doctor, then?"

"Yes."

"Vaska, you hear, the gentleman says you and me are just like frogs. How do you like that?"

"I'm afraid of them, of frogs," observed Vaska, a lad about seven, with hair as pale as flax, a gray smock with a stand-up collar, and bare feet.

"What are you afraid of? You think they bite?"

"Come on now, just wade into the water, you philosophers," said Bazarov.

Meanwhile, Nikolai Petrovich had also awakened and set off to see Arkady, whom he found already up and dressed. Father and son went onto the terrace under the awning; next to the railing on the table, between large bouquets of lilacs, a samovar was already bubbling. A young girl appeared, the one who'd been the first to greet the travelers on the porch the night before. She announced in a thin voice, "Fedosya Nikolaevna isn't feeling well and can't come; she told me to ask if you'll pour the tea yourself or should she send Dunyasha?"

"I'll pour it myself," Nikolai replied hurriedly. "Arkady, do you take your tea with cream or lemon?"

"Cream," answered Arkady; after a brief silence, he inquired, "Papa?"

Nikolai Petrovich looked at his son in embarrassment.

"What?" he asked.

Arkady lowered his eyes.

"Forgive me, Papa, if my question seems inappropriate," he began, "but you yourself, with your candor yesterday, invited mine . . . you won't get angry, will you? . . ."

"Go on."

"You give me the courage to ask . . . Is it perhaps that Fen . . . isn't it because I'm here that she won't come out to pour the tea?"

Nikolai Petrovich turned away slightly.

"Perhaps," he said at last, "she supposes . . . she's ashamed . . ."

Arkady cast a quick glance at his father.

"There's no reason for her to be ashamed. In the first place, you're well aware of my way of thinking [Arkady very much enjoyed uttering these words]; in the second place, why should I want to inhibit your life or habits in the least? Besides, I'm sure you couldn't have made a bad choice; if you've invited her to live here with you under one roof, she must deserve it. In any case, a son has no right to judge his father, especially me, especially a father such as you, who's never restricted my freedom in any way."

Arkady's voice was shaky at first: he perceived himself as magnanimous, but at the same time realized he was delivering something of a lecture to his father. But the sound of one's own words makes a powerful impact, and Arkady uttered his last words forcefully, even with emphasis.

"Thank you, Arkasha," Nikolai Petrovich began in a hollow voice, his fingers once again running over his brow and forehead. "Your assumptions are, in fact, accurate. Of course, if this young woman wasn't worth . . . This is no frivolous fancy. I find it awkward to talk about it with you; but you can understand why she finds it hard to come out with you here, especially the first day after your arrival."

"In that case, I'll go see her myself," cried Arkady with a new rush of magnanimous feeling, and he jumped up from his chair. "I'll explain to her there's nothing to be ashamed of in front of me."

Nikolai Petrovich also stood up.

"Arkady," he began, "do me a favor . . . how can you . . . there . . . I haven't told you . . ."

But Arkady, who wasn't listening to him anymore, rushed away from the terrace. Nikolai Petrovich looked after him and sank down on his chair in confusion. His heart began pounding . . . Did he imagine at that moment the inevitable strangeness of future relations between him and his son? Was he aware that his son might have shown him more respect if he'd never mentioned the subject? Did he reproach himself for his own weakness? It's hard to say. All these emotions were present, but in the form of sensations—and not very distinct ones at that; the flush didn't leave his face and his heart kept pounding.

There was a sound of hurried footsteps and Arkady returned to the terrace.

"We've become acquainted, Father!" he exclaimed with an expression of tender and good-natured triumph on his face. "Fedosya Nikolaevna really doesn't feel well today and will come out later. But why didn't you tell me I have a brother? I'd have gone in last night to cover him with kisses, as I did just now."

Nikolai Petrovich wanted to say something, to stand up and open his arms wide . . . Arkady threw himself into his father's embrace.

"What's this? Embracing again?" resounded the voice of Pavel Petrovich behind them.

Father and son rejoiced equally in his appearance at this moment; there are certain touching situations from which one nevertheless wants to escape as quickly as possible.

"Why are you so surprised?" Nikolai Petrovich began cheerfully. "I've been waiting ages for him to return . . . I haven't even had time to get a good look at him since yesterday."

"I'm not at all surprised," Pavel Petrovich replied. "I have nothing against embracing him myself."

Arkady went up to his uncle and once again felt the touch of his fragrant mustache against his cheek. Pavel Petrovich sat down at the table. He was wearing an elegant morning suit in the English style; his head was graced with a small fez. This fez and a casually knotted tie hinted at the freedom of country life, but the stiff collars of his shirt—true, not white, but striped, as befits morning attire—stood up as inexorably as ever against his well-shaved chin.

"Where's your new friend?" he asked Arkady.

"He's not home; he usually gets up early and goes off somewhere. The main thing is not to pay him too much attention: he doesn't like ceremony."

"Yes, that's obvious." Pavel Petrovich began, without hurrying, to spread some butter on his bread. "Is he going to stay here long?"

"Possibly. He stopped by on his way home to see his father."

"Where does his father live?"

"In our province, about sixty miles from here. They have a small estate. He used to be a regimental doctor."

"Yes, yes, yes . . . I've been asking myself where I'd heard the name Bazarov before . . . Nikolai, remember, in Father's division there was a doctor named Bazarov?"

"I think there was."

"Precisely, precisely. So that doctor was his father. Hmm!" Pavel Petrovich twitched his mustache. "Well, and what exactly is this Mr. Bazarov?" he asked slowly and deliberately.

"What is Bazarov?" Arkady grinned. "Would you like me to tell you, Uncle, what he really is?"

"If you please, Nephew."

"He's a nihilist."[2]

"How's that?" asked Nikolai Petrovich, while Pavel Petrovich raised

2. Note the way each character defines the term: Nikolai is neutral; Pavel, antagonistic; Arkady, approving.

his knife in the air with a piece of butter on the end of the blade and remained motionless.

"He's a nihilist," repeated Arkady.

"Nihilist," said Nikolai Petrovich. "That's from the Latin *nihil*, nothing, as far as I can tell; therefore, the word signifies a person who . . . acknowledges nothing?"

"Say, rather, who respects nothing," Pavel Petrovich put in, and once again set about spreading his butter.

"Who approaches everything from a critical point of view," observed Arkady.

"Isn't it all the same thing?" asked Pavel Petrovich.

"No, it isn't all the same thing. A nihilist is a person who doesn't bow down before authorities, doesn't accept even one principle on faith, no matter how much respect surrounds that principle."

"And is that a good thing?" Pavel Petrovich interrupted.

"That depends, Uncle. For some people, it's good; for others, it's not."

"So that's how it is. Well, I can see it's not our cup of tea. We're people of another age, we assume that without *principles*[3] [Pavel Petrovich articulated this word softly, in the French manner; Arkady, on the contrary, pronounced it *prínciples*, accenting the first syllable], without *principles* accepted, as you say, on faith, it's impossible to take a step, to draw a breath. V*ous avez changé tout cela*,[4] God grant you health and the rank of general;[5] we'll merely stand by and admire you, you gentlemen . . . how is it?"

"Nihilists," Arkady replied clearly.

"Yes. Before there were Hegelists,[6] and now we have nihilists. We'll see how you'll fare in a void, a vacuum; and now, Brother, Nikolai Petrovich, please ring for the servants because it's time for me to drink my cocoa."

Nikolai Petrovich rang and called, "Dunyasha!" But instead of Dunyasha, Fenechka came out onto the terrace. She was a young woman, about twenty-three years old, all fair and soft, with dark hair and eyes, full, red, childlike lips, and sweet little hands. She was wearing a neat cotton print dress; a new light blue scarf was resting softly on her rounded shoulders. She was carrying a large cup of cocoa, and, placing it in front of Pavel Petrovich, she became flustered: warm blood rushed in a crimson wave under the delicate skin of her attractive face. She dropped her eyes and stood near the table, resting lightly on her fingertips. She seemed ashamed that she'd come, yet at the same time seemed to feel she had a right to come.

---

3. Pavel uses the French word, while Arkady prefers the Russian borrowing.
4. "You've changed all that" (French).
5. A quotation from act 2 of the famous comedy *Woe from Wit* (1824) by A. S. Griboedov (1795–1829).
6. A derogatory reference to the followers of the German idealist philosopher Friedrich Hegel (1770–1831), usually called "Hegelians."

Pavel Petrovich knitted his brows sternly, while Nikolai Petrovich appeared embarrassed.

"Hello, Fenechka," he muttered through his teeth.

"Hello, sir," she replied in a low, but pleasant voice; with a sideways glance at Arkady, who was smiling at her in a friendly manner, she quietly withdrew. She walked with a slight waddle, but even that suited her.

Silence prevailed on the terrace in the course of the next few moments. Pavel Petrovich sipped his cocoa and suddenly raised his head.

"Here's our Mr. Nihilist come to grace us with his presence," he said in a low voice.

Bazarov was indeed coming through the garden, stepping over flowerbeds. His linen coat and trousers were spattered with mud; clinging marsh weed was twined around the crown of his old round hat; in his right hand he held a small sack; in it was something alive and moving. He approached the terrace rapidly and, nodding his head, said, "Hello, gentlemen. Excuse me for being late to tea; I'll be right back. I must take care of these captives of mine."

"What do you have there, leeches?" asked Pavel Petrovich.

"No, frogs."

"Do you eat them or breed them?"

"They're for experiments," replied Bazarov with indifference and went into the house.

"He plans to cut them up," Pavel Petrovich observed. "He doesn't believe in principles, but he believes in frogs."

Arkady looked at his uncle with pity, and Nikolai Petrovich shrugged his shoulders on the sly. Pavel Petrovich felt his witty remark had fallen flat, and began talking about the estate and the new steward who'd come to see him the night before to complain that the worker Foma "was deboshing" and had gotten out of hand. "Some Aesop[7] he is," he said among other things. "He passes himself off everywhere as a worthless fellow; he lives like a fool and will die the same way."

VI

Bazarov returned, sat down at the table, and began drinking his tea hurriedly. Both brothers watched him in silence, while Arkady glanced stealthily first at his father, then at his uncle.

"Did you go far from here?" Nikolai Petrovich asked at last.

"There's a little marsh not too far away, near the aspen grove. I startled half a dozen snipe there; you might want to go shooting, Arkady."

"You're not a hunter?"

"No."

"Is it physics you're studying?" Pavel Petrovich took a turn asking.

7. Traditional Greek author of animal fables, said to have been a slave on the island of Samos in the sixth century B.C.

"Yes, physics; natural sciences in general."

"They say the Teutons have enjoyed great success in that field of late."

"Yes, the Germans are our teachers in this regard," Bazarov replied casually.

Pavel Petrovich used the word *Teutons* instead of *Germans* for the sake of irony; no one, however, took any notice.

"Do you have such a high opinion of the Germans?" Pavel Petrovich asked with studied courtesy. He was beginning to feel a secret irritation. His aristocratic nature was disturbed by Bazarov's free-and-easy manner. This son of a doctor was not only unintimidated, but even replied abruptly and unwillingly; and, in the sound of his voice, there was something rude, almost insolent.

"Their scientists know what they're doing."

"Indeed. Well, and you probably have a much less flattering opinion of Russian scientists?"

"Perhaps I do."

"That's very praiseworthy self-effacement," Pavel Petrovich said, sitting up straight and throwing his head back. "But how is it that Arkady Nikolaevich told us just now you don't acknowledge any authorities? You don't believe in them?"

"Why should I acknowledge them? And what am I to believe in? They tell me what it's all about, I agree, and that's all there is to it."

"Do the Germans tell you what it's all about?" uttered Pavel Petrovich; his face took on such a detached, remote expression, as if he'd entirely withdrawn to some cloudy height.

"Not all of them," replied Bazarov with a short yawn; it was obvious he didn't want to continue the discussion.

Pavel Petrovich glanced at Arkady, as if wishing to say to him: "Polite, this friend of yours, isn't he?"

"As far as I'm concerned," he began again, not without some effort, "sinner that I am, I don't regard Germans with much favor. I'm not even talking about Russian Germans: it's well known what sort of creatures they are. Even German Germans aren't to my liking. Previously, there were some acceptable ones; they had their—well, there was Schiller, also Goethe . . . My brother here's especially fond of them . . . But now all they have is chemists and materialists . . ."

"A decent chemist is twenty times more useful than any poet," Bazarov interrupted.

"Is that so?" muttered Pavel Petrovich and, as if about to doze off, he raised his eyebrows slightly. "So you don't acknowledge art?"

"The art of making money or curing hemorrhoids!"[8] cried Bazarov with a contemptuous laugh.

---

8. Bazarov's joke probably refers to two translated works popular in Russia during the 1840s.

"Quite so, quite so. You do like to joke. Then you must reject everything? Let's assume so. That means you believe only in science."

"I've already explained that I don't believe in anything; besides, what is science—science in general? There are sciences, just like there are trades and vocations; but science in general doesn't exist."

"Very good, sir. And do you hold the same negative attitude concerning other conventions accepted in human society?"

"What's this, an interrogation?" asked Bazarov.

Pavel Petrovich paled slightly . . . Nikolai Petrovich considered it his obligation to intervene in the conversation.

"Some other time we'll talk about this subject in greater detail with you, my dear Evgeny Vasilich; we'll learn your opinions and express our own. For my part, I'm very glad you're studying the natural sciences. I've heard Leibig[9] has made some astonishing discoveries concerning the fertilization of fields. You could assist me in my agronomical work: you could give me some useful advice."

"I'm at your disposal, Nikolai Petrovich; but we have a long way to go to reach Leibig! First we need to study the alphabet and only later learn how to read books; we haven't even begun our ABCs."

"Well, I see you really are a nihilist," thought Nikolai Petrovich. "Nevertheless, I hope you'll allow me to consult you on occasion," he added aloud. "And now, Brother, I think it's time for us to chat with the steward."

Pavel Petrovich stood up from the table.

"Yes," he replied, without looking at anyone, "it's unfortunate to have lived these last five years out here in the country, far away from such great intellects! You become a fool in no time at all. You try not to forget what you've been taught, but then—all of a sudden—it turns out all to be nonsense; you're told that sensible people don't bother about that stuff anymore and that you are, so to speak, an old fogy. What's to be done? It's obvious that young people really are cleverer than we are."

Pavel Petrovich turned slowly on his heels and slowly withdrew; Nikolai Petrovich followed him.

"Well, is he always like that?" Bazarov asked Arkady coolly, as soon as the door closed behind the two brothers.

"Listen, Evgeny, you treated him too harshly," observed Arkady. "You offended him."

"Yes, and am I supposed to pander to them, these provincial aristocrats? Why, it's all vanity, society habits, foppishness. Well, he should've carried on his career in Petersburg, if that was his inclination . . . But, to hell with him! I've found a rather rare example of a water bug, *Dytiscus marginatus*, do you know it? I'll show it to you."

9. Baron Justus von Leibig (1803–73) was a German chemist and one of the founders of scientific agronomy.

"I promised to tell you his story," Arkady began.

"The story of the bug?"

"Enough of that, Evgeny. My uncle's story. You'll see he's not the sort of man you think he is. He's more deserving of compassion than mockery."

"I won't argue with that; but why're you so concerned about him?"

"One must be fair, Evgeny."

"How does that follow?"

"No, listen . . ."

And Arkady told him the story of his uncle. The reader will find it in the next chapter.

VII

Pavel Petrovich Kirsanov was educated first at home, like his younger brother, Nikolai, and subsequently in the Corps of Pages.[1] From childhood he was distinguished by his good looks; in addition, he was self-assured, somewhat sarcastic, and amusingly acrimonious—he couldn't help being liked. He began to appear everywhere as soon as he became an officer. He was lionized by many people, indulged himself, even played the fool, and put on airs; but this too suited him. Women were crazy about him, and men called him a dandy and envied him in secret. He lived, as has already been said, in the same apartment with his brother, whom he loved dearly, even though he didn't resemble him in the least. Nikolai Petrovich had a slight limp; small, pleasant, but rather gloomy features; small, dark eyes, and soft, sparse hair. He was fond of inactivity, also liked to read, and he shunned society. Pavel Petrovich rarely spent an evening at home; he was known for his audacity and agility (he was making gymnastics fashionable among young people in society) and had read a total of some five or six books in French. At the age of twenty-eight he'd already earned the rank of captain; a brilliant career lay ahead of him. Suddenly everything changed.

At that time in Petersburg society, there occasionally appeared a woman who's not been forgotten to this day, a certain Princess R. She had a well-educated and decent, but foolish, husband and no children. She would leave unexpectedly to go abroad, then return unexpectedly to Russia; in general, she led a strange life. She had a reputation as a frivolous coquette and devoted herself eagerly to all sorts of pleasures, dancing until she collapsed, laughing and joking with young people whom she received before dinner in a dimly lit drawing room; but at night she wept and prayed, finding no solace anywhere, often pacing her room until early morning, wringing her hands in anguish or sitting, cold and pale, over her Psalter. Day would come, and once again she was transformed into a society lady; she'd go out, laugh, chatter, and

1. An exclusive military school in Petersburg that enjoyed the tsar's patronage.

literally throw herself at anything that could afford her the least bit of pleasure. She had an astonishing figure; her braid of yellow hair, heavy as gold, fell below her knees, but no one would've called her beautiful. Her only good feature was her eyes, not really her eyes themselves—they were small and gray—but their gaze, quick and deep, uncaring to the point of audacity, pensive to the point of despondency—enigmatic. Something extraordinary shone in that gaze even when her tongue was uttering the emptiest phrases. She dressed elegantly. Pavel Petrovich met her at a ball, danced a mazurka with her in the course of which she uttered not one sensible word, and fell passionately in love with her. Accustomed to victory, he soon achieved his goal with her, too; but the ease of his victory didn't dampen his enthusiasm. On the contrary, he became even more agonizingly, more intimately attached to this woman, in whom there remained, even when she surrendered herself to him entirely, something secret and inaccessible, which no one could penetrate. God knows what was hidden away in her soul! She seemed to be in the power of some mysterious forces, unknown even to her; they toyed with her as they wished; her limited intellect couldn't withstand their whims. All her behavior presented a series of incongruities; she wrote the only letters that could've aroused her husband's justified suspicions to a man whom she hardly knew, and her love always retained a measure of sadness; she no longer laughed or joked with the man she'd chosen; she listened to him and looked at him in bewilderment. Sometimes, usually all of a sudden, this bewilderment would change into cold horror; her face would assume a wild, deathly expression; she'd lock herself up in her bedroom, and her maid, putting her ear to the keyhole, could hear her smothered sobs. On more than one occasion, upon returning home from a tender meeting with her, Kirsanov would experience that lacerating and bitter annoyance that overwhelms one's heart after a definitive failure. "What more do I want?" he'd ask himself, and his heart would ache. Once he gave her a present of a ring with a sphinx carved on a stone.

"What's this?" she asked. "A sphinx?"

"Yes," he replied, "and you're that sphinx."

"I am?" she asked, slowly raising her enigmatic gaze to him. "You know, that's very flattering," she added with a meaningless smile, and her eyes gazed at him with an equally strange look.

Pavel Petrovich found it difficult even when Princess R. was in love with him; but when she cooled, and that happened rather soon, he almost lost his mind. He was racked with pain and jealousy, gave her no peace, and followed her around everywhere; she was sick and tired of his persistent pursuit and left for abroad. He retired, in spite of entreaties by friends and pleas by superiors, and set out in search of the princess; he spent four years in foreign parts, first pursuing her, then deliberately losing sight of her; he was ashamed of himself, indignant at his own weakness . . . but nothing helped. Her image, an incomprehensible, almost meaningless, but enchanting image, had penetrated his soul too deeply. In Baden once again he somehow became as close to her as before; it seemed she'd never loved him so passionately . . . but a month later it was all over: the flame had flared up for the last time and gone out forever. Foreseeing an inevitable separation, he wanted to remain her friend at least, as if friendship with such a woman were possible . . . She left Baden quietly and thereafter constantly avoided meeting Kirsanov. He returned to Russia, tried to pick up his former life, but was unable to settle into his old routine. Like someone deranged, he wandered from place to place; he still appeared in society and maintained all the habits of a man about town; he could boast of two or three new conquests; but he no longer expected anything much from himself or other people and undertook no new ventures. He grew old, his hair turned gray; spending his evenings at the club, peevishly bored, arguing indifferently amidst bachelor society became essential to him, and this, as is well known, is a bad sign. Needless to say, he didn't even consider getting married. Ten years passed, colorlessly, fruitlessly, quickly, terribly quickly. Nowhere but in Russia does time pass so swiftly; they say it flies by even more quickly in jail. Once at dinner in the club Pavel Petrovich learned of Princess R.'s death. She'd died in Paris, in a condition bordering on insanity. He stood up from the table, paced the room for a long time, and then stopped next to the cardplayers, as if rooted to the spot; but he didn't go home any earlier than usual that evening. A little while later he received a parcel addressed to him: it contained the ring he'd given the princess. She'd drawn a pair of crossed lines over the sphinx and asked that he be informed that the cross was the solution to her enigma.

This occurred at the beginning of 1848, at the same time Nikolai Petrovich, having lost his wife, was setting off for Petersburg. Pavel Petrovich had hardly seen his brother since Nikolai had settled in the country: Nikolai's wedding had coincided with the beginning of Pavel's acquaintance with the princess. Having returned home from abroad, Pavel went to visit his brother with the intention of spending a month or two, to share his happiness, but he could stand no more than a week of it. The difference in the two brothers' situations was too great. By 1848 this difference had diminished: Nikolai Petrovich had lost his wife and Pavel Petrovich, his memories; after the princess' death he tried not to think about her anymore. But Nikolai was left with the feeling of a life well-spent, and his son was growing up before his very eyes; Pavel, on the other hand, a lonely bachelor, was entering into that troubled, twilight phase of life when regrets resemble hopes, and hopes, regrets, when youth has passed, but old age has not yet set in.

This time proved more difficult for Pavel Petrovich than for anyone else: when he'd lost his past, he'd lost everything.

"I won't invite you to come to Marino now," Nikolai Petrovich once said to him (he'd given that name to the village in honor of his late wife, Marya). "You were bored there even when my wife was still alive; now I think you'd die of boredom."

"I was still foolish and finicky," replied Pavel Petrovich. "Since then I've grown calmer, if not wiser. Now, on the contrary, if you'll allow me, I'm ready to settle down with you for good."

Instead of an answer Nikolai Petrovich embraced him; but a year and a half elapsed after this conversation before Pavel Petrovich actually decided to make good on his intention. On the other hand, once he settled in the country, he never left it again, even during the three winters Nikolai Petrovich spent with his son in Petersburg. He began reading, more and more in English; in general he arranged his entire life on the English model, rarely saw his neighbors, and came out only for the elections,[2] where, for the most part, he remained silent, only occasionally teasing and frightening landowners of the old school with his liberal witticisms; nor did he associate with representatives of the younger generation. Both the former and the latter considered him "arrogant"; both groups respected him for his superb aristocratic manners and the rumors surrounding his conquests; for the fact that he dressed so elegantly and always stayed in the best room of the best hotel; for the fact that he usually dined well, and once had even dined with Wellington at Louis Philippe's table;[3] for the fact that he always carried around a genuine silver dressing case and a portable bath; that he always smelled of some extraordinary, astonishingly "genteel" scent; that he played whist in a masterly fashion and always lost; and finally, they respected him for his incorruptible honesty. Women regarded him as a charming melancholic, but he didn't keep company with ladies . . .

"So you see, Evgeny," said Arkady, finishing his story, "how unfair you were to judge my uncle! I'm not even talking about the fact that on more than one occasion he's rescued my father from misfortune, given him all his money—perhaps you don't know, but their estate's never been divided[4]—he's glad to help anyone and, by the way, always stands up for the peasants; true, when he speaks to them he frowns and sniffs his eau de cologne . . ."

"His nerves, no doubt," Bazarov interrupted him.

"Perhaps, but he has a very kind heart. And he's by no means stupid. He's given me some very useful advice . . . especially . . . especially concerning relations with women."

---

2. The nobles in each province and district met every three years to elect officials called "marshals," who represented their interests as well as participated in local administration.
3. The duke of Wellington (1769–1852) was the English commander at the battle of Waterloo (1815), where Napoleon was finally defeated; Louis Philippe (1773–1850), king of France (1830–48), was deposed as a result of the revolution in Paris in 1848.
4. According to Russian law, each of the two brothers inherited half the father's estate; the Kirsanovs chose to maintain joint ownership of the entire property.

"Aha! He scalds himself on boiling milk and then tries to cool down someone else's hot water. We know the type!"

"Well, in a word," continued Arkady, "he's profoundly unhappy, believe me; it's a sin to despise him."

"Who despises him?" Bazarov objected. "Still I say that a man who stakes his whole life on a woman's love and, when that one card gets beaten, turns sour and sinks to the point where he's incapable of doing anything at all, then that person is no longer a man, not even a male of the species. You say he's unhappy: you ought to know; but all his foolishness still hasn't gone out of him. I'm certain that he earnestly regards himself as a worthwhile person because he reads *Galignani* once a month and saves an occasional peasant from corporal punishment."

"But remember his education, the age he lived in," observed Arkady.

"Education?" Bazarov broke in. "Every man should educate himself—just as I've done, for instance . . . And as regards the age— why should I depend on it? Let it rather depend on me. No, my friend, it's all that lack of discipline, shallowness! And what about those mysterious relations between a man and a woman? We physiologists understand all that. You just study the anatomy of the eye: where does that enigmatic gaze come from that you talk about? It's all romanticism, nonsense, rubbish, artifice. Let's go have a look at that beetle."

The two friends went off to Bazarov's room, which was already pervaded by a strong medicinal-surgical odor, mixed with the smell of cheap tobacco.

VIII

Pavel Petrovich wasn't present for long during his brother's conversation with the steward, a tall, thin man with a sugary, consumptive voice and deceitful eyes, who replied to all of Nikolai Petrovich's questions by saying, "Certainly, sir, everyone knows that, sir," and who tried to depict peasants as drunkards and thieves. The new system of estate management, introduced only recently, squeaked like an ungreased wheel, creaked like homemade furniture fashioned from unseasoned wood. Nikolai Petrovich didn't lose heart, but would frequently heave a sigh or sink into a reverie: he felt it wouldn't work without money, and he knew that almost all his money had been spent. Arkady was telling the truth: Pavel Petrovich had helped his brother on several occasions; seeing Nikolai struggling and racking his brains more than once, trying to think of a way out, Pavel would walk slowly up to the window and, thrusting his hands into his pockets, mutter through his teeth: *"Mais je puis vous donner de l'argent"*[5]—and he'd give him some money; but on this day he had none to give and preferred to withdraw. Annoyances stemming from running the household depressed him; it

5. "But I can give you some money" (French).

always seemed to him that Nikolai Petrovich, in spite of his zeal and love for hard work, didn't set about things in the right way, although he was unable to specify the exact nature of Nikolai's failings. "My brother isn't practical enough," he said to himself, "and he's being deceived." Nikolai Petrovich, on the other hand, had a high opinion of Pavel's practicality and always asked him for advice. "I'm a gentle man, weak, and have spent my life in the country," he used to say. "But you've benefited from living among so many people, you know them so well: you have an eagle eye." Pavel Petrovich merely turned away in response to these words, but did nothing to disabuse his brother of this opinion.

Leaving Nikolai Petrovich in his study, he headed along the corridor dividing the front part of the house from the rear, and, when reaching a low door, paused to reflect, then tugged at his mustache, and knocked.

"Who's there? Come in," Fenechka's voice rang out.

"It's I," Pavel Petrovich replied and opened the door.

Fenechka jumped up from the table where she'd been sitting with her child and, handing him to the girl, who carried him right out of the room, hurriedly adjusted her kerchief.

"Excuse me for disturbing you," Pavel Petrovich said without looking at her. "I only wanted to ask . . . today, it seems, they're going into town . . . Have them buy me some green tea."

"Certainly, sir," replied Fenechka, "how much would you like?"

"Half a pound will do, I think. I see you've made some changes in here," he added, casting a quick glance around, his eyes gliding past Fenechka's face. "Those curtains," he said, seeing she didn't understand him.

"Yes, sir, curtains; Nikolai Petrovich was kind enough to give them to me; they've been here for some time."

"But I haven't been here for some time. It's very nice here now."

"Thanks to Nikolai Petrovich," Fenechka whispered.

"Do you like it better here than in the wing where you were before?" asked Pavel Petrovich politely, but without the slightest smile.

"Of course, it's better here, sir."

"Who's been given your place?"

"The laundresses are there now."

"Ah!"

Pavel Petrovich fell silent. "He'll leave now," thought Fenechka, but he didn't, and she stood there before him as if rooted to the spot, her fingers fidgeting weakly.

"Why did you have your child taken away?" Pavel Petrovich said at last. "I love children: show him to me."

Fenechka blushed with embarrassment and joy. She was afraid of Pavel Petrovich: he almost never spoke to her.

"Dunyasha," she cried, "please bring Mitya here. [Fenechka used

formal address[6] with everyone in the house.] But wait a minute; I have
to get him dressed."

Fenechka headed for the door.

"It doesn't matter," said Pavel Petrovich.

"I'll be right back," Fenechka replied and left quickly.

Pavel Petrovich remained alone and this time looked around with
special attention. The small, low-ceilinged room in which he found
himself was very clean and comfortable. It smelled of a freshly painted
floor, as well as of camomile and melissa. Along the walls stood chairs
with backs in the shape of lyres; they'd been bought by the late general
in Poland, during one of his campaigns; in one corner was a little bed
under a muslin canopy, next to a trunk with forged clamps and a rounded
lid. In the opposite corner, a lamp was burning in front of a large dark
icon of St. Nikolai the miracle worker;[7] a tiny porcelain egg on a red
ribbon fastened to the saint's gold halo hung over his chest; there were
jars of last year's preserves on the windowsills, carefully arranged, glis-
tening bright green; on their paper lids Fenechka had written in large
letters: "Guzbery." Nikolai Petrovich was particularly fond of gooseberry
jam. From the ceiling on a long cord hung a cage containing a short-
tailed siskin; it chirped continuously, hopping around, its cage constantly
shaking and rocking: hempseeds were being scattered on the floor with
a light tapping sound. On the wall between two windows, above a small
washstand, hung some rather poor photographs of Nikolai Petrovich in
various poses taken by an itinerant artist; there was also a photograph of
Fenechka that was a complete failure: a face without eyes and a forced
smile staring out of a dark frame—it was impossible to make out anything
else—and above Fenechka, General Ermolov[8] in a Circassian cloak was
frowning menacingly toward distant Caucasian mountains, peering out
from under a little silk pincushion that had fallen over his forehead.

About five minutes passed; from the next room came the sounds of
bustling and whispering. Pavel Petrovich picked up a greasy book from
the washstand, an odd volume of Masalsky's *Streltsy*,[9] and flipped over
a few pages . . . The door opened and Fenechka entered with Mitya in
her arms. She'd dressed him in a red shirt with a lace collar, combed
his hair and washed his face: he was breathing heavily, his whole body
straining, and he was waving his little arms around just the way all
healthy babies do; but the fancy shirt obviously had an effect on him:
a feeling of pleasure was reflected in his plump little face. Fenechka
had fixed her own hair as well, and had arranged her kerchief better,

6. Russian distinguishes between informal (*ty*) and formal address (*vy*); cf. French *tous* and *vous*.
7. A patron saint in Russia venerated as the "miracle worker."
8. A. P. Ermolov (1772–1861) was a famous Russian general, hero of the war of 1812, and
   commander of the Russian army in the Caucasus; Circassians are a Moslem people inhabiting
   the greater Caucasus.
9. A lengthy historical novel (1832) by K. P. Masalsky (1802–61) about the musketeers formed
   by Ivan the Great in the sixteenth century and disbanded by Peter the Great at the end of the
   seventeenth century.

although she really could've stayed the way she was. In fact, is there anything on earth more charming than a beautiful young mother with a healthy child in her arms?

"What a chubby little fellow," Pavel Petrovich said indulgently and tickled Mitya's double chin with the tip of the long nail on his index finger; the child stared at the siskin and started to laugh.

"This is your uncle," said Fenechka, leaning over him and shaking him slightly, while Dunyasha quietly set a lighted aromatic candle on the windowsill, after placing a half-copeck piece under it.

"How old is he?" Pavel Petrovich asked.

"Six months; he'll be seven soon, on the eleventh."

"Isn't it eight, Fedosya Nikolaevna?" Dunyasha interrupted, not without timidity.

"No, seven; how could that be?" The child began laughing again, stared at the trunk, and suddenly grabbed hold of his mother's nose and mouth with his whole hand. "You mischief maker," said Fenechka without moving her face away from his fingers.

"He looks like my brother," said Pavel Petrovich.

"Who else should he look like?" wondered Fenechka.

"Yes," Pavel Petrovich continued, as if talking to himself, "there's an unmistakable resemblance." He looked at Fenechka carefully, almost mournfully.

"This is your uncle," she repeated, almost whispering.

"Ah! Pavel! So this is where you are!" Nikolai Petrovich's voice suddenly rang out.

Pavel Petrovich turned quickly and frowned; but his brother was looking at him so joyously, with such gratitude, he couldn't help but return a smile.

"What a fine little lad you have here," he said and looked at his watch. "I called in to see about my tea . . ."

And, assuming an air of indifference, Pavel Petrovich left the room at once.

"Did he come on his own?" Nikolai Petrovich asked Fenechka.

"Yes, sir; he knocked and came in."

"Well, and has Arkasha been here again?"

"No, he hasn't. Shall I move back to the wing of the house, Nikolai Petrovich?"

"What for?"

"I wonder if it might be better for the time being."

"N—no," Nikolai Petrovich stuttered and wiped his forehead. "It should've been done before . . . Hello, you little kid, you," he said with sudden animation and, drawing close to the child, kissed his cheek; then he bent over a little and put his lips to Fenechka's hand, which appeared white as milk against Mitya's red shirt.

"Nikolai Petrovich! What are you doing?" she asked, lowering her eyes, then quietly raising them . . . Her expression was lovely when she looked up at him from under her brows, chuckling affectionately and a little foolishly.

Nikolai Petrovich had made Fenechka's acquaintance in the following way. Once, about three years ago, he happened to spend a night at an inn in a remote district town. The cleanliness of his room and freshness of the bed linen made a pleasant impression on him. "Perhaps the mistress is German?" he wondered; but the mistress turned out to be Russian, a woman about fifty, neatly dressed, with a good-looking, intelligent face and a measured way of speaking. He struck up a conversation with her at tea; he liked her very much. At that time Nikolai Petrovich had just settled into his new manor house and, not wishing to keep serfs on as house staff, he was looking for hired laborers; the mistress, for her part, complained about the small number of travelers who came to town and about hard times; he suggested she come to work for him as a housekeeper; she agreed. Her husband had long since died, having left her only a daughter, Fenechka. Two weeks later Arina Savishna (that was the new housekeeper's name) arrived at Marino together with her daughter and settled in the lodge. Nikolai Petrovich's choice turned out to be successful. Arina introduced order into the household. No one said anything much about Fenechka, who'd just turned seventeen,[1] and she was rarely seen: she lived quietly, modestly, and only on Sundays Nikolai Petrovich would notice the delicate profile of her fair face in the parish church, sitting somewhere off on one side. A year or so passed.

One morning Arina came into his study and, after bowing deeply as usual, asked him if he could help her daughter, who had a spark from the stove in her eye. Like all homebodies, Nikolai Petrovich was able to care for the sick and had even ordered a collection of homeopathic remedies. He had Arina bring the patient to him at once. Upon learning that the master was summoning her, Fenechka grew very frightened, but followed her mother. Nikolai Petrovich led her up to the window and held her head in his hands. After examining her swollen red eye closely, he prescribed and prepared a lotion, and, tearing his own handkerchief into small pieces, showed her how to apply it. Fenechka listened to him and wanted to leave. "Kiss the master's hand, you silly girl," Arina said to her. Nikolai Petrovich didn't allow her to kiss his hand, and, feeling somewhat embarrassed, kissed her bent head, on the part of her hair. Fenechka's eye got better soon, but the impression she'd made on Nikolai Petrovich didn't fade quickly. He kept dreaming of this pure, tender, timid upturned face; he could feel her soft hair under the

---

1. Turgenev's text lists different ages for Fenechka. Above (p. 18), she is said to be "about twenty-three"; here, she is said to have been seventeen "about three years ago."

palms of his hands, see those innocent, slightly parted lips through which her moist, pearly white teeth glistened in the sunshine. He began paying more attention to her in church and tried to speak with her. At first she shunned him and once, toward evening, meeting him on a narrow footpath through a field, she turned off into the tall, thick rye, overgrown with wormwood and cornflowers, so as not to be seen by him. He spotted her head through the golden network of rye, from which she peered out like a little animal, and called to her affectionately, "Hello, Fenechka! I won't bite you!"

"Hello, sir," she whispered without leaving her hiding place.

Gradually she grew used to him, but was still timid in his presence, when suddenly her mother, Arina, died from cholera. What was to become of Fenechka? She'd inherited her mother's love of order, common sense, and propriety; but she was so young and lonely; Nikolai Petrovich was such a kind, modest man . . . There's no need to tell the rest.

"So my brother just dropped in on you?" Nikolai Petrovich asked. "Knocked and entered?"

"Yes, sir."

"Well, that's fine. Let me give Mitya a swing."

And Nikolai Petrovich began tossing him about, almost up to the ceiling to the child's great delight and the mother's considerable discomfort, who at every toss stretched out her own arms to catch his bare little legs.

Meanwhile Pavel Petrovich returned to his elegant study, its walls covered with attractive dark gray wallpaper and weapons displayed on a colorful Oriental rug, walnut furniture upholstered in dark green velveteen, a Renaissance-style bookcase made of dark, old oak, bronze statues on a magnificent writing desk, and a fireplace . . . He threw himself onto the sofa, put his hands behind his head, and sat there motionless, staring at the ceiling almost in despair. Whether he wanted to hide from the walls that which was being reflected in his face, or for some other reason, he got up, drew the heavy curtains across the windows, and threw himself down on the sofa again.

IX

Bazarov also made Fenechka's acquaintance that same day. He and Arkady were out walking together in the garden, and he was explaining to him why some of the trees, especially the young oaks, hadn't taken.

"You should plant more silver poplars here, and firs, and perhaps lindens, after you increase the loam. Now that arbor's done well," he added, "because it's all acacia and lilac—they're good boys and don't need much care. Bah! Why, there's someone over there."

In the arbor sat Fenechka with Dunyasha and Mitya. Bazarov stopped, while Arkady nodded to Fenechka as if they were old friends.

"Who's that?" Bazarov asked as soon as they'd gone past. "What a pretty girl!"

"Who're you talking about?"

"It's obvious: there was only one pretty girl."

Arkady, not without embarrassment, explained to him in a few words who Fenechka was.

"Aha!" muttered Bazarov. "Your father certainly has good taste. I like him, your father, I really do. He's a good man. But I must make her acquaintance."

"Evgeny!" Arkady called after him in fear. "Be careful, for heaven's sake."

"Don't worry," replied Bazarov. "I've got lots of experience; I've been around, you know."

He took off his cap as he approached Fenechka.

"Allow me to introduce myself," he began with a polite bow. "I'm a friend of Arkady Nikolaevich and a humble man."

Fenechka stood up from the bench and looked at him in silence.

"What a splendid child!" continued Bazarov. "Don't worry, I haven't given anyone the evil eye. Why are his cheeks so red? Is he cutting new teeth?"

"Yes, sir," Fenechka replied. "He's cut four new teeth already, and now his gums are swollen again."

"Let me have a look . . . You don't have to be afraid. I'm a doctor."

Bazarov picked up the child, who, to both Fenechka's and Dunyasha's surprise, offered not the least resistance and showed no fear.

"I see, I see . . . It's nothing; everything's in order: he'll have good teeth. If anything happens, just let me know. Are you in good health?"

"Yes, thank God."

"Thank God—that's the best thing of all. And you?" he added, turning to Dunyasha.

Dunyasha, a very stern young woman inside the house, but a real giggler outside, merely snorted in reply.

"Well, fine. Here's your little warrior back."

Fenechka took the child in her arms.

"He behaved so well with you," she said in a low voice.

"All children behave well with me," replied Bazarov. "I have a way with them."

"Children can tell who loves them," Dunyasha observed.

"Exactly," Fenechka agreed. "There're some people Mitya'd never go to."

"Will he come to me?" asked Arkady, who, having stood apart for some time, now approached the arbor.

He tried to get Mitya to come to him, but Mitya threw his head back and started whining, which upset Fenechka a great deal.

"Later, after he's grown used to me," Arkady said indulgently, and the two friends left.

"What did you say her name was?" asked Bazarov.

"Fenechka . . . Fedosya," replied Arkady.

"And her patronymic? One must know that, too."

"Nikolaevna."

"*Bene*.[2] I like the fact that she wasn't too shy. Other people might hold that against her. What nonsense! Why be shy? She's a mother—so she's right not to be shy."

"She is right," observed Arkady, "but as for my father . . ."

"And he's right," Bazarov interrupted.

"Well, no, I don't think so."

"Perhaps you don't like the idea of having an extra heir?"

"You should be ashamed to attribute such ideas to me!" Arkady replied heatedly. "It's not from that point of view I consider my father wrong; I think he should marry her."

"Oho!" Bazarov said serenely. "How very generous we are! So you still attach significance to marriage; I never expected that from you."

The friends took several steps in silence.

"I've seen your father's entire establishment," Bazarov began again. "The cattle are poor, the horses, run-down. The buildings are in bad shape and the workers look like confirmed loafers; the steward's either a fool or a thief, I still can't tell which."

"You're being rather harsh today, Evgeny Vasilevich."

"And the good little peasants are taking your father for all he's worth. You know the saying, 'The Russian peasant would devour God Himself.' "

"I'm beginning to agree with my uncle," said Arkady. "You really do have a poor opinion of Russians."

"What difference does that make? The only good point about a Russian is that he has a very low opinion of himself. What's important is that two times two makes four; all the rest's nonsense."

"And is nature nonsense?" asked Arkady, looking thoughtfully across the multicolored fields, gently and beautifully illuminated by the setting sun.

"Nature's nonsense too in the sense you understand it. Nature's not a temple, but a workshop where man's the laborer."

At that moment the slow, drawn-out notes of a cello reached them from the house. Someone was playing Schubert's *Erwartung*[3] with feeling, although with an inexperienced touch, and the sweet melody flowed through the air like honey.

"What's that?" Bazarov asked in astonishment.

"It's my father."

---

2. "Fine" (Latin).
3. "Expectation" (1815) is a lyrical song by the romantic Austrian composer Franz Schubert (1797–1828).

"Your father plays the cello?"

"Yes."

"How old's your father?"

"Forty-four."

Bazarov suddenly burst out laughing.

"What're you laughing at?"

"Imagine! A forty-four-year-old man, a *pater familias*,[4] living in such-and-such district—and plays the cello!"

Bazarov continued laughing; but Arkady, as much as he revered his mentor, this time didn't even smile.

X

About two weeks passed. Life in Marino flowed along in the usual way: Arkady lived a life of luxury while Bazarov worked. Everyone in the house had gotten used to him, his offhand manner, his laconic and abrupt way of speaking. Fenechka in particular felt so comfortable with him that one night she even summoned him: Mitya was having convulsions. He came and, in his usual manner, half-joking, half-asleep, spent two hours sitting with her and helping the child. On the other hand, Pavel Petrovich came to despise Bazarov with all the strength he could muster: he considered him arrogant, impudent, a cynic, and a plebian; he suspected that Bazarov didn't respect him, that he might even despise him—Pavel Kirsanov! Nikolai Petrovich was afraid of the young "nihilist" and had some doubts about his influence on Arkady; but he listened to him eagerly and attended his experiments in chemistry and physics willingly. Bazarov had brought along a microscope and spent hours using it. The servants also grew accustomed to him, even though they made fun of him: they felt that he was almost one of them, not a master. Dunyasha giggled with him gladly and would give him sidelong, meaningful glances as she ran by "like a little quail"; Peter, an extremely vain and stupid man whose brow was eternally furrowed under the strain, a man whose entire merit consisted in the fact that he looked respectful, could read haltingly, and frequently brushed his jacket—even he would smirk and brighten up as soon as Bazarov paid him any attention; the peasant boys ran after the "doktur" like little puppies. Only old man Prokofich didn't like him, served him his food at the table with a gloomy expression, referred to him as a "swindler" and a "knave," and asserted that with his side whiskers he looked just like a pig in a poke. Prokofich, in his own way, was just as much of an aristocrat as Pavel Petrovich.

The best time of year arrived—the first days of June. The weather was magnificent; true, there was a distant threat of cholera, but the inhabitants of the province had managed to accustom themselves to its

4. "The father of a family" (Latin).

visitations. Bazarov would get up very early and head off two or three miles, not for a stroll—he couldn't stand strolls without a purpose—but to collect grasses and insects. Sometimes he took Arkady along with him. On their return they usually got into an argument; Arkady was usually demolished, even though he spoke far more than his comrade.

Once for some reason they lingered quite a while; Nikolai Petrovich went out to meet them in the garden and, upon approaching the arbor, suddenly overheard the rapid footsteps and voices of the two young men. They were walking on the other side of the arbor and couldn't see him.

"You don't know my father well enough," said Arkady.

Nikolai Petrovich hid.

"Your father's a good man," Bazarov said, "but he's antiquated; his song's been sung."

Nikolai Petrovich listened more intently . . . Arkady made no reply.

The "antiquated" man stood there without moving for a few minutes and then slowly made his way home.

"A few days ago I looked over and he was reading Pushkin," Bazarov continued meanwhile. "Tell him, if you would, that it's of no use. After all, he's no longer a young boy: it's time to toss that rubbish aside. Just imagine the desire to be a romantic in this day and age! Give him something more substantial to read."

"What should I give him?"

"Well, I think Büchner's *Stoff und Kraft*[5] to begin with."

"I think so, too," Arkady observed approvingly. "*Stoff und Kraft* is written in a popular style . . ."

"So you see," Nikolai Petrovich said to his brother after dinner that same day while sitting in his study, "you and I've become antiquated; our song's been sung. Well, what of it? Perhaps Bazarov's even right; but, I must confess, one thing hurts: this was precisely when I'd hoped to become closer to Arkady. Now it turns out I've been left behind while he's moved ahead, and we can't understand each other."

"How is it he's moved ahead? How's he so different from us?" Pavel Petrovich exclaimed impatiently. "It's that *signor*, that nihilist who's been stuffing his head full of these things. I hate that so-called doctor; in my opinion, he's simply a charlatan; I doubt he knows that much about physics, even with all his frogs."

"No, Brother, don't say that: Bazarov's clever and he knows his stuff."

"His conceit's repulsive," Pavel Petrovich said, interrupting him.

"Yes," said Nikolai Petrovich. "He is conceited. But there seems to be no way around that; here's what I don't understand. I seem to do all I can to keep up with the times: I've made arrangements for my peasants, established a farm, with the result that I'm called a "Red" throughout

5. The actual title of the famous work by the German philosopher and physician Ludwig Büchner (1824–99) is *Kraft und Stoff* (Force and matter) (1855). This controversial book, which provided a materialist interpretation of the universe, was first translated into Russian in 1860.

the province; I read, study, and try to respond in general to the require-
ments of our day—but they say my song's been sung. You know, Brother,
I'm beginning to think perhaps it really has been sung."

"Why so?"

"Here's why. Today I was sitting and reading Pushkin . . . as I recall,
it happened to be *The Gypsies* . . . [6] Suddenly Arkady comes up to me
and silently, with an expression of such tender compassion, very gently,
as if I were a little child, takes my book away and places another one
in front of me, a German one . . . he smiles and then leaves, carrying
away my Pushkin."

"You don't say! What book did he give you?"

"Here it is."

Nikolai Petrovich took from the back pocket of his frock coat a copy
of the notorious treatise by Büchner in its ninth edition.

Pavel Petrovich turned it over in his hands.

"Hmm!" he muttered. "Arkady Nikolaevich's worried about your education. Well, have you tried to read it?"

"I have."

"And, what do you think?"

"Either I'm stupid or it's all rubbish. I must be stupid."

"You haven't forgotten your German?" asked Pavel Petrovich.

"I understand German."

Pavel Petrovich once again turned the book over in his hands and
glanced at his brother from under his brows. They were both silent.

"Oh, by the way," Nikolai Petrovich began, obviously eager to change
the subject of conversation. "I received a letter from Kolyazin."

"Matvei Ilich?"

"Yes. He's come to town to inspect the province. He's a person of
consequence now and writes that, as a relative, he wants to see us and
has invited us and Arkady to town."

"Are you going?" asked Pavel Petrovich.

"No. What about you?"

"I'm not going either. Why drag myself thirty miles for no good reason
at all. Mathieu wants to show himself to us in all his glory: to hell with
him! The whole province'll be singing his praises—he can do without
us. What a great honor: a privy councillor! If I'd continued in the civil
service, engaged in such drudgery, why I'd be an adjutant-general by
now. Besides, you and I are antiquated people."

"Yes, Brother; clearly it's time to order our coffins and lay our arms
across our chests," Nikolai Petrovich observed with a sigh.

"Well, I won't give up so easily," his brother muttered. "We'll still
have a skirmish with that doctor fellow; I feel it coming."

The skirmish occurred that very day at evening tea. Pavel Petrovich
entered the living room ready for battle, irritable and determined. He

6. A narrative poem (1824) by Pushkin that treats the themes of passion and freedom in the
context of gypsy life.

merely waited for a pretext to attack his enemy; but for a long time no
pretext presented itself. In general Bazarov said very little in the presence
of the "little old Kirsanov men" (as he called the two brothers), but that
evening he was in a bad mood and sat in silence drinking cup after cup
of tea. Pavel Petrovich burned with impatience; at last his wishes were
fulfilled.

The conversation turned to one of the local landowners. "He's trash,
a lousy little aristocrat," Bazarov observed indifferently; he'd met him
in Petersburg.

"Allow me to inquire," Pavel Petrovich began, his lips trembling, "in
your understanding are the words *trash* and *aristocrat* synonymous?"

"I said 'lousy little aristocrat,' " replied Bazarov, lazily sipping his tea.

"Indeed you did, sir; but I'm assuming you hold the same opinion of
'aristocrats' that you do of 'lousy little aristocrats.' I consider it my obligation to inform you that I do not share that opinion. I dare say everyone
knows me to be a liberal who advocates progress; but that's precisely
why I respect aristocrats—genuine ones. Remember, my dear sir [at
these words Bazarov raised his gaze to Pavel Petrovich's face], remember,
my dear sir," he repeated bitterly, "the English aristocrats. They don't
retreat one iota from their rights, and consequently, they respect the
rights of others; they demand the fulfillment of obligations owing to
them, and consequently, fulfill their own obligations. The aristocracy
gave England its freedom and supports it."

"We've heard that tune many times," Bazarov replied, "but what do
you hope to prove by that?"

"By *that* I hope to prove, my dear sir [When he was angry, Pavel
Petrovich deliberately mispronounced the words *this* and *that*, although
he knew he was violating the rules of grammar. This whim of his was
left over from the reign of Alexander I.[7] The notables of that time, in
the rare instances when they spoke their native language, mispronounced
this and *that*, as if to say, "We're genuine Russians, and at the same
time, we're grandees who're allowed to ignore schoolboy rules of grammar"], by *that* I hope to prove that without a sense of one's own worth,
without respect for oneself—in aristocrats these feelings are very well-
developed—there's no secure foundation for social . . . *bien public*,[8]
for the social structure. Personality, my dear sir, that's the main thing;
human personality must be solid as a rock because everything's built
upon it. I know very well, for example, that you find my habits amusing,
my apparel, even my neatness, but all this comes from my own sense
of self-respect, a sense of duty, yes, sir, duty. I live in the country, the
backwoods, but I don't let myself go, I respect the human qualities in
myself."

"Allow me, Pavel Petrovich," said Bazarov, "you say you respect

7. Alexander (1777–1825) ruled Russia from 1801 until his death, during which time France
   continued to exert a strong cultural and linguistic impact on Russian society.
8. "Public welfare" (French).

yourself, yet you sit here with your arms crossed; what use is that to the *bien public*? You'd be better off not respecting yourself, but doing something."

Pavel Petrovich grew pale.

"That's a completely different question. There's no need for me to explain to you at this time why I sit here with my arms crossed, as you so kindly put it. I merely want to say that aristocratism is a principle, and in these times only immoral or frivolous people can live without principles. I said this to Arkady the day after he arrived here and I say it again. Isn't that so, Nikolai?"

Nikolai Petrovich nodded his head.

"Aristocratism, liberalism, progress, principles," Bazarov was saying meanwhile, "just think, how many foreign . . . and useless words! A Russian has no need of them whatsoever."

"What, then, in your opinion, does he need? According to you, we stand outside humanity, beyond its laws. For heaven's sake, the logic of history demands . . ."

"What good's that logic? We can get along without that, too."

"How so?"

"Just so. You, I trust, don't need logic to put a piece of bread in your mouth when you're hungry. What do we need all these abstractions for?"

Pavel Petrovich wrung his hands. "After that I don't understand you. You insult the Russian people. I don't see how it's possible to reject principles and rules! On what basis can you act?"

"I've already told you, Uncle, we don't accept any authorities," Arkady intervened.

"We act on the basis of what we recognize as useful," Bazarov replied. "Nowadays the most useful thing of all is rejection—we reject."

"Everything?"

"Everything."

"What? Not only art and poetry . . . but even . . . it's too awful to say . . ."

"Everything," Bazarov repeated with indescribable composure.

Pavel Petrovich stared at him. He hadn't expected this, and Arkady even blushed from delight.

"But allow me," Nikolai Petrovich began. "You reject everything, or, to put it more precisely, you destroy everything . . . But one must also build."

"That's not for us to do . . . First, the ground must be cleared."

"The present condition of the people demands it," Arkady added pompously. "We must respond to these demands; we have no right to give in to the satisfaction of our personal egoism."

Apparently Bazarov didn't like this last phrase; it smacked of philosophy, that is, romanticism, since Bazarov referred to all philosophy as romanticism; but he considered it unnecessary to correct his young disciple.

"No, no!" Pavel Petrovich exclaimed with a sudden burst of emotion. "I don't want to believe that you gentlemen really know the Russian people and represent their needs and aspirations! No, the Russian people isn't as you imagine it to be. It holds tradition sacred; it's a patriarchal people and can't live without faith . . ."

"I won't argue with that," Bazarov said, interrupting. "I'm even ready to agree that you're correct *in this regard*."

"But if I'm right . . ."

"It still doesn't prove anything."

"Precisely, it doesn't prove anything," Arkady repeated with the certainty of an experienced chess player who's foreseen an apparently dangerous move by his opponent and therefore isn't in the least perturbed.

"What do you mean it doesn't prove anything?" asked the astonished Pavel Petrovich. "Then you're going against your own people?"

"What if that were true?" cried Bazarov. "The people believe that when they hear thunder, it's the prophet Elijah riding across the sky in his chariot. What then? Am I supposed to agree with that? Besides, they're Russian and I'm Russian, too, aren't I?"

"No, after what you've just said, you're not Russian! I can't acknowledge you as Russian."

"My grandfather ploughed the earth," Bazarov replied with arrogant pride. "Ask any of your peasants which of us—you or me—he recognizes as his fellow countryman. You don't even know how to talk to them."

"While you speak to them and despise them at the same time."

"So what, if they deserve to be despised? You condemn my course, but whoever said it was accidental, that it wasn't occasioned by that same national spirit in whose name you protest?"

"Is that so? Much we need nihilists!"

"Needed or not—it's not for us to decide. Why, you don't consider yourself useless."

"Gentlemen, gentlemen, please, let's not get personal!" Nikolai Petrovich exclaimed, rising to his feet.

Pavel Petrovich smiled and, placing his hand on his brother's shoulder, made him sit down again.

"Don't worry," he said. "I won't forget myself precisely because of that feeling of self-worth that was so cruelly mocked by Mister . . . by Mister Doctor. Allow me to ask," he continued, addressing Bazarov once more, "do you perhaps think your doctrine is something new? If so, you're quite mistaken. The materialism you preach has been in fashion more than once before and has always turned out to be insubstantial . . ."

"Another foreign word!" Bazarov interrupted. He was beginning to get angry and his face turned a particular rough coppery color. "In the first place, we're not preaching anything; that's not our custom . . ."

"Then what are you doing?"

"I'll tell you what we're doing. Previously, in recent times, we acknowledged that our civil servants take bribes, that we lack roads, commerce, true justice . . ."

"Well, yes, so, you're denouncers—that's what it seems to be called. I agree with many of your denunciations, but . . ."

"Then we realized that talking, simply talking all the time about our open sores isn't worth the trouble, that it leads only to being vulgar and doctrinaire; we saw that even our intelligent men, our so-called progressives and denouncers, served no purpose at all, that we were preoccupied with a lot of nonsense, arguing over some form of art, unconscious creativity, parliamentarianism, legal profession, and the devil knows what else, while it was really a question of our daily bread, when we were being oppressed by the most primitive superstitions, when all our joint stock companies were collapsing merely as a result of a lack of honest men, while the emancipation, about which the government was so concerned, will hardly do any good because our peasants are happy to steal from themselves, as long as they can get stinking drunk in the tavern."

"Yes," Pavel Petrovich said, interrupting him, "I see: you've become convinced of all this and now have decided not to do anything serious about it."

"We've decided not to do anything serious about it," Bazarov repeated grimly.

He was suddenly annoyed with himself for having been so expansive with this gentleman.

"And merely curse everything?"

"And curse everything."

"And this is called nihilism?"

"And this is called nihilism," Bazarov repeated again, this time with particular rudeness.

Pavel Petrovich wrinkled his face slightly.

"So that's how it is!" he said in a strangely serene voice. "Nihilism is supposed to relieve all our ills, and you, you're our saviors and heroes. But then why do you abuse others, even those very denouncers? Aren't you doing a lot of talking, too, just like all the rest?"

"We're guilty of many sins, but not that one," Bazarov said through his teeth.

"Well, then? Are you taking action or what? Are you preparing to take action?"

Bazarov made no reply. Pavel Petrovich gave a little shudder, but then gained control of himself.

"Hmmm! To act, destroy . . . ," he continued. "But how can one destroy without even knowing why?"

"We destroy because we're a force," Arkady observed.

Pavel Petrovich looked at his nephew and smiled.[9]

"Yes, a force—one that doesn't need to account for itself," Arkady said and sat up straighter.

"You unfortunate lad!" cried Pavel Petrovich; he was positively unable to restrain himself any longer. "If only you'd consider what it is you're supporting in Russia with your vulgar maxim! Why, it's enough to try the patience of a saint! A force! There's force in a wild Kalmuck[1] and a Mongol—but what's the good of that to us? Our road's one of civilization, yes, sir, yes, my kind sir; its fruits are dear to us. And don't you tell me these fruits are insignificant: the worst dauber, *un barbouilleur*,[2] a ballroom pianist who gets five copecks to play for an entire evening, all of them are more useful than you because they're representatives of civilization, not some primitive Mongol force! You imagine you're progressive, but you're only fit to sit in some Kalmuck's cart! A force! Just you remember once and for all, you mighty gentlemen, that there're only four and a half of you, while there're millions of others who won't let you trample their most sacred beliefs underfoot and who'll crush you!"

"If they crush us, so be it," said Bazarov. "But we'll see what we shall see. There aren't as few of us as you think."

"What? Do you seriously think you can take on, cope with a whole people?"

"Moscow, you know, burned down from a candle that cost only one copeck," replied Bazarov.

"Yes, I see. First there's almost Satanic pride, then ridicule. That's how our young people amuse themselves, that's what wins the inexperienced hearts of young lads! There, just look, one of them's sitting there next to you; why, he almost worships you. Look at him. [Arkady turned away and frowned.] And this infection's already spread quite far. I've heard that in Rome our artists won't set foot in the Vatican. They consider Raphael[3] a fool because, they say, he's an authority; and they themselves are disgustingly impotent and sterile; their imagination goes no further than *Girl at the Fountain*[4] no matter how hard they try! And that girl's very poorly depicted. According to you, they're fine fellows, isn't that so?"

"According to me," Bazarov objected, "Raphael isn't worth a damn and they're no better than he is."

"Bravo! Bravo! Listen, Arkady . . . that's the way contemporary young

---

9. In the original version of the novel, Pavel Petrovich replies to Arkady, "A fine thing, force—without any content."
1. The Kalmucks (or Kalmyks) were an Asian people and a branch of the Mongols.
2. "Dabbler" (in writing or painting) (French).
3. Major Italian Renaissance painter (1483–1520).
4. This does not refer to any specific painting, but merely indicates a total lack of talent among young Russian artists.

people should express themselves! Just think, how can they resist following you? Previously, young people were required to study; they didn't want to be viewed as ignorant, so they worked whether they wanted to or not. But now all they have to say is, 'Everything on earth's nonsense!'—and that's all there is to it. Young people are delighted. The fact is that before they were simply blockheads, but these days they've suddenly become nihilists."

"Now your vaulted sense of self-dignity has betrayed you," Bazarov observed phlegmatically, while Arkady flared up, his eyes flashing. "Our argument's gone too far . . . I think it's better to stop here. I'll be prepared to agree with you later," he said standing up, "when you present me with a single institution of contemporary life, either in the family or in the social sphere, that doesn't deserve absolute and merciless rejection."

"I can present you with millions of such institutions," cried Pavel Petrovich, "millions of them! Why, there's the peasant commune,[5] for example."

A cold smirk distorted Bazarov's lips.

"Well, as far as the peasant commune's concerned," he said, "you really ought to talk to your brother. I think he's found out by now what sort of thing the commune is, with its collective responsibility, sobriety, and other such customs."

"The family, then, the family as it exists among our peasants!" cried Pavel Petrovich.

"I suggest you'd better not look into that question in too much detail either. No doubt you've heard about a father-in-law's rights with his daughter-in-law?[6] Listen to me, Pavel Petrovich, give yourself some time to think about it; it's difficult to come up with something on the spot. Sort through all the levels of our society and think carefully about each; meanwhile Arkady and I will . . ."

"You must ridicule everything," Pavel Petrovich interrupted.

"No, we must dissect frogs. Let's go, Arkady; good-bye, gentlemen!"

The two friends left. The brothers remained alone and at first merely looked at one another.

"There," began Pavel Petrovich at last, "there's our contemporary young people for you! There they are—our heirs!"

"Heirs," repeated Nikolai Petrovich with a mournful sigh. During the course of the entire argument, he sat as if on tenterhooks, stealthily casting painful glances at Arkady from time to time. "Do you know what I remembered, Brother? Once I had an argument with our late mother: she was shouting and didn't want to listen to me . . . Finally, I told her she couldn't understand me; I said we belonged to two different generations. She was terribly offended, and I thought to myself: what's to be done? It's a bitter pill—but one must swallow it. Well, now our

5. *Mir*, a form of peasant self-government that is regarded as uniquely Russian.
6. That is, to have sexual relations with his son's wife.

turn's come, and our heirs can say to us: 'We belong to a different generation; swallow that pill.' "

"You're being much too generous and modest," Pavel Petrovich objected. "On the contrary, I'm sure you and I are far more in the right than these young fellows, although perhaps we express ourselves in rather archaic language, *vielli*,[7] and lack that arrogant self-assurance . . . The haughtiness of these young people nowadays! You ask one of them, 'Which wine would you like, red or white?' 'It's my custom to prefer red!' he answers in a bass voice and with such a pompous expression, as if the entire universe were observing him at that very moment . . ."

"Would you care for some more tea?" Fenechka inquired, sticking her head in the door: she'd decided not to enter the living room as long as she heard voices arguing there.

"No, you can tell them to take the samovar away," Nikolai Petrovich replied and stood up to meet her. Pavel Petrovich abruptly said *bon soir*[8] to him and retired to his study.

XI

Half an hour later Nikolai Petrovich went into the garden to his favorite pavilion. He was sunk in gloomy meditation. This was the first time he'd become aware of any distance between him and his son; he felt that with each passing day this distance would increase. Consequently, those winters in Petersburg when he'd spent endless days studying the latest works had all been in vain; in vain had he listened in on those young people's conversations; in vain had he rejoiced when he managed to insert a word or two into their heated discussions. "My brother says we're right," he thought, "and, setting aside all vanity, it also seems to me that they're farther from the truth than we are; but at the same time, I feel they have something we lack, some advantage over us . . . Youth? No, it's not only youth. Perhaps their advantage consists in the fact that there're fewer traces of gentry mentality left in them than in us?"

Nikolai Petrovich hung his head and wiped his hand across his face.

"But to reject poetry?" he thought again, "to have no feeling for art, nature . . . ?"

He looked around, as if wishing to understand how it was possible to have no feeling for nature. It was almost evening; the sun was hidden behind a small grove of aspens that stood about half a verst[9] from the garden: its shadow stretched endlessly across motionless fields. A little peasant on a white nag was trotting along a dark, narrow path next to the grove; he was clearly visible, all of him, including the patch on his shoulder, even though he was in the shadows; the horse's hooves could

7. "Old-fashioned" (Italian).
8. "Good evening" (French).
9. A unit of linear measure (3,500 feet).

be seen plainly rising and falling in a pleasant fashion. The sun's rays,
for their part, made their way into the grove; penetrating the thickets,
they bathed the aspen trunks in such warm light that they began to
resemble pine trees, and their leaves looked almost dark blue, while
above them stretched the pale blue sky, slightly reddened by the sunset.
The swallows were flying very high; the wind had died down completely;
some tardy bees were lazily and sleepily buzzing amidst the lilac blos-
soms; a swarm of midges hung over a single outstretched branch. "My
God, how nice it all is!" thought Nikolai Petrovich, and just as his
favorite lines of poetry were about to come to his lips, he remembered
Arkady and his *Stoff und Kraft*—and remained silent; but he continued
sitting there, giving way to melancholy and the comforting play of solitary
reflection. He loved to dream; country life had fostered this tendency
in him. It was not all that long ago he'd engaged in such dreaming while
waiting for his son at the carriage inn; but since then such a change
had occurred, and their relations, which had at that time been so unclear,
had now become quite well-defined . . . how well-defined they were!
He thought once again about his late wife, not as he'd known her through
many years, not as a good, domestic housewife, but rather as a young
girl with her slim figure, her innocent, inquisitive look, and her tightly
knotted braid over her slender, childish neck. He remembered seeing
her for the first time. He was still a student then. He'd met her on the
stairs of the apartment where he lived; accidentally bumping into her,
he turned around to apologize, but could mutter only, *"Pardon, monsieur,"* while she bent her head, started laughing, and suddenly, as if
frightened, scurried away. At the bend in the stairs, she glanced back
at him quickly, assumed a serious look, and blushed. Then he recalled
his first timid visits, half-words, half-smiles, and the embarrassment,
sadness, upheavals, and finally the breathless rapture . . . Where had
it all gone? She became his wife; he was happy as few people on earth
ever are . . . "But," he thought, "those first, sweet moments, why can't
a person live an eternal, immortal life in them?"

He didn't try to clarify his own thoughts, yet felt he wanted to preserve
that blessed time with something stronger than memory; he wanted to
feel once more the presence of his Marya, experience her warmth and
breath, and he could already imagine above him . . .

"Nikolai Petrovich," Fenechka's voice rang out nearby. "Where are
you?"

He shuddered. He felt neither pain nor shame . . . He'd never even
allow the possibility of comparison between his wife and Fenechka, but
regretted that she'd come to look for him. Her voice summoned him
back at once: his gray hair, his age, his present . . .

The magical world he'd already entered, arising from dim mists of
the past, was shaken and then vanished.

"Over here," he replied. "I'm coming. You go on ahead." "There

they are, those traces of gentry mentality" flashed through his mind.
Fenechka looked into the pavilion and glanced at him in silence, then
disappeared; meanwhile he was surprised to notice that night had fallen
while he was sitting there dreaming. Everything around him had grown
dark and quiet, and Fenechka's face appeared before him, so small and
pale. He stood up, wanting to return home, but the emotions stirring
in his heart couldn't be calmed; he began pacing slowly around the
garden, first gazing sadly at the ground under his feet, then raising his
eyes to the sky, where swarms of stars were already twinkling. He paced
a great deal, until he was quite exhausted, but his agitation, a vague,
searching, mournful agitation, couldn't be appeased. Oh, how Bazarov
would've made fun of him, if only he'd known what he was feeling at
that moment! Arkady too would judge him harshly. He, a forty-four-
year-old man, an agronomist and landowner, with tears welling up in
his eyes, senseless tears; this was a hundred times worse than playing
the cello.

Nikolai Petrovich continued to pace and couldn't resolve to return
home, to that peaceful and comfortable nest that looked at him so
invitingly with all its illuminated windows; he was unable to part with
the darkness, the garden, the fresh air in his face, and his grief, his
agitation. . . .

At a bend in the path he met Pavel Petrovich.

"What's wrong?" he asked Nikolai Petrovich. "You're pale as a ghost;
you must be ill. Why don't you go to bed?"

Nikolai Petrovich explained his state of mind briefly, then moved on.
Pavel Petrovich walked to the end of the garden, also grew thoughtful,
and also raised his gaze to the sky. But nothing was reflected in his
handsome dark eyes except the stars. He hadn't been born a romantic,
and his fastidiously dry and passionate soul, with its touch of French
misanthropy, didn't even know how to dream . . .

"Do you know what?" Bazarov said to Arkady that very evening.
"I've just had a splendid idea. Today your father said he's received an
invitation from your illustrious relative. Your father isn't going; why
don't you and I set off for ***; you know, that gentleman's invited you,
too. You see how fine the weather is now; let's go for a ride and have
a look at the town. We'll spend five or six days there, and that's that!"

"Will you come back here afterward?"

"No, I'll have to go see my father. You know, he's only about thirty
versts from ***. I haven't seen him or my mother for a long time; one
must console the old folks. They're good people, especially my father;
he's so amusing. I'm all they have."

"Will you stay there long?"

"I don't think so. I'll probably get bored."

"Will you come to see us on your way back?"

"I don't know . . . we'll see. Well, so, how about it? Shall we go?"

"All right," Arkady replied lazily.

In his heart and soul he was delighted with his friend's proposal, but he considered it his obligation to conceal his emotions. It was not for nothing he was a nihilist!

The next day he left with Bazarov for ***. The young people in Marino regretted their departure; Dunyasha even shed a few tears . . . but the old folks breathed a sigh of relief.

XII

The town of ***, to which our friends were heading, came under the jurisdiction of a youngish governor who was both a progressive and a despot, as happens all too often in Russia. During the first year of his administration, he managed to quarrel not only with the marshal of the nobility, a retired captain of the horse guards who ran a stud farm and entertained frequently, but also with his own subordinates. The squabbles arising from this situation finally grew to such proportions that the ministry in Petersburg found it necessary to dispatch a trusted personage to investigate the entire matter on the spot. The authorities' choice fell upon Matvei Ilich Kolyazin, son of the Kolyazin whose patronage the Kirsanov brothers once enjoyed. He was also "youngish," that is, recently turned forty, but already aspiring to an important government position and sporting stars on both sides of his chest. It's true that one was a foreign decoration, and not all that distinguished. Just like the governor he'd come to review, he was considered a progressive and, being a person of consequence already, didn't resemble the majority of such people. He thought very highly of himself; his vanity knew no bounds, but he behaved simply, looked approvingly, listened indulgently, and laughed so generously that at first glance he might even be taken for a "good fellow." However, on important occasions, he knew quite well how to throw his weight around, as the saying goes. "Energy is essential," he used to say at such times, "*l'énergie est la première qualité d'un homme d'état*";[1] but for all that, he was usually made a fool of, and any relatively experienced civil servant could wrap him around his little finger. Matvei Ilich used to express his great respect for Guizot[2] and tried to impress each and every person with the idea that he didn't belong to the ranks of ordinary officials and backward bureaucrats and that he didn't neglect any important aspect of social life . . . Such phrases were most customary to him. He even followed the development of contemporary literature, though with casual condescension, it's true: in the same way a grown man who meets a line of young boys on the street will sometimes fall in behind it. In essence, Matvei Ilich hadn't progressed much beyond

---

1. "Energy is the primary quality of a statesman" (French).
2. François Guizot (1787–1874), a French statesman and historian.

those statesmen of Alexander I, who, to prepare themselves for an evening at Madame Svechina's[3]—living in Petersburg at the time—would read a page or two of Condillac[4] that very morning; but his methods were different, more up-to-date. He was a shrewd courtier, a great schemer, and nothing more; he didn't know a thing about business and had zero intelligence; but he knew how to handle his own affairs: no one could outsmart him there, and that was the most important thing.

Matvei Ilich received Arkady with the generosity—we might even say, playfulness—characteristic of an enlightened higher official. However, he was surprised to learn that the relatives he'd invited had chosen to remain in the country. "Your father always was a bit of an eccentric," he observed, playing with the tassels of his magnificent velvet dressing gown. Suddenly turning to a young civil servant attired in a smart uniform, he exclaimed with a worried expression, "What?" The young man, whose lips were stuck together as a result of his prolonged silence, rose to attention and regarded his superior with perplexity. But, after so confounding his subordinate, Matvei Ilich no longer paid him any attention. Our higher officials are quite fond of confounding their subordinates; the means to which they resort for accomplishing this goal are rather diverse. The following method, among many others, is rather popular, "quite a favorite," as the English would say: the high official suddenly ceases to understand even the simplest words, feigning total deafness. He asks, for example, "What day is it?"

He's informed most respectfully: "Today's Friday, Your Exc-c-cellency."

"Eh? What? What's that? What did you say?" the high official repeats in annoyance.

"Today's Friday, Your Exc-c-cellency."

"How's that? What? What's Friday? Which Friday?"

"Friday, Your Exc-c-c-c-cellency, the day of the week."

"So, you've decided to teach me a lesson, have you?"

Matvei Ilich was just this sort of higher official, even though he was considered a liberal.

"I advise you, my friend, to pay a visit to the governor," he said to Arkady. "You understand, I'm urging you to do this not because I subscribe to old-fashioned ideas about the need to pay one's respects to the authorities, but simply because the governor's a decent chap; besides, you probably want to make the acquaintance of local society . . . After all, you're not a bear, I hope? And, the day after tomorrow he's giving a grand ball."

"Will you be there?" asked Arkady.

3. Sofiya Svechina (1782–1859) was a popular Russian writer and proponent of fashionable religious mysticism.
4. Étienne Bonnot de Condillac (1715–80) was a French philosopher who developed a theory of sensationalism.

"He's giving it for me," said Matvei Ilich, almost pityingly. "Do you know how to dance?"

"I do, rather badly."

"That's a shame. There're some pretty girls around here and a young man should be ashamed if he doesn't know how to dance. Once again, I'm not saying this in support of any old ideas; by no means do I assume that a man's intelligence resides in his feet, but Byronism[5] is rather ridiculous, *il a fait son temps.*"[6]

"But, Uncle, it's not because of Byronism that I . . ."

"I'll introduce you to our local young ladies, I'll take you under my wing," Matvei Ilich said, interrupting him and giving a self-satisfied chuckle. "You'll find it warm here, eh?"

The servant entered and informed him that the chairman of the provincial revenue department had arrived, an old man with sugarsweet eyes and wrinkled lips, who loved nature deeply, especially on a summer's day, when, in his own words, "every little bee takes a little bribe from every little flower . . ." Arkady left.

He found Bazarov at the inn where they were staying and spent a long time persuading him to visit the governor. "There's no way out!" said Bazarov at last. "If we've come this far, we might as well go through with it. We wanted to have a look at the landowners—well, then, let's have a look at them!" The governor received the young people cordially, but didn't ask them to sit down and remained standing himself. He was constantly fussing and hurrying; in the morning he'd put on a snug uniform and an extremely tight necktie; he never had time to finish eating or drinking, and was always giving orders. In the province he was nicknamed Bourdaloue,[7] not after the reknowned French preacher, but after the Russian word *burda*—"slops." He invited Kirsanov and Bazarov to the ball and a few minutes later invited them again, taking them for brothers and referring to them as the Kaisarovs.

They were just returning home from the governor's, when suddenly a rather short man jumped from a passing carriage; wearing a Slavophile jacket,[8] shouting, "Evgeny Vasilich!" he threw himself at Bazarov.

"Ah! It's you, Herr Sitnikov," said Bazarov, continuing along the sidewalk. "What brings you here?"

"Just imagine, it's pure chance," he replied; turning to his carriage, he waved his hand five times or so and shouted, "Follow us, follow us! My father has some business here," he continued, jumping over a ditch, "so he asked me . . . I learned of your arrival today and have already

---

5. A romantic worldview and lifestyle based on the life and works of the great English romantic poet Lord Byron (1788–1824).
6. "It's had its day" (French).
7. Louis Bourdaloue (1632–1704) was a French Jesuit preacher and famous orator whose works were translated into Russian.
8. An affected "native" style of dress, worn to demonstrate nationalist feeling. The Slavophiles, as opposed to the Westernizers, sought to preserve the originality of Russian culture.

been to your room . . . [In fact, when the friends returned to their room they found a visiting card with bent corners and Sitnikov's name, in French on one side, Cyrillic on the other.] I hope you're not just coming from the governor's?"

"Don't hope: that's exactly where we were."

"Ah! Well, in that case, I'll visit him, too . . . Evgeny Vasilich, introduce me to your . . . to him . . ."

"Sitnikov, Kirsanov," Bazarov grumbled without stopping.

"I'm very flattered," began Sitnikov, walking sideways, grinning, and hurriedly pulling off his overly elegant gloves. "I've heard so much about . . . I'm an old friend of Evgeny Vasilich and can even say—his disciple. I owe him my regeneration . . ."

Arkady looked at Bazarov's disciple. A restless and vacant expression appeared on the small, though pleasant features of his pampered face; his little eyes, looking as if they'd been squeezed into his face, stared intently and uneasily, and he laughed nervously, in an abrupt, wooden manner.

"Would you believe it?" he went on. "When Evgeny Vasilevich first told me that one needn't acknowledge any authorities, I felt such delight . . . it was as if I suddenly saw the light! 'There,' I thought, 'at long last I've found a man!' By the way, Evgeny Vasilevich, you really must drop in on a certain lady who's completely capable of understanding you, for whom your visit will be a real treat; I think you may've heard something about her."

"Who is it?" Bazarov asked unwillingly.

"Kukshina, Eudoxie, Evdoksiya Kukshina. She's a remarkable character, *émancipée* in the true sense of the word, a progressive woman. Do you know what? Let's drop in on her together right now. She lives only a little way from here. We'll have some lunch there. You haven't had lunch yet, have you?"

"Not yet."

"Well, splendid. She's separated from her husband, you understand, and is completely independent."

"Is she good-looking?" Bazarov asked, interrupting him.

"N . . . no, one couldn't say that."

"Then why the devil are you taking us to see her?"

"Ah, you're making fun . . . She'll treat us to a bottle of champagne."

"So that's it! Now I see what a practical fellow you are. By the way, is your father still tax farming?"[9]

"Yes, indeed," Sitnikov replied quickly, emitting a shrill laugh. "Well then? Shall we go?"

"I don't really know."

---

9. Individuals hired by the state to collect liquor taxes often managed to increase their personal wealth in the performance of their official duties.

"You wanted to have a look at people, go on," Arkady said in a low voice.

"What about you, Mr. Kirsanov?" Sitnikov resumed. "You come too; we won't go without you."

"How can we all descend on her at once?"

"Never mind! Kukshina's a marvelous person."

"Will there really be a bottle of champagne?" asked Bazarov.

"Three of them!" cried Sitnikov. "I swear to it!"

"Swear on what?"

"My own head."

"It'd be better to swear on your father's moneybags. Well, let's go."

XIII

The small nobleman's house built in the Moscow style where Avdotya (or Evdoksiya) Nikitishna Kukshina lived, stood on one of the recently burnt-out streets in the town of ***; it's a well-known fact that our provincial towns burn down every five years or so. At the door, above a visiting card nailed at an angle, was a bell handle; in the entryway visitors were greeted by someone who wasn't exactly a servant, but not quite a companion, wearing a cap—obvious signs of the mistress's progressive tendencies. Sitnikov asked whether Avdotya Nikitishna was at home.

"Is that you, Victor?" a shrill voice rang out from the next room. "Come on in."

The woman in the cap disappeared at once.

"I'm not alone," Sitnikov replied, boldly removing his jacket, under which he was wearing something like a jerkin or sackcoat, and casting a brazen glance at Arkady and Bazarov.

"Never mind," answered the voice. "*Entrez.*"[1]

The young men went in. The room in which they found themselves looked more like a study than a drawing room. Papers, letters, thick Russian journals, for the most part with their pages uncut, lay strewn about on dusty tables; cigarette butts were scattered everywhere. On a leather-covered sofa a lady was half-reclining; she was still young, had fair hair, a bit disheveled, and was wearing a silk dress, not altogether tidy, with large bracelets on her short arms, a lace kerchief on her head. She got up from the sofa; casually pulling a velvet cape trimmed with yellowed ermine over her shoulders, she said languidly, "Hello, Victor," and shook Sitnikov's hand.

"Bazarov, Kirsanov," he said abruptly, imitating Bazarov.

"Welcome," replied Kukshina and, fixing Bazarov with her round eyes between which was a forlorn, turned-up, very little red nose, she added, "I know you," and she shook his hand, too.

1. "Come in" (French).

Bazarov frowned. There was nothing ugly in the small, unprepossessing figure of this emancipated woman, but the expression on her face made a bad impression on the viewer. One felt inclined to ask: "What's the matter? Are you hungry? Bored? Afraid? Why so tense?" Just like Sitnikov, she was always anxious. She spoke and moved in a rather casual, though awkward, manner: she obviously considered herself a good-natured, simple creature; at the same time, no matter what she did, it always seemed that she didn't want to be doing that. Everything she did appeared to be done on purpose, as children say, that is, neither simply nor naturally.

"Yes, yes, I know you, Bazarov," she repeated. (She had the habit, like many of our provincial and Moscow ladies, of calling men by their surname from the moment she met them.) "Would you like a cigar?"

"A cigar's all well and good," said Sitnikov, who was already sprawling in an armchair and sticking one leg up in the air, "but do give us some lunch; we're awfully hungry. And have them open a bottle of champagne for us."

"You sybarite," muttered Evdoksiya and began laughing. (When she laughed, the gums above her upper teeth showed.) "Isn't it true, Bazarov, he's a sybarite?"

"I love the comforts of life," Sitnikov intoned pompously. "That doesn't prevent me from being a liberal."

"Yes, it does, it does prevent you!" cried Evdoksiya, but she still gave her maid orders for lunch and a bottle of champagne. "What do you think?" she asked, turning to Bazarov. "I'm certain you share my opinion."

"Well, no," Bazarov replied. "A piece of meat's better than a piece of bread, even from the chemical point of view."

"Do you study chemistry? It's my passion. I've even invented a new resin."

"A resin? You?"

"Yes, me. Do you know what it's for? To make dolls' heads that won't break. I'm also practical. But it's not quite finished. I must still read Leibig.[2] By the way, have you read Kislyakov's article about women's labor in the *Moscow News*?[3] Do read it. You must be interested in the women's question. And in schools, too? What's your friend studying? What's his name?"

Madame Kukshina scattered her questions one after another with casual disregard, without waiting for answers; it's just the way spoiled children talk to their nannies.

"My name's Arkady Nikolaevich Kirsanov," Arkady replied, "and I'm not studying anything."

2. See above, p. 21, n. 9.
3. A newspaper published between 1756 and 1917. The author's name, Kislyakov (lit. "sourpuss"), is probably invented.

Evdoksiya burst out laughing.

"How nice! Well, do you smoke? Victor, you know I'm angry with you."

"What for?"

"I'm told you've begun singing the praises of George Sand.[4] She's a retrograde woman and nothing more! How can one compare her to Emerson?[5] She has no ideas whatever about education, physiology, nothing. I'm sure she's never even heard of embryology, and in our day and age—what can one do without it? [Evdoksiya even threw up her hands.] Ah, what a splendid article Elisevich[6] wrote on this score. He's such a brilliant gentleman! [Evdoksiya constantly used the word *gentleman* instead of *man*.] Bazarov, come over here and sit down on the sofa next to me. Perhaps you don't know it, but I'm very much afraid of you."

"Why so? Allow me to inquire."

"You're a dangerous gentleman; you're such a critic. Oh, my God! It's so absurd, but I'm talking like a country landowner. In fact, I really am a landowner. I manage my own estate, and, just imagine, have a steward named Erofey—he's a wonderful character, just like Cooper's Pathfinder:[7] there's something so spontaneous about him! I've settled down here once and for all; the town's unbearable, isn't that so? But what's to be done?"

"It's a town like any other," Bazarov remarked coolly.

"Petty interests all the time, that's what makes it so awful! I used to spend winters in Moscow . . . but now my lawful spouse, Monsieur Kukshin, resides there. Besides, Moscow nowadays . . . well, I don't know—it's not quite the same as it was. I'm thinking about going abroad; last year I was just about to set off."

"To Paris, naturally?" asked Bazarov.

"Paris and Heidelberg."

"Why Heidelberg?"

"Good Lord, because Bunsen's[8] there!"

Bazarov could find nothing to say in reply to this.

"Pierre Sapozhnikov . . . do you know him?"

"No, I don't."

"Good Lord, Pierre Sapozhnikov . . . why he's always at Lidiya Khostakova's."

---

4. French feminist writer (1804–76) whose eighty or so novels treat primarily women's issues, especially romantic love.
5. Ralph Waldo Emerson (1803–82), one of the United States's most influential writers and philosophers and founder of the transcendentalist movement.
6. A name probably invented by combining those of two radical journalists, G. Z. Eliseev and M. A. Antonovich, major contributors to *The Contemporary*.
7. James Fenimore Cooper (1789–1851), the first American novelist. His narratives about the frontier often idealized the life of the American Indian. *The Pathfinder* was published in 1840.
8. Robert Wilhelm Bunsen (1811–99), a German scientist, pioneer in the field of chemistry, and inventor of the Bunsen burner.

"I don't know her either."

"Well, he's the one who agreed to accompany me. Thank God, I'm free, I have no children . . . What was that I just said? '*Thank God*'! Well, it doesn't matter."

Evdoksiya rolled a cigarette with her tobacco-stained fingers, licked the edge of it with her tongue, sucked on it, and then lit it. The maid entered carrying a tray.

"Ah, here's our lunch! Would you like something to eat? Victor, open the bottle; that's in your line of work."

"Yes, it is, it is indeed," muttered Sitnikov, once again emitting a shrill laugh.

"Are there any pretty women around here?" asked Bazarov, as he downed a third glass.

"There are," replied Evdoksiya, "but they're all so empty-headed. For example, *mon amie*[9] Odintsova isn't bad looking. It's a pity her reputation's so . . . That wouldn't matter, though, but she has no independent views, no breadth, nothing of that sort. We must reform the entire educational system. I've given it some thought already; our women are very badly educated."

"You can't do anything with them," Sitnikov said. "One ought to despise them, and I do, absolutely and completely! [The possibility of despising someone and expressing that feeling was a most pleasant sensation for Sitnikov; he attacked women most of all, never suspecting that in a few months he'd be groveling before his wife, simply because she'd been born a Princess Durdoleosova.] Not a single one of them could understand our conversation; not one even deserves being talked about by serious men like us!"

"But they've no need to understand our conversation," said Bazarov.

"Who're you talking about?" Evdoksiya interrupted.

"Pretty women."

"What? Then you must share Proudhon's[1] opinion?"

Bazarov drew himself up arrogantly.

"I don't share anyone's opinion: I have my own."

"Down with authorities!" cried Sitnikov, delighted with the chance to express himself incisively in the presence of the man before whom he fawned.

"But Macaulay[2] himself," Kukshina started to say.

"Down with Macaulay!" thundered Sitnikov. "Are you going to defend those silly females?"

"Not those silly females, but women's rights, which I've sworn to defend with my last drop of blood."

9. "My friend" (French).
1. Pierre Joseph Proudhon (1809–65), radical French social theorist, founder of anarchism, and opponent of feminism.
2. Thomas Babington Macaulay (1800–59), famous English historian and essayist.

"Down with them!" But Sitnikov stopped there. "I don't reject them," he said.

"No, I can see you're a Slavophile!"[3]

"No, I'm not, although, of course . . ."

"No, no, no! You *are* a Slavophile. You're a proponent of the *Domostroi*.[4] You should carry a whip in your hand!"

"A whip's a fine thing," observed Bazarov, "but we're down to the last drop . . ."

"Of what?" asked Evdoksiya.

"Champagne, most esteemed Evdoksiya Nikitishna, champagne—not your blood."

"I can't listen with indifference when women are attacked," continued Evdoksiya. "It's awful, just awful. Instead of attacking them, you ought to read Michelet's *De l'amour*.[5] It's wonderful! Gentlemen, let's talk about love," added Evdoksiya, lowering her arm languorously onto the rumpled cushion of the sofa.

There suddenly followed a moment of silence.

"No, why talk about love?" Bazarov asked. "But you just said something about Odintsova . . . That's what you called her, right? Who is that lady?"

"She's lovely, simply lovely," squeaked Sitnikov. "I'll introduce you to her. She's clever, rich, and a widow. Unfortunately, she's still not very enlightened: she needs to become better acquainted with our Evdoksiya. I drink to your health, Eudoxie! Let's clink glasses! '*Et toc, et toc, et tin-tin-tin! Et toc, et toc, et tin-tin-tin!!*' "[6]

"Victor, you're a naughty boy."

Lunch lasted a very long time. The first bottle of champagne was followed by a second, then a third, even a fourth . . . Evdoksiya chattered without stopping; Sitnikov echoed her. They talked a great deal about the meaning of marriage—whether it was a prejudice or a crime, whether people are born equal or not, and the nature of individualism. It finally reached the point that Evdoksiya, flushed from all the wine she'd drunk, banging her blunt nails on the keys of an out-of-tune piano, began singing in a hoarse voice, first some gypsy songs, then Seymour Schiff's romance "Grenada lies slumbering,"[7] while Sitnikov tied a scarf around his head and imitated a dying lover at the words:

> And thy lips to mine
> In burning kiss entwine.

3. See above, p. 48, n. 8.
4. A product of sixteenth-century Russian culture, expounding a rigid system of household management.
5. *On Love* (1859), a work by the great French romantic historian Jules Michelet (1798–1874).
6. A line quoted from a song entitled "*L'ivrogne et sa femme*" (The drunkard and his wife) by the French lyrical poet Pierre Jean de Béranger (1780–1857).
7. A reference to a romance entitled "Night in Grenada" by K. A. Taranovsky, set to music by the pianist and composer Seymour Schiff.

Finally Arkady could stand no more. "Gentlemen, this has begun to resemble bedlam," he observed aloud.

Bazarov, who from time to time merely inserted a sarcastic word or two into the conversation—he was more interested in the champagne —yawned loudly, stood up, and, without saying good-bye to the hostess, walked out with Arkady. Sitnikov ran after them.

"So then, what do you think?" he asked, skipping obsequiously first to the right, then to the left. "I told you, didn't I: she's a remarkable person! If we only had more women like her! In her own way she's a highly moral phenomenon."

"What about *your* father's establishment? Is that also a moral phenomenon?" asked Bazarov, pointing to the tavern they were passing that very moment.

Sitnikov once again emitted a shrill laugh. He was very ashamed of his background and didn't know whether to feel flattered or offended by Bazarov's unexpected familiarity in addressing him.

XIV

A few days later there was a ball at the governor's house. Matvei Ilich was the real "hero of the occasion"; the Marshal of the Nobility[8] declared to each and every one that he'd come simply out of respect for the governor; while the governor, even at the ball, even while standing motionless, continued to "govern." The cordiality of Matvei Ilich's demeanor could only be equaled by his stateliness. He was nice to everyone—to some with a trace of antipathy, to others with a trace of respect. To ladies he appeared *"en vrai chevalier français,"*[9] and constantly broke into a strong, sonorous, solitary laugh, appropriate for a dignitary. He slapped Arkady on the back and loudly called him "my little nephew"; to Bazarov, who was attired in a rather old dress coat, he gave an absentminded, but condescending sidelong glance, and an indistinct, but affable grunt, from which one could only make out the words "I" and "terribly"; he extended a finger or two to Sitnikov and smiled, but he'd already turned away; even to Kukshina, who appeared at the ball wearing no crinolines whatever, a pair of dirty gloves, and a bird of paradise in her hair, even to Kukshina he said, *"Enchanté."*[1] There were hordes of people and no lack of dancing partners; the civilians tended to crowd along the walls, but the military men danced enthusiastically, especially one who'd spent six weeks in Paris, where he'd learned various devil-may-care exclamations such as, *"Zut,"* *"Ah, fichtrre,"* *"Pst, pst, mon bibi,"*[2] and so on. He pronounced them perfectly, with genuine Parisian *chic;* yet at the same time he said, *"si j'aurais"*

---

8. See above, p. 25, n. 2.
9. "Like a true French cavalier" (French).
1. "Delighted" (French).
2. Various nonsensical exclamations in French.

instead of "*si j'avais*," and used the word "*absolument*" in the sense of "certainly."[3] In brief, he expressed himself in that Great Russo-French dialect that the French love to mock when they have no need to assure us that we speak their language like angels, "*comme des anges.*"

Arkady danced badly, as we already know, while Bazarov didn't dance at all. They both stood in a corner; Sitnikov joined them there. Having assumed a look of contemptuous scorn and letting venomous remarks fall where they may, he looked around insolently and seemed to be enjoying himself immensely. Suddenly his expression changed and, turning to Arkady, he said as if with some embarrassment, "Odintsova's just arrived."

Arkady turned around and saw a tall woman in a black dress standing near the door of the room. He was struck by her dignified bearing. Her bare arms lay gracefully alongside her slender figure; light sprays of fuchsia hung tastefully from her shiny hair onto her slanting shoulders; from under a slightly protruding white forehead her bright eyes peered out serenely and quietly—it was precisely serenely, not pensively, and her lips curled into a scarcely noticeable smile. Some sort of tender, gentle strength emanated from her face.

"Are you acquainted with her?" Arkady asked Sitnikov.

"Intimately. Do you want me to introduce you?"

"Please . . . after this quadrille."

Bazarov also turned his attention to Odintsova.

"And who might that be?" he asked. "She doesn't resemble the other hags."

Waiting until the end of the quadrille, Sitnikov led Arkady to Odintsova. He was hardly intimately acquainted with her: he became confused as he spoke, and she regarded him with some astonishment. But her face assumed a cordial expression when she heard Arkady's surname. She asked if he was Nikolai Petrovich's son.

"Precisely."

"I've met your father on two occasions and have heard a great deal about him," she continued. "I'm very glad to make your acquaintance."

At that moment an adjutant came rushing up and asked her to dance a quadrille. She agreed.

"So you dance?" Arkady inquired politely.

"I do. Why did you think I didn't? Do I seem too old to you?"

"I beg your pardon, how could I . . . In that case, allow me to ask you for the mazurka."

Odintsova smiled indulgently.

"If you wish," she said and looked at Arkady, not exactly as a superior, but as married sisters regard their much younger brothers.

Odintsova was a little older than Arkady; she'd already turned twenty-

---

3. Matvei Ilich makes mistakes in his French grammar here, saying "if I should have" (conditional) instead of "if I had" (imperfect). He also makes mistakes in his French diction, using the adverb *absolutely* to mean "certainly."

nine, but in her presence he felt like a schoolboy, a student, as if the difference in their ages was much greater. Matvei Ilich came up to her with an imposing air and obsequious phrases. Arkady moved aside, but continued watching her; he didn't take his eyes off her all during the quadrille. She chatted just as casually with her partner as with the dignitary; she quietly turned her head and eyes, and laughed softly once or twice. Her nose was a little broad, like almost all Russian noses, and her complexion was not entirely clear; nevertheless, Arkady was sure he'd never met such a lovely woman. He couldn't get the sound of her voice out of his ears; the very folds of her dress seemed to hang in a special way, more gracefully and elegantly than all the rest, and her movements were particularly smooth, yet natural at one and the same time.

Arkady felt some timidity in his heart when, at the first sounds of the mazurka, he sat down next to his partner; preparing to engage her in conversation, he merely passed his hand through his hair, unable to think of anything to say. But he didn't feel timid or agitated for very long; Odintsova's serenity was communicated to him as well. Within a quarter of an hour he was telling her all about his father, his uncle, life in Petersburg, and in the country. Odintsova listened with polite attention, gently opening and closing her fan; his chatter was interrupted when she was asked to dance quadrilles; Sitnikov, by the way, asked her twice. She'd come back, sit down again, pick up her fan, and wouldn't even be breathing more rapidly; meanwhile Arkady would resume his chatter, suffused with happiness by being so near her, talking to her, looking into her eyes, at her beautiful forehead, at her pleasant, imposing, intelligent face. She said very little, but her words revealed her knowledge of life; from several of her remarks Arkady gathered that this young woman had already managed to feel and think a great deal . . .

"Who was that man you were just with," she asked him, "when Mr. Sitnikov introduced you to me?"

"Oh, so you noticed him?" Arkady asked in turn. "He has a fine face, doesn't he? His name's Bazarov; he's a friend of mine."

Arkady began telling her about "his friend."

He spoke about him in such detail and with such enthusiasm that Odintsova turned and looked at him very carefully. Meanwhile the mazurka was coming to an end. Arkady felt sad at having to part from her: he had so enjoyed spending nearly an hour with her! True, during the whole time he constantly felt she was indulging him, that he ought to feel grateful to her . . . but young hearts aren't burdened much by this feeling.

The music ended.

"*Merci*," Odintsova said and stood up. "You promised to visit me; bring your friend with you. I'd be very curious to meet a man who's bold enough not to believe in anything."

The governor went up to Odintsova and announced that supper was served and, with a preoccupied look, offered her his arm. As she left she turned around to smile and nod to Arkady for the last time. He bowed deeply and watched her go (her figure seemed so graceful to him, draped in the grayish sheen of black silk!); he thought, "By this time she's forgotten entirely about my existence," and in his soul he felt a sense of exquisite humility . . .

"Well, so?" Bazarov asked Arkady, as soon as the latter had returned to the corner. "Did you enjoy yourself? One gentleman here just told me she's quite a woman—*ooh là là*; then again, that gentleman seems to be a bit of a fool. Well, what do you think, is she—*ooh là là*, or not?"

"I don't quite understand what you mean," replied Arkady.

"Is that so! What innocence!"

"In that case I really don't understand that gentleman. Odintsova is very nice—no doubt, but her behavior's so cold and severe that . . ."

"Still waters run deep, you know!" Bazarov interrupted. "You say she's cold. That provides special flavor. You like ice cream, don't you?"

"Perhaps," muttered Arkady. "I can't judge such things. She wants to make your acquaintance and has asked me to bring you along to meet her."

"I can just imagine how you described me! However, you did very well. Take me along. Whoever she may be—simply a provincial lioness or 'an emancipated woman' like Kukshina—she still has the nicest pair of shoulders I've seen in a long time."

Arkady was offended by Bazarov's cynicism, but—as is often the case—reproached his friend for something other than what he disliked in him . . .

"Why are you so unwilling to allow women to be freethinkers?" he asked in a low voice.

"Because, my little friend, as far as I've observed, the only female freethinkers are ugly monsters."

Their conversation ended here. Both young men left right after supper. Kukshina, in a nervously spiteful way, but not without timidity, began laughing after they left: her vanity was deeply offended by the fact that neither of them had paid her any attention. She stayed at the ball later than everyone else; at three o'clock in the morning she was still dancing a polka-mazurka in the Parisian style with Sitnikov. The governor's fête concluded with this edifying spectacle.

XV

"Let's see what species of Mammalia this person belongs to," Bazarov said to Arkady the next day as they both climbed the stairs of the hotel where Odintsova was staying. "My nose tells me something's not quite right."

"I'm surprised at you!" cried Arkady. "What? You, you, Bazarov, clinging to such narrow-minded morality, that . . ."

"What a strange fellow you are!" Bazarov said, cutting him off abruptly. "Don't you know in our language, when we say 'not quite right,' that means 'quite all right'? In other words, there's something to be gained. Wasn't it you who said today that she married peculiarly, although, in my opinion, marriage to a wealthy old man—isn't peculiar at all; on the contrary, it's very sensible. I don't believe all those rumors heard in town; but I do like to think, as our educated governor says, that they're well-founded."

Arkady made no reply and knocked on the door of the room. A young servant dressed in livery led the two friends into a large room, badly furnished, like all rooms in Russian hotels, but well supplied with flowers. Odintsova soon appeared in a simple morning dress. She seemed even younger in the light of the springtime sun. Arkady introduced Bazarov to her and was secretly astonished to notice that he seemed embarrassed, while Odintsova remained completely serene, just as she had yesterday. Bazarov was aware of his embarrassment and became annoyed. "Well, I'll be! Afraid of a woman!" he thought. Sprawling in an armchair just as Sitnikov had, he began talking in an exaggeratedly casual manner, while Odintsova never took her clear eyes off him.

Anna Sergeevna Odintsova was the daughter of Sergei Nikolaevich Loktev, known as a handsome man, a speculator and gambler, who, after hanging on for fifteen years or so and becoming famous in both Petersburg and Moscow, ended up by losing everything. He was forced to settle in the country, where he soon died, leaving a tiny inheritance to his two daughters, Anna, who was twenty, and Katerina, twelve. Their mother, who'd come from an impoverished line of Princes Kh., passed away in Petersburg, when her husband was at the peak of his powers. After her father's death, Anna's situation became very difficult. The splendid education she'd received in Petersburg hadn't prepared her to assume responsibility for the household and estate—or for life in the remote countryside. She knew absolutely no one in the entire neighborhood, and there was no one to turn to. Her father had managed to avoid all contact with his neighbors; he despised them and they, him, each in his own way. She didn't lose her head, however, and promptly summoned her mother's sister, the Princess Avdotya Stepanovna Kh., a nasty, arrogant old woman, who, after taking up residence in her niece's house, appropriated all the best rooms for herself, growled and grumbled from morning to night, and wouldn't even go out for walks in the garden unless accompanied by her one servant, a gloomy footman in worn, pea-green livery with light blue braid, and a three-cornered hat. Anna patiently endured all her aunt's whims, gradually assumed responsibility for her sister's education, and, it seemed, had already reconciled herself to the idea of wasting away in the remote countryside.

. . . But fate had decreed otherwise for her. A certain Odintsov happened to notice her; he was a very wealthy man, about forty-six years old, eccentric, hypochondriac, portly, ponderous, and sour, but neither stupid nor mean; he fell in love with her and proposed marriage. She agreed to become his wife; he lived with her almost six years and, when he died, left her all his property. For about a year after his death Anna Sergeevna didn't leave the country; then she went abroad with her sister, but only to Germany; she grew bored and returned to live on her beloved estate of Nikolskoe, about forty versts from the town of ***. There she had a magnificent, splendidly furnished house and a lovely garden with a conservatory: the late Odintsov had denied himself nothing. Anna Sergeevna rarely went into town; when she did, it was only on business and she never stayed long. She wasn't loved in the province; there was a great deal of fuss over her marriage to Odintsov, and all sorts of unbelievable stories circulated about her: it was claimed she'd helped her father with his cardsharping, had good reasons for going abroad, and had to conceal some unfortunate consequences[4] . . . "You know what I mean," the indignant narrators would conclude their tale. "She's gone through fire and water," they used to say about her; and a well-known local wit would add, "And through copper pipes as well."[5] All these rumors reached her, but she didn't pay any attention to them: she had an independent and rather resolute character.

Odintsova was seated, leaning against the back of an armchair, and, with one hand resting on the other, was listening to Bazarov. Contrary to his normal behavior, he spoke a great deal and made an obvious effort to interest his interlocutor, which also surprised Arkady. He couldn't tell whether Bazarov had achieved his goal. It was hard to guess from Anna Sergeevna's face what sort of impression he was making: her face retained one and the same expression—cordial and elegant; her lovely eyes shone with attention, but that attention was completely composed. Bazarov's affectation in the first moments of their meeting had an unpleasant effect on her, like a foul odor or a shrill sound; but she understood at once that he was embarrassed, and even found that flattering. Vulgar mediocrity was the only thing that repulsed her, and no one could accuse Bazarov of that. Arkady continued to be surprised all that day. He expected Bazarov would talk to an intelligent woman like Odintsova about his convictions and views: she'd declared her desire to meet a man "bold enough not to believe in anything." But instead, Bazarov talked about medicine, homeopathy, and botany. It turned out Odintsova hadn't been wasting her time in solitude: she'd read several good books and expressed herself in excellent Russian. She directed the conversation to music, but when she learned that Bazarov didn't acknowledge art, she quietly returned to the subject of botany, although Arkady

4. Perhaps an unwanted pregnancy.
5. The pregnancy might have ended in an illegal abortion.

was just about to launch into a disquisition on the significance of folk melodies. Odintsova continued to treat him as if he were her younger brother: she seemed to value his youthful generosity and good nature—but nothing more. Their conversation lasted a little over three hours—it was unhurried, free-ranging, and animated.

At last the friends stood up and began to take their leave. Anna Sergeevna looked at them cordially, extended her beautiful white hand to each, and, after reflecting a moment, said with some hesitation, but with a pleasant smile, "Gentlemen, if you're not afraid of being bored, do come visit me in Nikolskoe."

"If you like, Anna Sergeevna," cried Arkady, "I'd consider it a great honor . . ."

"And you, Monsieur Bazarov?"

Bazarov merely bowed—and Arkady was surprised for one last time: he noticed his friend had blushed.

"Well?" he said to him on the street. "Do you still think she's—*ooh là là?*"

"Who knows? Just see how frigid she's made herself!" Bazarov replied. After a brief silence he added: "She's a duchess, a regal personage. All she needs is a train out behind her and a crown on top of her head."

"Our duchesses don't speak Russian that well," Arkady observed.

"She's been through many changes, my dear boy; she's tasted the common bread."

"All the same, she's lovely!" said Arkady.

"What a delectable body!" continued Bazarov. "Perfect for the dissecting table."

"Stop it, Evgeny, for God's sake! That's unspeakable."

"Well, don't get angry, my little one. What I meant was—she's first-rate. We'll have to pay her a visit."

"When?"

"Why not the day after tomorrow? What's there to do here? Drink champagne with Kukshina? Listen to your relative, that liberal official? . . . We'll leave the day after tomorrow. By the way—my father's small estate isn't too far from there. This Nikolskoe's along the *** road, isn't it?"

"It is."

"*Optime.*[6] There's no need to dawdle; only fools and know-it-alls do that. I tell you: she has a delectable body!"

Three days later the two friends were on their way to Nikolskoe. The day was bright and not too hot, the well-fed little posthorses trotted along smoothly, gently switching their twisted and braided tails. Arkady looked at the road and smiled without knowing why.

"Congratulate me," Bazarov cried suddenly, "today, June twenty-

6. "Perfect" (Latin).

second, is my guardian angel's day.[7] Let's see how he takes care of me. My parents e:pect me home today," he added, lowering his voice . . . "Well, they'll wait. What difference does it make?"

XVI

Anna Sergeevna's estate stood on the slope of a bare hill, not far from a yellow stone church with a green roof, white columns, and a fresco over the main entrance depicting the "Resurrection of Christ" in the "Italian" style.[8] A swarthy warrior wearing a helmet and reclining in the foreground was particularly noteworthy for his rounded contours. Behind the church a large village extended for some distance in two rows of cottages with chimneys visible here and there over thatched roofs. The manor house was built in the same style as the church, known here as Alexandrine;[9] the house was also painted yellow, had a green roof, white columns, and a gable with a coat of arms. The provincial architect had erected both buildings with the approval of the late Odintsov, who couldn't stand any frivolous or extemporaneous innovations, as he referred to them. The house was flanked on both sides by dark trees in an old garden; an avenue of pruned firs led to the entrance.

Our friends were met in the hall by two tall footmen in livery; one ran off to fetch the butler immediately. The butler, a portly man wearing a black frockcoat, appeared at once and directed the guests up a carpeted staircase to a special room already provided with two beds and all the prerequisites for their toilette. It was clear that order prevailed in this house: everything was clean and sweet-smelling, just like in a minister's reception room.

"Anna Sergeevna requests that you come see her in half an hour," the butler informed them. "Is there anything you require at present?"

"Nothing at present, most esteemed sir," replied Bazarov. "Would you be so kind as to bring me a glass of vodka?"

"Yes, sir," replied the butler, somewhat bewildered, and left, his boots squeaking.

"What grand style!" observed Bazarov. "That's what it's called by your sort, isn't it?"

"A fine duchess she is," Arkady retorted. "At the first acquaintance she invites such mighty aristocrats as you and me to come visit her."

"Especially me, a future medic, a medic's son, and a sexton's grandson . . . Did you know I'm the grandson of a sexton? Like Speransky,"[1] he

---

7. The birthday of one's patron saint, also known as one's name day.
8. That is, presumably, Renaissance style.
9. Pertaining to the reign of Alexander I; see above, p. 37, n.7.
1. Mikhail Mikhailovich Speransky (1772–1839), a leading statesman and liberal reformer under Alexander I. He was the son of a village priest and one of the first to rise to a position of great power from such humble origins.

added, pursing his lips after a brief silence. "Still, she has pampered herself; oh, how this lady's pampered herself! Maybe we should put on our frockcoats?"

Arkady merely shrugged his shoulders . . . but he too felt slightly embarrassed.

Half an hour later Bazarov and Arkady entered the drawing room. It was a spacious, lofty room, furnished rather elegantly, but without any particular taste. Heavy, expensive furniture stood in the usual formal arrangement along walls covered in brown paper with a gold design; the late Odintsov had ordered the wallpaper from Moscow through his friend and agent, a wine merchant. Over the middle sofa hung a portrait of a corpulent, fair-haired man who seemed to be looking down at the guests inhospitably. "That must be *him*," whispered Bazarov to Arkady, and, wrinkling up his nose, added, "Maybe we should get out of here?" But at that very moment the mistress appeared. She was wearing a light beige dress; her hair was combed smooth behind her and lent a girlish expression to her clear, fresh face.

"Thank you so much for keeping your word," she began. "You must stay a while: it really isn't too bad here. I'll introduce you to my sister; she plays the piano very well. That won't make any difference to you, Monsieur Bazarov; but it seems that you, Monsieur Kirsanov, love music; besides my sister, I also have an old aunt living here with me, and a neighbor of ours sometimes comes over to play cards: that's our entire society. And now, let's sit down."

Odintsova uttered this entire short speech with particular precision, as if she'd learned it all by heart; then she turned to Arkady. It turned out that her mother had known Arkady's mother and had even been aware of her love for Nikolai Petrovich. Arkady began talking about his late mother with enthusiasm; meanwhile, Bazarov set about examining picture albums. "What an unassuming fellow I've become," he thought.

A beautiful borzoi with a blue collar came running into the drawing room, paws tapping the floor, followed by a girl about eighteen,[2] with black hair and dark skin, a roundish, but pleasant face, and small dark eyes. In her hands she held a basket filled with flowers.

"Here's my Katya," said Odintsova, nodding her head toward her.

Katya made a slight curtsey, took up a position next to her sister, and began sorting the flowers. The borzoi, whose name was Fifi, went up to each visitor in turn, wagging her tail, and thrust her cold nose into their hands.

"Did you pick them all yourself?" Odintsova asked.

"I did," Katya replied.

"Is Auntie coming to tea?"

"She is."

---

2. Turgenev's text lists different ages for Katya: here she is "about eighteen"; above (p. 59) she is described as eight years younger than Anna, who is said to be twenty-nine.

When Katya spoke, she smiled very sweetly, both timidly and openly, and glanced up in an amusingly stern way. Everything about her was still green and fresh: her voice, the light down on her face, her pink hands with white circles on her palms, and her slightly narrow shoulders . . . She was constantly blushing and hastily catching her breath.

Odintsova turned to Bazarov.

"You're looking at those pictures out of politeness, Evgeny Vasilich," she began. "They really don't interest you. Come and join us and let's argue about something or other."

Bazarov moved closer.

"What shall we talk about?" he asked.

"Whatever you like. I must warn you, I love to argue."

"You?"

"Yes. Does that surprise you? Why?"

"Because as far as I can tell, you have a cold, serene manner; one must have passion to argue."

"How did you manage to find me out so soon? In the first place, I'm impatient and insistent—just ask Katya; in the second, I get excited very easily."

Bazarov looked at Anna Sergeevna.

"Perhaps; you know best. So, you'd like to have an argument—by all means. I was examining some views of Saxony in your album, and you observed that such an activity couldn't interest me. You said that because you assume I have no feeling for art whatsoever—yes, in fact I lack such feeling; but these views could've interested me from a geological point of view, for example, the formation of mountains."

"Excuse me; as a geologist you'd be more likely to resort to a book, a special work on the subject, rather than these drawings."

"A drawing can show me at one glance what might take ten pages in a book to describe."

Anna Sergeevna was silent for a moment.

"All the same, you haven't the least bit of artistic feeling?" she asked, resting her elbows on the table, and in so doing, brought her face close to Bazarov's. "How do you get along without it?"

"What good is it, may I ask?"

"Well, if only to know how to study and understand people."

Bazarov smiled.

"In the first place, one's life experience serves that purpose; in the second, I can tell you it isn't worth the trouble to study separate individuals. All people resemble each other, in soul as well as body; each one of us has a brain, spleen, heart, and lungs, all made similarly. So-called moral qualities are also shared by everyone: small variations don't mean a thing. A single human specimen's sufficient to make judgments about all the rest. People are like trees in a forest; no botanist would study each birch individually."

Katya, who was arranging her flowers without hurrying, raised her eyes to Bazarov in perplexity; meeting his swift and careless glance, she blushed to her ears. Anna Sergevna shook her head.

"Trees in a forest," she repeated. "Then in your opinion there's no difference between a stupid person and a clever one, between a good person and a bad one?"

"Yes, there is. Just like between a sick person and a healthy one: the lungs of a consumptive patient aren't in the same condition as your lungs and mine, although they're built similarly. We know more or less what causes physical ailments; moral illnesses result from bad upbringing, all the nonsense that gets stuffed into people's heads from childhood, in a word, the deformed condition of society. If you correct society, you won't have any more illness."

Bazarov said all this with a look on his face as if he were thinking: "You can believe me or not, it's all the same to me!" He was slowly stroking his long side whiskers while his eyes were roaming around the room.

"And you assume," Anna Sergeevna said, "that when society is cured, there won't be any more stupid or bad people?"

"At least in a properly organized society it won't make any difference whether a person's stupid or clever, bad or good."

"Yes, I understand; everyone will have the same spleen."

"Precisely, madame."

Odintsova turned to Arkady.

"What's your opinion, Arkady Nikolaevich?"

"I agree with Evgeny," he replied.

Katya looked at him from under her brows.

"You amaze me, gentlemen," Odintsova said, "but we'll talk with you further. As for now, I see that Auntie's coming for tea; we must spare her ears."

Anna Sergeevna's auntie, the Princess Kh., a short, slender woman with a face pinched like a fist and nasty, steady eyes under a gray wig, came in. Scarcely greeting the guests, she lowered herself into a large velvet-covered armchair, in which no one else had any right to sit. Katya placed a little bench under her feet; the old woman didn't thank her and didn't even glance up; she merely placed her hands underneath the yellow shawl covering almost her entire feeble body. The princess loved the color yellow: she was also wearing a cap with bright yellow ribbons.

"Did you have a good rest, Auntie?" Odintsova inquired, raising her voice.

"That dog's in here again," the old woman muttered in reply. Noticing that Fifi had made a few hesitant steps in her direction, she cried, "Shoo, shoo!"

Katya called Fifi and opened the door for her.

Fifi gladly ran out in the hope that someone would take her for a walk, but when left alone on the other side of the door, she began scratching and whining. The princess frowned and Katya was about to leave . . .

"I think tea's ready," Odintsova announced. "Gentlemen, if you please; Auntie, let's go have tea."

The princess stood up from her armchair and was the first to leave the drawing room. Everyone followed her into the dining room. A servant boy in livery pulled an armchair stacked with cushions away from the table with a loud scrape—she sank into this chair, which was also reserved exclusively for her use; Katya was pouring tea and handed her the first cup decorated with a coat of arms. The old woman put some honey into the cup (she considered it sinful and expensive to drink tea with sugar, even though she never spent a copeck on anything); she suddenly asked in a hoarse voice, "What does *Preence* Ivan write?"

No one answered her. Bazarov and Arkady quickly surmised that no one paid her any attention, although she was treated with respect. "It's all *for the sake of appearance* they keep her, because she comes from a princely line," thought Bazarov . . . After tea Anna Sergeevna suggested they go for a walk; but it began to drizzle and everyone, except for the princess, returned to the drawing room. The neighbor who loved to play cards arrived; his name was Porfiry Platonych. He was a portly, gray-haired man with short, pointy legs that looked as if they'd been sharpened, and he was very polite and entertaining. Anna Sergeevna, who chatted mostly with Bazarov, asked him whether he'd like to play an old-fashioned game of preference[3] with them. Bazarov agreed, saying he really needed to prepare himself in advance for a career as a country doctor.

"Be careful," remarked Anna Sergeevna, "Porfiry Platonych and I will beat you. And you, Katya," she added, "play something for Arkady Nikolaevich; he loves music, and we'll listen, too."

Katya went to the piano unwillingly; Arkady, although he really did love music, followed her unwillingly. Odintsova seemed to be sending him away; like every young man of his age, he felt in his heart the welling up of a vague, painful sensation, resembling the forebodings of love. Katya raised the cover of the piano and, without looking up at Arkady, asked in a low voice, "What would you like me to play?"

"Whatever you like," Arkady replied indifferently.

"What kind of music do you prefer?" Katya repeated, without changing her position.

"Classical," replied Arkady in the same tone of voice.

"Do you like Mozart?"

"Yes."

Katya took out Mozart's Sonata-Fantasia in C Minor. She played very

---

3. A card game similar to whist.

well, although her rendition was a bit stiff and dry. Without taking her eyes off the music and pressing her lips together firmly, she sat upright and motionless; only at the end of the sonata did her face flush and a little curl of hair fall down over her dark brow.

Arkady was particularly struck by the last part of the sonata, that part where, in the midst of the enchanting gaiety of a carefree melody, there suddenly burst forth strains of such mournful, almost tragic grief . . . But the reflections aroused in him by the sounds of the Mozart didn't refer to Katya. Looking at her, he merely thought: "This young lady doesn't play too badly, and she's not bad-looking either."

After finishing the sonata, Katya, without lifting her hands from the keyboard, asked, "Is that enough?" Arkady declared that he dare not trouble her further and began chatting with her about Mozart. He asked whether she'd chosen that sonata herself, or someone had recommended it to her. Katya answered him in monosyllables: she was *hiding*, having retreated into herself. When this happened, she didn't emerge very quickly; her face would assume a stubborn, almost dull-witted expression. She wasn't exactly shy, merely distrustful and a little intimidated by her sister, who'd provided her with an education, and who, of course, had no suspicion of all this. Arkady wound up calling Fifi, who'd come back in; to maintain appearances, he began petting the dog's head with a gracious smile. Katya returned to her flowers.

Meanwhile, Bazarov kept losing round after round. Anna Sergeevna played cards like a master; Porfiry Platonych could also hold his own. Bazarov wound up losing a sum of money that, though insignificant, was still not altogether pleasant for him. During supper Anna Sergeevna once again turned the conversation to botany.

"Let's go for a walk tomorrow morning," she said to him. "I want to learn the Latin names of the wildflowers and all their characteristics."

"Why do you want to know the Latin names?" asked Bazarov.

"Order is needed in all things," she replied.

"What a splendid woman Anna Sergeevna is," exclaimed Arkady, when left alone later with his companion in the room reserved for them.

"Yes," answered Bazarov, "that lady has a head on her shoulders. And she's been around as well."

"In what sense do you mean that, Evgeny Vasilich?"

"In a good sense, my dear boy, Arkady Nikolaevich, in a good sense! I'm sure she also does a fine job managing her estate. But she's not the splendid one—it's her sister."

"What? That swarthy girl?"

"Yes, that swarthy girl. She's so fresh, unspoiled, timid, taciturn, anything you like. That's someone to take an interest in. You could make anything you like of her; while the other one's an old warhorse."

Arkady said nothing in reply to Bazarov, and each of them lay down to sleep with his own thoughts.

That evening Anna Sergeevna also thought about her guests. She liked Bazarov—the absence of flirtatiousness and the very harshness of his judgments. She saw something novel in him, something she'd never encountered before, and was curious.

Anna Sergeevna was a rather strange creature. Without any prejudices, without even any strong convictions, she never yielded to anyone or deviated from her path. She saw a great deal very clearly, took an interest in many things, but nothing completely satisfied her; she scarcely desired complete satisfaction. Her mind was both inquisitive and indifferent at the same time: her doubts never subsided into oblivion or expanded to anxiety. If she hadn't been so rich and independent, she might have thrown herself into the struggle, might have come to know real passion . . . But she had an easy life, though boring at times, and continued passing day after day, without hurrying and only occasionally getting agitated. The colors of the rainbow would sometimes dance before her eyes, but she was always relieved when they faded and had no regrets. Her imagination even exceeded the boundaries of what's considered permissible according to the laws of conventional morality; but even then her blood flowed as quietly as ever in her charmingly graceful and tranquil body. Sometimes, upon emerging from a fragrant bath, all warm and soft, she'd fall to musing about the insignificance of life, its sadness, travail, and evil . . . Her soul would be filled with unexpected boldness and seethe with noble aspiration; but a draught of wind would blow in from a half-opened window and Anna Sergeevna would retreat into herself, complain, and feel almost angry; the only thing she needed at that moment was for the nasty wind to stop blowing on her.

Like all women who never managed to fall in love, she longed for something without knowing precisely what it was. Strictly speaking, she didn't want anything, although it seemed to her she wanted everything. She could hardly stand the late Odintsov (she married him out of calculation, although she probably wouldn't have agreed to become his wife if she hadn't considered him a good man), and she harbored a secret disgust for all men whom she considered to be nothing more than slovenly, ponderous, flaccid, feebly tiresome creatures. Once while abroad she met a handsome young Swede with a chivalrous expression and honest blue eyes under a broad forehead; he made a strong impression on her, but that didn't prevent her from returning to Russia.

"This doctor's a strange man!" she thought, lying in her magnificent bed on lace cushions under a light silk coverlet . . . Anna Sergeevna had inherited from her father a share of his penchant for luxury. She'd loved her sinful, but kindhearted father very dearly, and he'd adored her, joked with her in a friendly way as with an equal, and trusted her entirely, consulted her. She could scarcely remember her mother.

"That doctor's strange!" she repeated to herself. She stretched, smiled, put her hands behind her head, then ran her eyes over a few pages of a silly French novel, threw down the book—and fell fast asleep, feeling all clean and cool, in sweet, fragrant bed linen.

The next morning right after breakfast Anna Sergeevna set off botanizing with Bazarov and returned before dinner; Arkady didn't go anywhere and spent about an hour with Katya. He wasn't bored with her, and she offered to repeat yesterday's performance of the sonata; but when at last Odintsova returned and he saw her, his heart instantly felt a pang . . . She was coming through the garden at a somewhat tired pace; her cheeks were red, her eyes shining brighter than usual under her round straw hat. She was twisting the thin stem of a wildflower in her fingers, her light shawl had slipped down to her elbows, and the broad gray ribbons of her hat were clinging to her chest. Bazarov walked alongside, in a confident, carefree manner, as always, but the expression on his face, although cheerful and even affectionate, was not at all to Arkady's liking. After muttering through his teeth, "Hello!" Bazarov headed to his room, while Odintsova shook Arkady's hand absentmindedly and also walked right past him.

"Hello?"[4] wondered Arkady. "As if we hadn't seen each other already today?"

XVII

Time (as is well known) sometimes flies by like a bird, while at other times it crawls like a worm; but a person is particularly fortunate when he doesn't even notice whether it's passing swiftly or slowly. In precisely this way Arkady and Bazarov spent about two weeks at Odintsova's. This was facilitated in part by the order she'd established in her house and in her life. She adhered to it very strictly and forced others to submit as well. Everything in the course of a day was done at a certain time. At exactly eight o'clock in the morning everyone assembled for tea; between tea and breakfast each person did as he wished; the mistress herself was busy with the steward (the estate was run on the quitrent system),[5] with the butler, and the main housekeeper. Before dinner everyone gathered again to converse or read; evenings were devoted to walks, cards, or music; at half past ten Anna Sergeevna retired to her room, gave orders for the following day, and went to bed. Bazarov didn't care for this regimented, somewhat imperious punctuality in everyday life; "it's as if everything moved along rails," he said. The footmen in livery and the formal butlers offended his democratic sentiments. He believed that if things had gone that far, it was fitting to dine entirely in the English style—frockcoats and white ties. Once he aired his views on this subject to Anna Sergeevna. She behaved in such a way so that everyone, without a moment's hesitation, would express his opinions to

4. Russians typically greet each other only once a day.
5. See above, p. 8, n. 4.

her. She heard him out and replied: "From your point of view, you're correct—perhaps, in this case, I am an aristocratic lady; but in the country it's impossible to live with disorder; the boredom would be overwhelming." And she continued in her own ways. Bazarov complained, but it was precisely because "everything moved along rails" that he and Arkady lived so comfortably in Odintsova's house.

Nevertheless, a change had occurred in both young men since the first days of their stay at Nikolskoe. Bazarov, toward whom Anna Sergeevna was obviously well-inclined, though she rarely agreed with him, began to display unprecedented signs of anxiety: he was easily irritated, spoke unwillingly, looked angry, and couldn't sit still, as if he felt provoked; meanwhile Arkady, who'd decided all by himself that he was in love with Odintsova once and for all, began to give way to quiet despondency. This feeling, however, didn't prevent him from drawing closer to Katya; it even helped him establish affectionate, friendly relations with her. "*She* doesn't appreciate me! So be it! . . . But this kind creature doesn't reject me," he thought, and his heart once again experienced the sweetness of magnanimous emotion. Katya vaguely understood that he was seeking some consolation in her company; but she didn't deny either him or herself the innocent pleasure of a half-bashful, half-trusting friendship. They didn't talk much in Anna Sergeevna's presence: Katya always retreated under her sister's sharp gaze, while Arkady, as is typical for a person in love when in the presence of his beloved, couldn't pay attention to anything else; but he was only happy with Katya. He felt he wasn't exciting enough to interest Odintsova; he became timid and confused when left alone with her. Nor did she know what to say to him: he was too young for her. On the other hand, Arkady felt at home with Katya; he treated her indulgently, didn't prevent her from expressing those impressions aroused in her by music or reading tales, verse, and other trifles, without noticing or realizing himself that these very *trifles* interested him as well. For her part, Katya didn't prevent him from feeling despondent.

Arkady felt comfortable with Katya; Odintsova, with Bazarov; therefore it often happened that the two couples, after spending some time together, would each go their separate ways, especially during their walks. Katya *adored* nature, and Arkady loved it, though dared not admit it; Odintsova was rather indifferent to it, just like Bazarov. The almost constant separation of the two friends had its consequences: relations between them began to change. Bazarov stopped talking to Arkady about Odintsova and even ceased mocking her "aristocratic ways"; it's true, he continued to praise Katya as before, merely advising Arkady to restrain her sentimental tendencies, but his praise was hurried, his advice, dry; in general he talked with Arkady much less than before . . . as if avoiding him, feeling ashamed of something . . .

Arkady noticed all this, but kept his opinions to himself.

The real cause of all this "newness" was the feeling in Bazarov inspired by Odintsova—a feeling that tormented and enraged him, one that he'd have denied immediately with scornful laughter and cynical abuse, had anyone ever remotely suggested the possibility of what was actually taking place. Bazarov was a great lover of women and feminine beauty, but love in the ideal sense, or, as he expressed it, in the romantic sense, he called rubbish or unforgivable stupidity; he considered chivalrous feelings something akin to deformity or disease and had expressed his amazement more than once: why hadn't Toggenburg[6] been locked away in an asylum with all those minstrels and troubadors? "If you like a woman," he used to say, "try to gain your end; if that's impossible—well, never mind, turn your back on her—there's plenty of fish in the sea." He liked Odintsova: the rumors circulating about her, the freedom and independence of her thought, her indisputable fondness for him—all this, it seemed, was in his favor; but he soon realized that with her he wouldn't "gain his end"; to his own amazement, however, he lacked the strength to turn his back on her. His blood caught fire as soon as he thought about her; he could've easily coped with his blood, but something else had taken root in him that he'd never been able to admit, something he'd always mocked, something that irritated his pride. In conversations with Anna Sergeevna he expressed even more strongly than before his careless contempt of everything romantic; but when left alone he acknowledged with indignation the romantic in himself. At such times he headed for the woods and walked with long strides, breaking any branches that got in his way, cursing both her and himself under his breath; or else he took to the hayloft in the barn and, stubbornly closing his eyes, forced himself to sleep, which, naturally, he couldn't always do. He imagined those chaste arms wrapping around his neck, those proud lips responding to his kisses, those clever eyes coming to rest on his with tenderness—yes, tenderness—and his head would start spinning; for a moment he'd forget where he was until his indignation would flare up once again. He caught himself having all sorts of "shameful" thoughts, as if the devil were teasing him. Sometimes it seemed to him that a change was also taking place in Odintsova, that something special had appeared in her expression, that perhaps . . . But at this point he usually stamped his foot or clenched his teeth and shook a fist in his own face.

Meanwhile, Bazarov wasn't entirely mistaken. He'd appealed to Odintsova's imagination; he interested her and she thought about him a great deal. She wasn't bored in his absence and didn't wait for him to come, but his appearance enlivened her at once; she willingly remained alone with him and gladly conversed with him, even when he angered her or offended her taste, her elegant habits. It was as if she wished to test him and come to know herself.

6. The romantic hero of a literary ballad (1797) by the German writer Friedrich von Schiller (1759–1805), entitled "*Ritter Toggenburg*" (The knight Toggenburg).

Once while walking with her in the garden, he suddenly announced in a sullen voice that he intended to leave soon and visit his father in the country . . . She turned pale, as if something had caused her great pain, so much pain that she herself was surprised and thought for a long time afterward about what it might mean. Bazarov had informed her of his impending departure with no intention of testing her or to see what might happen: he never "fabricated." That morning he'd talked with his father's steward, Timofeich, who used to take care of him. This Timofeich, an experienced and clever old man with faded yellow hair, a weather-beaten reddish face, and tiny teardrops in his squinting eyes, had appeared before Bazarov unexpectedly, wearing his shortish coat of thick blue-gray cloth, tied with a leather belt, and tarred boots.

"Ah, hello, old man," cried Bazarov.

"Good day, Evgeny Vasilevich, sir," the old fellow began with a broad grin, so that his whole face was covered in wrinkles.

"What're you doing here? Have they sent for me, or what?"

"For goodness sake, sir, how could we?" Timofeich muttered (recalling the strict orders he'd received from his master before departure). "I was on my way to town on the master's business and heard you were here, sir, so I turned in along the way, that is—to have a look at you, sir . . . how could we think of disturbing you?"

"Come on now, don't lie," Bazarov said, interrupting him. "The road to town doesn't pass anywhere near here."

Timofeich hesitated and made no reply.

"Is father well?"

"Thank God, sir."

"And mother?"

"And Arina Vlasevna, glory be to God."

"I suppose they're waiting for me?"

The old man leaned his small head to one side.

"Ah, Evgeny Vasilevich, I'll say they're waiting, sir! So help me God, my heart aches just looking at your parents."

"Well, all right, all right! Don't carry on. Tell them I'll be there soon."

"Yes, sir," Timofeich replied with a sigh.

As he left the house, he pulled his cap down over his head with both hands, climbed into the dilapidated racing carriage left at the gate, and set off at a trot, not toward town.

That evening Anna Sergeevna was sitting in her room with Bazarov, while Arkady was pacing the hall listening to Katya's playing. The princess had retired to her own room upstairs; she couldn't stand guests in general, especially these "new wild-looking ones," as she called them. In the public rooms she merely sulked; but in her own room, in her maid's presence, she expressed her irritation in such abusive language, that her cap would bounce up and down on her head together with her wig. Odintsova had heard all about this.

"Why do you plan to leave us?" she began. "What about your promise?"

Bazarov was startled.

"What promise, madam?"

"You've forgotten. You offered to give me lessons in chemistry."

"What's to be done, madam? My father's waiting for me; it's impossible for me to remain here any longer. Besides, you can read Pelouse et Frémy, *Notions générales de chimie*;[7] it's a good book and very clearly written. You'll find everything you need in it."

"Don't you remember: you assured me a book could never replace . . . I forget exactly what you said, but you know what I mean . . . do you remember?"

"What's to be done, madam?" Bazarov repeated.

"Why must you leave?" Odintsova repeated, lowering her voice.

He looked at her. She'd rested her head on the back of the armchair and folded her arms, bare to the elbow, across her chest. She seemed pale in the light of one lamp covered by a perforated paper shade. Her ample white dress hid her completely beneath its gentle folds; her legs were crossed, and the ends of her feet could hardly be seen.

"Why stay?" replied Bazarov.

Odintsova turned her head slightly.

"What do you mean, why? Aren't you enjoying yourself here? Perhaps you think you won't be missed?"

"I'm sure about that."

Odintsova was silent.

"You're wrong. Besides, I don't believe you. You couldn't have said that seriously." Bazarov continued sitting there without moving. "Evgeny Vasilevich, why don't you say something?"

"What can I say? In general it's not worth missing people, especially me."

"Why so?"

"I'm an unimaginative, uninteresting man. I don't even know how to converse."

"You're fishing for compliments, Evgeny Vasilevich."

"That's not one of my habits. You know, don't you, the elegant side of life is inaccessible to me, that side you value so highly."

Odintsova bit the corner of her handkerchief.

"Think whatever you like, but I'll be bored after you leave."

"Arkady will be here," Bazarov remarked. Odintsova shrugged her shoulders slightly.

"I'll be bored," she repeated.

"Really? In any case, you won't be bored for long."

"Why do you think that?"

"Because you yourself told me you're bored only when your normal

---

7. *General Principles of Chemistry*, a work published in Paris in 1853 by Theophile Pelouse (1807–67) and Edmond Frémy (1814–94).

routine's disturbed. You've organized your life with such infallible precision, there's no room in it for boredom or depression . . . no painful feelings."

"You think I'm infallible . . . that is, I've organized my life in such a way?"

"I'll say! Here's an example: in a few minutes it'll be ten o'clock and I know full well you'll chase me out."

"No, I won't, Evgeny Vasilich. You may stay. Open that window . . . it's stuffy in here."

Bazarov stood up and pushed the window. It flew open with a loud noise . . . He hadn't expected it to move so easily; besides, his hands were trembling. The soft, dark night peered into the room with its almost black sky, its lightly rustling trees, and the fresh aroma of pure, free air.

"Lower the curtain and sit down," Odintsova said. "I'd like to talk to you before you leave. Tell me something about yourself; you never talk about yourself."

"I try to converse about useful matters, Anna Sergeevna."

"You're so modest . . . But I'd like to find out something about you, your family, your father—for whom you're forsaking us."

"Why does she say such things?" Bazarov wondered.

"All that isn't the least bit interesting," he said aloud, "especially for you; you and I are somber people . . ."

"And, in your opinion, I'm an aristocrat?"

Bazarov raised his eyes and looked at Odintsova.

"Yes," he replied with exaggerated abruptness.

She smiled.

"I see you don't know me very well, even though you're sure all people resemble one another and it's not worth studying them. Sometime I'll tell you the story of my life . . . but first you must tell me yours."

"I don't know you well," replied Bazarov. "Perhaps you're right; perhaps it's true that every person's a mystery. Take you, for example: you avoid society, feel oppressed by it—yet you've invited two students to visit you here. Why, with your intellect and beauty, do you choose to live in the country?"

"What? How did you put that?" Odintsova asked briskly. "With my . . . beauty?"

Bazarov frowned.

"It doesn't matter," he muttered. "I wanted to say that I really don't understand why you've settled down in the country."

"You don't understand . . . But you must explain it to yourself somehow."

"Yes . . . I suppose you choose to remain in one place because you've spoiled yourself, because you love comfort and convenience a great deal, and you're indifferent to all the rest."

Odintsova smiled again.

"You really don't want to believe I can be carried away?"

Bazarov glanced at her from under his brow.

"By curiosity, perhaps; but nothing else."

"Really? Well, now I can understand why we've become friends; you're just like me."

"Become friends . . ." Bazarov repeated hollowly.

Bazarov stood up. A lamp burnt dimly in the darkened, fragrant, solitary room; through the curtain, which billowed occasionally, the irritating freshness of night air flowed in and mysterious whispering could be heard. Odintsova didn't move a muscle, but a secret excitement was gradually overtaking her . . . It was communicated to Bazarov. He suddenly felt he was all alone with a beautiful young woman . . .

"Where're you going?" she asked slowly.

He made no reply and sank onto a chair.

"So, you consider me a placid, pampered, spoiled creature," she continued in the same voice, without taking her eyes off him. "While all I know about myself is I'm very unhappy."

"Unhappy! Why? Surely you can't attribute any significance to those idle rumors?"

Odintsova frowned. She was annoyed at the way he understood her.

"Those rumors don't even amuse me, Evgeny Vasilevich, and I'm too proud to let them disturb me. I'm unhappy because . . . I have no desire, no will to live. You're looking at me incredulously and thinking: here's an 'aristocrat' speaking, all dressed up in lace, sitting on a velvet armchair. I'm not hiding anything: I love what you call comfort, and at the same time I have little desire to live. Explain that contradiction as best you can. Besides, in your eyes it's all romanticism."

Bazarov shook his head.

"You're healthy, independent, rich; what else is there? What do you want?"

"What do I want?" Odintsova repeated and sighed. "I feel very tired and old; it seems as if I've been living for a long time. Yes, I'm old," she added, gently pulling the ends of her mantilla over her bare arms. Her eyes met Bazarov's and she blushed slightly. "There're so many memories behind me: life in Petersburg, wealth, then poverty, my father's death, marriage, then a trip abroad, just as it should be . . . Many memories, but nothing to remember, while ahead of me—a long, long path, but no goal . . . I really don't want to go on."

"Are you that disenchanted?" Bazarov asked.

"No," Odintsova replied slowly and deliberately, "but I'm not satisfied. It seems that if I could form a strong attachment to something . . ."

"You want to fall in love," Bazarov said, interrupting her, "but you can't: that explains your unhappiness."

Odintsova began examining the sleeves of her mantilla.

"Is it true I can't fall in love?" she asked.

"Hardly! But I wouldn't have called that unhappiness. On the contrary, a person to whom it happens is more deserving of pity."

"What happens?"

"Falling in love."

"How do you know that?"

"By hearsay," Bazarov replied angrily.

"You're flirting," he thought, "you're bored and teasing me because you've nothing better to do, while I . . . ." His heart was about to burst.

"Besides, perhaps you're too demanding," he said, leaning his whole body forward and playing with the fringe on the chair.

"Perhaps. In my opinion, it's either all or nothing. A life for a life. You take mine, you give up yours, without regrets, without turning back. Or else, why bother?"

"Well," remarked Bazarov, "those are fair conditions. But I'm surprised that up to now . . . you haven't found what you're looking for."

"Do you think it's easy to surrender yourself completely to whatever you want?"

"Not easy if you begin to reflect, waiting and assigning value to yourself, that is, appreciating yourself; but if you don't reflect, then it's easy to surrender yourself."

"How can you help but appreciate yourself? If I have no value, then who needs my devotion?"

"That's not really my business; it's someone else's job to determine my value. The main thing is, you must know how to surrender yourself."

Odintsova leaned forward in her chair.

"Don't talk like that," she began, "as if you've experienced it all."

"Incidentally, Anna Sergeevna: you should know that all this isn't in my line."

"But you'd know how to surrender yourself?"

"I don't know; I don't want to boast."

Odintsova didn't say anything and Bazarov fell silent. The sounds of the piano reached them from the drawing room.

"Why's Katya playing so late?" Odintsova inquired.

Bazarov stood up.

"Yes, it really is late and time for you to get some rest."

"Wait, where are you going? . . . I have one more thing to say to you."

"What's that?"

"Wait," she whispered.

Her eyes rested on Bazarov; she seemed to be scrutinizing him closely.

He walked around the room, then all of a sudden approached her, hurriedly said, "Good-bye," squeezed her hand so hard she almost cried, and left the room. She brought her crushed fingers to her lips, blew on them, and then, suddenly, stood up abruptly from her chair and headed to the door with rapid steps, as if wishing to call Bazarov back . . . The maid came into the room carrying a pitcher on a silver tray. Odintsova stopped, told her to go away, sat down again, and once more sank into thought. Her braid became undone and curled around her shoulder like a dark snake. A lamp remained lit for a long time in Anna Sergeevna's room, and she remained motionless for a long time, only occasionally rubbing her hands, which were being lightly nipped by the cold night air.

Meanwhile, two hours later, Bazarov returned to his room, his boots damp from the dew, looking disheveled and dismal. He found Arkady at the writing table with a book in his hands, his jacket buttoned up to his neck.

"You still haven't gone to bed?" he asked, as if annoyed.

"You were with Anna Sergeevna a long time today," Arkady said, without replying to his question.

"Yes, I was with her all the while you and Katya Sergeevna were playing the piano."

"I wasn't playing," Arkady began and then fell silent. He felt tears welling up in his eyes and didn't want to cry in front of his sarcastic friend.

XVIII

The next day when Odintsova appeared at tea, Bazarov sat leaning over his cup for some time, then suddenly looked up at her . . . She turned to him as if prodded; her face seemed to have become paler overnight. She soon returned to her own room and reappeared only at breakfast. The weather that morning was rainy, so there was no possibility of an outing. Everyone gathered in the drawing room. Arkady picked up the latest issue of a journal and began reading aloud. The princess's face expressed surprise at first, as was her custom, as if he were doing something indecent; then she began glaring at him angrily; he didn't pay her any attention.

"Evgeny Vasilevich," said Anna Sergeevna, "come to my room . . . I want to ask you something . . . Yesterday you mentioned a particular manual . . ."

She stood up and headed for the door. The princess looked around as if to say: "Look, see how amazed I am!" Once more she glared at Arkady, but he raised his voice and, exchanging glances with Katya, who was sitting next to him, continued reading.

Odintsova reached her study with hurried steps. Bazarov followed her quickly, without raising his eyes, merely catching the whispering and rustling sounds of her silk dress as it glided ahead of him. Odintsova lowered herself into the same armchair where she'd been sitting the night before, while Bazarov took up the same position he'd occupied yesterday.

"So what was the name of that book?" she began after a brief silence.

"Pelouse et Frémy, *Notions générales . . .*" Bazarov replied. "In addition, I can recommend Ganot, *Traité élémentaire de physique expérimentale.*[8] The drawings are clearer in that work, and in general the text's more . . ."

Odintsova stretched out her hand.

"Evgeny Vasilich, forgive me, but I didn't ask you here to discuss textbooks. I wanted to renew the conversation we began yesterday. You left so suddenly . . . Will it bore you?"

"I'm at your service, Anna Sergeevna. But what were we talking about yesterday?"

Odintsova threw a sidelong glance at Bazarov.

"It seems we were talking about happiness. I was telling you about myself. By the way, I just mentioned the word *happiness.* Tell me why it is that even when we're enjoying music, for example, or a pleasant evening, conversation with sympathetic people, why does all that seem more like an intimation of some immeasurable happiness that exists somewhere or other, rather than actual happiness, that is, the kind we ourselves possess? Why is this so? Perhaps you've never experienced this feeling?"

"You know the saying, 'The grass is always greener,' " replied Bazarov. "Besides, you yourself told me yesterday you weren't satisfied. It's true, though, such thoughts never enter my head."

"Perhaps you find them ridiculous?"

"No, but they never enter my head."

"Really? You know I'd really like to know what you do think about."

"What? I don't understand you."

"Listen, for some time now I've been wanting to have a frank conversation with you. There's no need to tell you—you know it all too well—you're not an ordinary sort of person; you're still young—your whole life's ahead of you. What're you preparing yourself for? What sort of future awaits you? I mean to say—what goal do you hope to achieve, where are you headed, what do you have in mind? In short, who are you and what are you?"

"You surprise me, Anna Sergeevna. You know I'm studying natural science, and as for who I am . . ."

"Yes, who are you?"

"I've already told you I'm a future district doctor."

Anna Sergeevna made an impatient movement.

"Why do you say that? You don't believe it. Arkady could answer me like that, but not you."

"What's Arkady got to do with this . . . ?"

"Stop it! Is it really possible you could be satisfied with such a modest

8. *Elementary Treatise of Experimental Physics*, a work published in Paris in 1851 by A. Ganot (1804–87).

occupation? Aren't you always maintaining that for you medicine doesn't exist? You—with your ambition—a district doctor! You're just saying that to escape from me, because you don't trust me. But you know, Evgeny Vasilich, I've managed to figure you out: I was poor and ambitious like you; I may have gone through the same trials as you."

"That's all splendid, Anna Sergeevna, but you must forgive me . . . In general I'm not accustomed to such frank pronouncements and there's such a distance separating you and me . . ."

"What kind of distance? Are you going to tell me once again that I'm an aristocrat? Enough of that, Evgeny Vasilich; I thought I'd proved to you that . . ."

"Yes, and besides that," Bazarov said, interrupting her, "why do you have such a desire to think and talk about the future, which, for the most part, doesn't depend on us? If the chance of doing something turns up, then fine; if not, then at least I can be content that I didn't prattle on about it needlessly."

"You call a friendly conversation 'prattle'? . . . Perhaps you don't consider me as a woman worthy of your confidence? Why, you despise all of us."

"I don't despise you, Anna Sergeevna, and you know that."

"No, I don't know anything . . . but let's suppose: I understand your disinclination to talk about your future; but as for what's transpiring within you now . . ."

" 'Transpiring!' " repeated Bazarov. "As if I were some state or society! In any case, it's not at all interesting; besides, is it really possible for a person always to say what's 'transpiring' within him?"

"I don't see why it isn't possible to say everything you have in mind."

"Can *you?*" Bazarov asked.

"I can," Anna Sergeevna replied after a brief hesitation.

Bazarov bowed his head.

"You're more fortunate than I."

Anna Sergeevna looked at him questioningly. "As you wish," she continued. "Something still tells me we've not come together in vain, that we'll become good friends. I'm sure that your—how shall I say?— your reticence, reserve will eventually disappear."

"So you've noticed my reserve . . . how else did you put it . . . my reticence?"

"I have."

Bazarov stood up and went over to the window.

"And you'd like to know the reason for my reserve; you'd like to know what's transpiring within me?"

"Yes," Odintsova repeated with some apprehension that she didn't quite comprehend.

"And you won't get angry?"

"I won't."

"You won't?" Bazarov stood with his back to her. "Then you should know that I love you, stupidly, madly . . . Now see what you've extracted."

Odintsova stretched out both her arms, while Bazarov pressed his forehead against the window. He was breathing hard; his whole body was trembling visibly. But it was not the trembling of youthful timidity or the sweet fretting over a first declaration of love that overcame him: it was passion struggling within him—powerful and painful—passion that resembled malice and was perhaps even related to it . . . Odintsova was both afraid of him and felt sorry for him.

"Evgeny Vasilich," she said with a touch of unintended tenderness in her voice.

He turned around quickly, threw her a devouring look—and, seizing both her hands, suddenly drew her to his chest.

She didn't free herself from his embrace immediately; but a moment later she was standing far away in the corner, looking at Bazarov from there. He rushed toward her.

"You've misunderstood me," she whispered in hurried alarm. It seemed that if he took another step, she'd scream . . . Bazarov bit his lips and left the room.

Half an hour later the maid brought Anna Sergeevna a note from Bazarov; it consisted of only one line: "Must I leave today—or may I stay until tomorrow?" "Why leave? I didn't understand you—you didn't understand me," Anna Sergeevna replied, and thought to herself: "I didn't even understand myself."

She didn't appear until dinner and kept pacing her room, arms behind her back, stopping from time to time in front of the window or the mirror, slowly wiping her handkerchief over her neck where she still seemed to feel a burning spot. She kept asking herself what had compelled her to "extract," as Bazarov had put it, his candor; hadn't she suspected something of that sort? . . . "I'm to blame," she muttered aloud, "but I couldn't have foreseen it." She became pensive and then blushed, remembering Bazarov's almost savage face as he threw himself at her . . .

"Or else?" she suddenly said aloud, stopped, and tossed back her curls . . . She looked at herself in the mirror; her head thrown back, a mysterious smile on her half-closed, half-open lips, and at that moment her eyes seemed to tell her something she found embarrassing . . .

"No," she decided once and for all, "God knows where it might have led; one mustn't fool around with this kind of thing; serenity is still better than anything else on earth."

Her composure wasn't shaken, but she felt sad, even shed a few tears, not knowing why, but not from any insult inflicted on her. She didn't feel insulted: instead she felt guilty. Under the influence of various vague emotions, an awareness of life passing by, a desire for novelty, she'd forced herself to reach a certain point, to look beyond it—and there she glimpsed not even an abyss, but emptiness . . . or formless hideousness.

XIX

No matter how great Odintsova's self-control, how distanced she was from every sort of prejudice, she still felt uncomfortable at dinner in the dining room. But the meal passed rather smoothly. Porfiry Platonych arrived and told various anecdotes; he'd just returned from town. Among other things, he said that the governor, Bourdaloue,[9] had issued a special order to all his subordinates to wear spurs, just in case he should have to dispatch them on horseback in a great hurry. Arkady was conversing with Katya in a low voice and diplomatically attending to the princess. Bazarov was stubbornly and morosely silent. Two or three times Odintsova glanced—directly, not stealthily—at his face, which was stern and irritable, his eyes downcast, signs of contemptuous resolution visible in every feature, and she thought, "No . . . no . . . no . . ." After dinner she went into the garden with all the assembled guests; noticing that Bazarov wished to speak with her, she took several steps to one side and stopped. He drew near, but even then didn't raise his eyes and said in a hollow voice, "I must apologize, Anna Sergeevna. You must be furious with me."

"No, I'm not angry, Evgeny Vasilich," replied Odintsova, "but I am chagrined."

"So much the worse. In any case, I've been punished enough. My position, as you'll doubtless agree, is ridiculous. You wrote, 'Why leave?' I can't stay and don't care to. I'll be gone by tomorrow."

"Evgeny Vasilich, why are you . . ."

"Leaving?"

"No, that's not what I wanted to say."

"You can't bring back the past, Anna Sergeevna . . . sooner or later this was bound to happen. Therefore, I must leave. I can imagine only one condition under which I could stay, but that condition can never be. Excuse my audacity, but you don't love me and never will, isn't that so?"

Bazarov's eyes glittered for an instant from under his dark brows.

Anna Sergeevna didn't reply. "I'm afraid of this man" flashed through her mind.

"Farewell, madame," Bazarov said, as if guessing her thought, and headed back to the house.

Anna Sergeevna walked behind him slowly and, after calling Katya, took her by the hand. She didn't part from her until evening. She didn't play cards and kept laughing frequently, in marked contrast to her pale and worried look. Arkady didn't understand and kept an eye on her as

9. See above, p. 48 and n. 7.

young people tend to do, that is, constantly wondering what it all meant. Bazarov locked himself in his room, but came down for tea. Anna Sergeevna wanted to say a kind word or two to him, but didn't know where to begin . . .

An unexpected coincidence rescued her from the difficult situation: the butler announced Sitnikov's arrival.

It's difficult to convey in words exactly how the young progressive came bursting into the room like a quail. He'd decided, with his characteristic impudence, to set out for the country and visit a woman he hardly knew and who'd never invited him, but with whom, according to his various sources of information, many of his intelligent and intimate friends were staying. Still, he felt timid through and through; instead of using all the apologies and greetings he'd prepared in advance, he mumbled some nonsense to the effect that Evdoksiya, that is, Kukshina, had sent him to inquire about Anna Sergeevna's health and that Arkady Nikolaevich had always sung the highest praises of . . . At this point he hesitated and became so confused he sat on his hat. However, when no one turned him away and Anna Sergeevna even introduced him to her aunt and sister, he quickly recovered and began chatting merrily. The appearance of mediocrity is sometimes a useful thing in life: it soothes strings that have been stretched too taut and it sobers emotions that have become too self-confident or forgetful, suggesting their own close proximity to the mediocre. With Sitnikov's arrival everything became somehow duller—and simpler; everyone even ate a heartier supper and toddled off to bed half an hour earlier than usual.

"Now I can repeat to you," Arkady said, as he got into bed, to Bazarov, who was undressing, "something you once said to me: 'Why are you so depressed? Did you just carry out some sacred duty?' "

For some time now an artificially casual banter had been established between the two friends, a sure sign of secret dissatisfaction or unstated suspicion.

"Tomorrow I'm going home to see my old man," Bazarov replied.

Arkady raised himself up and rested on his elbow. He was both surprised and, for some reason or other, delighted.

"Ah!" he said. "Is that why you're depressed?"

Bazarov yawned. "If you know too much, you'll grow old too soon."

"What about Anna Sergeevna?" continued Arkady.

"What about Anna Sergeevna?"

"I mean, will she really let you go?"

"I'm not her hired hand."

Arkady became pensive, while Bazarov lay down and turned his face to the wall.

A few moments of silence passed.

"Evgeny!" cried Arkady suddenly.

"What?"

"I'm going with you tomorrow."

Bazarov made no reply.

"But I'll head for home," Arkady continued. "We can travel together as far as the Khokhlovsky settlement, and there you can get fresh horses from Fedot. I'd like to meet your parents, but I'm afraid to trouble them and you. You'll come back to us later, won't you?"

"I've left my things there," Bazarov answered, without turning over.

"How come he doesn't ask me why I'm leaving, and just as suddenly as he is?" wondered Arkady. "Come to think of it, why am I leaving and why is he?" he continued his reflections. He couldn't answer his own question satisfactorily, and his heart filled with bitterness. He felt it would be hard for him to part from this life to which he'd grown so accustomed; but it would also be awkward for him to stay on alone. "Something's happened between them," he said to himself. "Why should I hang around here in her presence after he's gone? She'll get sick and tired of me once and for all; I'll lose what little remains." He began to think about Anna Sergeevna, but then someone else's features gradually eclipsed the image of the lovely young widow.

"I also feel sorry for Katya!" Arkady said softly into his pillow, on which a tear had already fallen . . . Suddenly he tossed back his hair and said aloud, "Why on earth did that idiot Sitnikov turn up here?"

At first Bazarov stirred in his bed, then replied, "My boy, I can see you're still a fool. Sitnikovs are indispensable to us. Understand this: I need dolts like him. Not God, but man makes pot and pan!"

"Oho!" Arkady thought; it was then and only for a moment that the broad expanse of Bazarov's conceit was revealed to him. "Are you and I gods, then? That is, if you're a god, I must be a dolt?"

"Yes," repeated Bazarov gloomily, "you're still a fool."

Odintsova displayed no particular surprise the next day when Arkady told her he'd be leaving with Bazarov; she seemed absentminded and tired. Katya gave him a silent, serious look; the princess even made the sign of the cross under her shawl, so he couldn't see it; on the other hand, Sitnikov was completely disconcerted. He'd only just come down to breakfast wearing a fashionable new outfit, this time not in the Slavophile style; the previous evening he'd astonished the servant assigned to him by the amount of linen he'd brought along. And now, all of a sudden, his comrades were deserting him! He took a few dainty steps, then rushed around like a hunted hare at the edge of the woods—and suddenly, almost in fear, almost in a wail, announced that he too intended to leave. Odintsova made no attempt to detain him.

"I have a very smooth carriage," the young man added, turning to Arkady. "I can give you a ride. Evgeny Vasilich can take your coach, so it'll be even more comfortable."

"But wait a minute, it's out of your way and quite far to my place."

"Never mind, it's no trouble; I've lots of time. Besides, I have some business in that area."

"Tax farming?" asked Arkady, rather too contemptuously.

But Sitnikov was so desperate he didn't even laugh as usual. "I assure you the carriage is extremely smooth," he muttered, "and there's room for everyone."

"Don't offend Mr. Sitnikov by refusing," Anna Sergeevna said . . .

Arkady glanced at her and lowered his head in agreement.

The guests departed after breakfast. Saying good-bye to Bazarov, Odintsova stretched out her hand and said, "We'll see each other again, won't we?"

"As you wish," replied Bazarov.

"In that case, we will."

Arkady was the first to emerge onto the porch; he climbed into Sitnikov's carriage. The butler rendered polite assistance, but Arkady would gladly have hit him or else burst into tears. Bazarov took his place in the coach. Having reached the Khokhlovsky settlement, Arkady waited until Fedot, the proprietor of the coaching inn, had harnessed the fresh horses; then, going up to the coach, he said to Bazarov with his previous grin, "Evgeny, take me with you; I want to visit your house."

"Get in," Bazarov replied through his teeth.

Sitnikov, who'd been walking around whistling boldly near the wheels of his carriage, merely gaped in surprise when he heard these last words. Arkady coolly removed his things from the carriage and climbed in next to Bazarov. Bowing politely to his former traveling companion, he cried, "Let's go!" The coach started up and soon vanished from sight . . . Sitnikov, completely bewildered, looked at his coachman, but he was busy flicking his whip above the tail of the tracehorse.[1] Then Sitnikov jumped into his carriage and, after bellowing at two passing peasants, "Put on your caps, you idiots!" drove back to town, where he arrived very late and where, at Kukshina's the following day, he didn't mince his words about those two "repulsive, arrogant, stupid louts."

Sitting next to Bazarov in the coach, Arkady squeezed his hand warmly and for a long time said nothing. Bazarov seemed to understand and appreciate both the gesture and the silence. He hadn't slept at all the previous night, hadn't smoked, and had hardly eaten anything for the last few days. His spare profile stood out glumly and sharply from under the cáp pulled way down on his head.

"Well, my boy," he said at last, "give me a cigar, will you? Have a look: is my tongue yellow?"

"It is," replied Arkady.

"Well, yes . . . and the cigar doesn't taste very good. The machine's falling apart."

"You've really changed of late," observed Arkady.

"Never mind! We'll recover. One thing's a nuisance—my mother's so tenderhearted: if your belly doesn't swell and you don't eat ten times

1. See above, p. 7, n. 3.

a day, she gets very upset. But my father's all right; he's been around, had his ups and downs. No, I can't smoke," he added, tossing the cigar onto the dusty road.

"Is it about twenty-five versts to your estate?" asked Arkady.

"Yes. But you can ask this sage here."

He pointed to the peasant sitting on the box, one of Fedot's workers.

But the sage replied, "How in 'ell should I know—versts ain't counted 'ereabouts," and continued in a low voice to abuse the shafthorse for "kickin' with his headpiece," by which he meant jerking his head.

"Yes, yes," said Bazarov, "let it be a lesson to you, my young friend, an instructive example. The devil only knows what sort of nonsense it all is! Every man hangs by a thread, an abyss can open up beneath him at any moment, he can create all sorts of unpleasantness for himself, spoil his whole life."

"What are you hinting at?" asked Arkady.

"I'm not hinting at anything. I'm saying plainly that you and I behaved very foolishly. What's to explain? But as I've already observed in the hospital, a person who gets angry at his own illness is sure to overcome it."

"I don't quite understand you," Arkady said. "It seems to me you've nothing to complain about."

"Since you don't quite understand me, let me inform you of the following: in my opinion, it's better to break rocks on a roadway than to let a woman gain control of even the tip of one's little finger. That's all . . ." Bazarov almost uttered his favorite word *romanticism*, but restrained himself and said, "nonsense." "You won't believe me now, but let me say this: you and I fell into the society of women and found it very pleasant; forsaking society of that sort is just like splashing yourself with cold water on a hot day. Men have no time to waste on such trifles. A man must be fierce, says a splendid Spanish proverb. Why, you," he added, turning to the peasant sitting on the box, "you know-it-all, do you have a wife?"

The peasant turned his dull and weak-sighted face to the two friends.

"A wife? Sure, I do. Why not?"

"Do you beat her?"

"My wife? Anything can happen. I don't beat her for no reason."

"Splendid. And does she beat you?"

The peasant tugged at the reins.

"What a thing to say, sir. You do like to have a joke . . ." He was obviously offended.

"You hear, Arkady Nikolaevich? You and I were given a beating . . . that's what it means to be educated men."

Arkady gave a forced laugh, but Bazarov turned away and didn't open his mouth all the rest of the way.

Those twenty-five versts seemed like fifty to Arkady. But then, on the slope of a gently rising hill at long last there appeared a small village where Bazarov's parents lived. Next to it, in a grove of young birch trees, they could see a small manor house with a thatched roof. Two peasants wearing caps stood in front of the first hut and traded insults. "You're a big pig," one said to the other, "worse than a little piglet." "And your wife's a witch," the other retorted.

"From the lack of restraint in their mode of address," Bazarov observed to Arkady, "and by the playfulness of their expressions, you can tell my father's peasants aren't overly oppressed. Here he comes himself onto the porch of the house. He must've heard the bells. That's him, that's him—I recognize his figure. Hey! how gray he's become, the poor old fellow!"

XX

Bazarov leaned out of his carriage, while Arkady poked his head around his comrade's back and saw on the little porch of the manor house a tall, gaunt man with disheveled hair and a thin aquiline nose, dressed in an old, unfastened military jacket. He stood there, legs wide apart, smoking a long pipe, his eyes squinting from the sun.

The horses stopped.

"Home at last," said Bazarov's father, continuing to smoke, although the pipe was bobbing up and down in his fingers. "Well, get out, get out, let me give you a hug."

He began embracing his son . . . "Enyusha, Enyusha,"[2] a trembling woman's voice exclaimed The door flew open and on the threshold appeared a squat, short old woman, wearing a white cap and a short colorful blouse. She cried out, swayed a bit, and certainly would've collapsed if Bazarov hadn't caught her. Her plump arms were instantly entwined around his neck, her head pressed to his chest, and there was complete silence. The only sound was that of her intermittent sobbing.

Old man Bazarov was breathing deeply and squinting even more than before.

"Well, enough, enough, Arisha! Stop it," he said, exchanging glances with Arkady, who was standing near the carriage while even the peasant sitting on the box had turned away. "That's not necessary at all! Please, stop it."

"Ah, Vasily Ivanych," the old woman muttered, "it's been so long, my dear, darling boy, my Enyushenka . . ." and, without letting him go, moved her gentle, tender, tear-stained face away, looked at him with her blissful, comical eyes, and once again fell on him.

"Well, yes, of course, it's all in the nature of things," Vasily Ivanych said, "but we'd better go inside. Look, a guest has come with Evgeny.

---

2. One of several affectionate diminutive forms of Evgeny used by his mother (cf. below "En-yushenka" and "Enyushechka").

Forgive me," he added, turning to Arkady, and shuffled one foot a little. "You understand, it's a woman's weakness; well, and a mother's heart . . ."

But his own lips and eyebrows were also twitching, his chin trembling . . . obviously he was trying to control his emotions and appear almost indifferent. Arkady bowed.

"Let's go in, Mother, really," said Bazarov and led the weakened old woman into the house. After sitting her in an armchair, he gave his father another quick hug and then introduced Arkady to him.

"Delighted to make your acquaintance," said Vasily Ivanovich. "You mustn't be too hard on us: everything here's very plain and simple, like the military. Calm down, Arina Vlasevna, do me a favor. Why so fainthearted? What will our distinguished visitor think?"

"Sir," the old woman said through her tears, "I haven't the honor of knowing your first name and patronymic . . ."

"Arkady Nikolaich," Vasily Ivanych prompted her solemnly in a loud whisper.

"Forgive a stupid old woman like me." She blew her nose and, leaning her head first to the right, then to the left, carefully wiped one eye after the other. "You'll excuse me. Why, I thought I might even die before ever getting to see my da-a-arling little boy again."

"Now you've seen him, madame," Vasily Ivanovich inserted. "Tan-yushka," he said, turning to a barefoot girl of thirteen, wearing a bright red cotton dress, timidly peeking in at the door. "Bring the mistress a glass of water—on a tray, you hear? And you, gentlemen," he added with old-fashioned playfulness, "allow a retired old veteran to invite you into his study."

"Just let me hug you once more, Enyushechka," Arina Vlasevna moaned. Bazarov leaned over to her. "What a handsome man you've become!"

"Well, handsome or not," observed Vasily Ivanovich, "still a man, as they say, *ommfay*.[3] Now I hope, Arina Vlasevna, having satisfied your maternal heart, you'll begin to worry about satisfying the appetites of your dear guests because, as you know, even nightingales can't live on fairy tales alone."

The old woman stood up from her chair.

"Right away, Vasily Ivanych, the table will be set, I'll run to the kitchen myself and have the samovar heated. Everything'll be ready, everything. I haven't seen him for three years, haven't served him any food or drink. Do you think it's been easy?"

"Well, go on then, little housewife, get busy, don't disgrace us; mean-while, gentlemen, I invite you to follow me. Here's Timofeich come

3. *Homme fait*: "a real man" (French).

to pay his respects to you, Evgeny. He's happy, too, the old dog, I can tell. What? Happy, aren't you, you old dog? Please follow me."

Vasily Ivanovich bustled on ahead, shuffling and scraping his worn-out slippers.

His entire abode consisted of six little rooms. One of them, where he led our friends, was called the study. A thick-legged table, piled high with papers black from dust, looking as if they'd been smoked, occupied all the space between the two windows; on the walls hung Turkish guns, whips and sabers, two maps, some anatomical drawings, a portrait of Hufeland,[4] a monogram made of hair in a black frame, and a mounted diploma; a leather sofa, worn and torn in places, stood between two enormous cupboards of Karelian birchwood; the shelves were crowded with books, boxes, stuffed birds, jars, and vials in disarray; in one corner stood some broken electric gadget.

"I warned you, my dear guest," Vasily Ivanych began, "we live here, so to speak, in a bivouac . . ."

"Stop it! Why are you apologizing?" Bazarov said, interrupting him. "Kirsanov knows full well we're no Croesuses[5] and you don't own a palace. Where will we put him, that's the question?"

"Yes, of course, Evgeny; there's an excellent room in the wing next to me: he'll be fine there."

"So you've added a wing, have you?"

"Yes, sir; where the bathhouse is, sir," Timofeich inserted.

"That is, next to the bathhouse," Vasily Ivanovich added hurriedly. "It's summer now . . . I'll go over there right away and arrange things myself; meanwhile, Timofeich, you bring their things. Evgeny, you'll take my study, of course. *Suum cuique.*"[6]

"That's my father! An amusing old man and very kind," Bazarov added as soon as Vasily Ivanovich had left. "Just as eccentric as your father, but in a different way. He chatters a great deal."

"And your mother seems to be a wonderful woman," Arkady remarked.

"Yes, lacking all guile. Just see what kind of dinner she'll fix us."

"They weren't expecting you today, sir; no beef's been delivered," said Timofeich, who'd just dragged in Bazarov's case.

"We'll manage without beef; where nothing is, nothing can be had. Poverty, they say, is no sin."

"How many serfs does your father own?" Arkady asked suddenly.

"The estate belongs to my mother, not him; if I remember correctly, they have fifteen serfs."

"Twenty-two in all," Timofeich observed with some dissatisfaction.

---

4. Chistoph Wilhelm Hufeland (1762–1836), a well-respected German physician famous for his treatise entitled *On Extending the Human Life Span* (1796).
5. Croesus, the last king of Lydia (c. 560–546 B.C.), ruled a large part of Asia Minor. He had a reputation among the Greeks for incredible wealth.
6. "To each his own" (Latin).

They heard slippers shuffling, and Vasily Ivanovich appeared once again.

"Your room'll be ready for you in a little while," he exclaimed triumphantly. "Arkady . . . it's Nikolaich, isn't it? Here's a servant for you," he added, pointing to a closely cropped young boy wearing a blue caftan with worn-out elbows and someone else's boots. "His name's Fedka. Once more, I repeat, though my son forbids it, you mustn't expect too much. But he knows how to fill a pipe. You smoke, don't you?"

"Mostly cigars," Arkady replied.

"That's very sensible of you. I prefer cigars, too, but it's extremely difficult to obtain them in remote areas like this."

"Stop bemoaning your fate," Bazarov said, interrupting him again. "Why don't you sit here on the sofa and let me get a good look at you."

Vasily Ivanovich laughed and sat down. He looked a great deal like his son, but his brow was lower and narrower, his mouth somewhat wider, and he was constantly in motion, shrugging his shoulders as if his coat cut him under the arms, blinking, coughing, wiggling his fingers, while his son was marked by his casual immobility.

"Bemoaning my fate!" repeated Vasily Ivanovich. "Evgeny, don't think I'm trying to win our guest's sympathy by telling him we live in the boondocks. On the contrary, I'm of the opinion that for a thinking man there's no such thing as boondocks. At least I try, as far as possible, not to let any grass grow under my feet, as they say, not to fall behind the times."

Vasily Ivanovich pulled from his pocket a new yellow handkerchief that he'd managed to pick up when he ran to Arkady's room; waving it in the air, he continued, "I'm not even alluding to the fact that I, for example, not without considerable sacrifice on my part, put my peasants on the quitrent system and have given them land for sharecropping.[7] I considered this my duty; common sense dictates as much in this case, although other landowners don't even dream of such a solution. I'm talking about science, education."

"Yes. I see you have here the 1855 edition of *The Friend of Health*,"[8] remarked Bazarov.

"An old comrade sends it to me out of friendship," Vasily Ivanovich said hurriedly, "but even we, for example, have some idea of phrenology," he added, turning, however, more to Arkady and pointing toward the cupboard housing a small plaster head divided into numbered squares. "We've heard about Schönlein[9] and Rademacher[1] as well."

---

7. The technical term is *métayage*: a system of land cultivation under which peasants farmed the landowner's estate in return for a share of the crop.
8. A newspaper for doctors published in Petersburg from 1833 to 1869.
9. Johann Lukas Schönlein (1793–1864), a German doctor and professor of medicine.
1. Johann Gottfried Rademacher (1772–1849), a German doctor and follower of Philippus Paracelsus (1493?–1541), Swiss physician and alchemist who advocated the use of specific remedies for specific diseases.

"Do people out in this province of ours still believe in Rademacher?" Bazarov inquired.

Vasily Ivanovich cleared his throat.

"In this province of ours . . . Of course, you gentlemen know better; how could we possibly keep up with you? Why, you've come along to replace us. In my own time some humoralist named Hoffmann[2] and some vitalist called Brown[3] seemed ridiculous to us, but they too had their day. Someone new has taken Rademacher's place and you idolize him; but in twenty years or so, perhaps, they'll probably be making fun of him."

"I'll say this to console you," said Bazarov. "Nowadays we make fun of medicine in general and don't bow down before anyone."

"How can that be? Don't you want to become a doctor?"

"Yes, but one thing doesn't prevent the other."

Vasily Ivanovich poked his middle finger into his pipe, where a small amount of burning ash still remained.

"Well, perhaps, perhaps—I don't want to argue. Besides, what am I? A retired army doctor, *voyla-too*;[4] and now I've become an agronomist. I served in your grandfather's regiment," he said, turning once again to Arkady. "Yes, sir; yes, sir; I've seen quite a bit in my time, I have. I've been in society, known all sorts of people! I myself, the man you see before you now, have shaken hands and felt the pulse both of Prince Wittgenstein[5] and Zhukovsky![6] They were in the southern army, on the fourteenth of December,[7] you understand [here Vasily Ivanovich pursed his lips knowingly]. I knew each and every one of them. But my work lay elsewhere: know your lancet, and that's that! Your grandfather was a well-respected man, a true soldier."

"Confess, he was a real blockhead," Bazarov said lazily.

"Oh, Evgeny, don't say things like that! Mercy! . . . Of course, General Kirsanov wasn't one of those who . . ."

"Well, never mind him," Bazarov said, interrupting him. "As I was approaching the house, I was glad to see your birch grove; it's taken nicely."

Vasily Ivanovich grew animated.

"Just wait 'til you see my little garden! I planted each and every tree myself. There are fruit trees, berries, all sorts of medicinal herbs. No

2. Friedrich Hoffmann (1660–1742), a German doctor and humoralist who believed that illness was the result of an imbalance in the body's fluids or "humors."
3. John Brown (1735–88), an English doctor and vitalist who maintained that life is sustained by a vital principle distinct from all physical and chemical forces.
4. *Voilà tout*: "that's all" (French).
5. Prince Peter Wittgenstein (1768–1842), a field marshal in the Russian army who participated in the War of 1812 against Napoleon and commanded the southern army from 1818 to 1828.
6. Vasily Zhukovsky (1783–1852), a leading preromantic poet and translator.
7. A reference to the rebellion staged in Petersburg on December 14, 1825, by the members of the Society of Decembrists, a group of army officers.

matter how smart you young fellows are, old man Paracelsus[8] spoke the truth when he said: *in herbis, verbis et lapidibus*[9] . . . You know, I don't practice anymore, but two or three times a week I'm obliged to relive the past. Folks come to me for advice—I can't chase them away. Sometimes the poor come for my help. There aren't any doctors around here. Imagine, one of my neighbors, a retired major, also treats patients. So I asked whether he'd ever studied medicine . . . They reply, 'No, he hasn't; he does it more out of philanthropy . . . ' Ha, ha! Philanthropy! Eh? That's something! Ha, ha! Ha, ha!"

"Fedka! Fill me a pipe!" Bazarov said harshly.

"There used to be another doctor around here who once visited a patient," Vasily Ivanovich continued in some desperation, "but the patient was already *ad patres*;[1] the servant wouldn't let the doctor in, saying it was no longer necessary. The doctor hadn't expected that, was embarrassed and asked, 'Did your master hiccup before he died?' 'Yes, sir.' 'Did he hiccup a great deal?' 'A great deal.' 'Well, that's good,' he said and turned to leave. Ha, ha, ha!"

The old man was the only one laughing; Arkady managed to smile. Bazarov merely inhaled on his pipe. The conversation went on like this for about an hour; Arkady was able to slip away temporarily to his little room, which did turn out to be attached to the bathhouse, but was very clean and comfortable. At last Tanyusha came in and announced that dinner was served.

Vasily Ivanovich was the first to stand up.

"Let's go, gentlemen! Forgive me if I've bored you. Perhaps the mistress will satisfy you better."

Dinner, even though hastily prepared, turned out to be very good, even sumptuous; only the wine could be found wanting: it was almost dark sherry, purchased by Timofeich from a merchant he knew in town. It tasted not quite like copper, not quite like resin; the flies were also a bother. On ordinary days a servant boy used to chase them off by waving a large green branch; but on this occasion Vasily Ivanovich had sent him away for fear of being condemned by the younger generation. Arina Vlasevna had had time to dress up; she'd put on a tall cap with silk ribbons and a light blue patterned shawl. She began to cry once again as soon as she set eyes on her Enyusha, but her husband didn't even have to admonish her: she quickly wiped away her tears so as not to stain her shawl. Only the young people ate: the master and mistress had eaten their dinner some time before. Fedka served the meal, obviously encumbered by unfamiliar boots; he was aided by a woman named Anfisushka, who had a masculine face and only one eye, who performed the duties of housekeeper, poultry keeper, and laundress. All during

8. See above, p. 89, n. 1.
9. "In herbs, words and minerals" (Latin).
1. "To [one's] fathers," i.e., dead (Latin).

dinner Vasily Ivanovich paced the room with a completely happy, even blissful expression, talking about his serious misgivings concerning Napoleon's policies and the complexity of the Italian question.[2] Arina Vlasevna paid no attention to Arkady, failing to regale him with her hospitality. She supported her round face on her small closed fist. Her full, cherry red lips and the moles both on her cheeks and over her brows imparted a good-natured expression to her face. She never took her eyes off her son and sighed constantly; she desperately wanted to know how long he was going to stay, but was afraid to ask. "Well, what if he says only two days," she thought, and her heart almost stopped. After the main course Vasily Ivanovich disappeared for a minute and returned with an opened half-bottle of champagne. "Here," he exclaimed, "even though we live in the boondocks, we still have ways to celebrate special occasions!" He filled three goblets and a little wineglass, toasted the health of their "inestimable visitors," immediately downed his glass military style, and forced Arina Vlasevna to drink hers to the very last drop. When time came for preserves, Arkady, who didn't care for sweets, thought it his duty to sample four different kinds, all freshly made, all the more so since Bazarov flatly refused and promptly lit up a cigar. Tea was served—with cream, butter, and biscuits; then Vasily Ivanovich led them all into the garden to admire the beauty of the evening. Walking past a bench he whispered to Arkady, "This is where I love to sit and philosophize while watching the sun set: it suits an old hermit like me. Over there I planted a few of the trees beloved by Horace."

"What kind of trees?" Bazarov asked, overhearing.

"Why acacias . . . of course."

Bazarov began to yawn.

"I suppose it's time our travelers were nestled in the arms of Morpheus," observed Vasily Ivanovich.

"That is, it's time for bed!" Bazarov interjected. "That's a fair judgment. It *is* time."

Saying good night to his mother, he kissed her forehead; she embraced him and stealthily crossed him three times behind his back. Vasily Ivanovich accompanied Arkady to his room and wished him "the same kind of refreshing repose I enjoyed when I was your tender age." As a matter of fact, Arkady slept very well in his little room attached to the bathhouse: it smelled of mint, and two crickets took turns chirping soporifically behind the stove. Vasily Ivanovich left Arkady and returned to his study. Perching on the sofa at his son's feet, he hoped to have a nice chat with him, but Bazarov sent him away at once, saying that he wanted to sleep; but he didn't fall asleep until morning. Eyes wide open, he stared vindictively into the darkness: childhood memories had no

---

2. Italy's struggle for independence from Austria and for national unification was frequently discussed in the Russian press during the 1850s.

power over him; however, he still hadn't managed to rid himself of recent bitter impressions. Arina Vlasevna first prayed to her heart's content, then had a very long chat with Anfisushka, who stood as if rooted to the spot before her mistress, her solitary eye fixed on her, conveying in a mysterious whisper all her observations and speculations about Evgeny Vasilevich. The old woman's head was spinning from joy, the wine, and cigar smoke; her husband tried speaking with her, but gave up.

Arina Vlasevna was a genuine Russian noblewoman of the old school; she should have lived some two hundred years earlier, in the days of old Muscovy.[3] She was very devout and emotional, believing in all sorts of omens, fortune-telling, charms, and dreams; she believed in holy fools, house spirits, forest spirits, unlucky meetings, the evil eye, folk remedies, Maundy salt,[4] and the imminent end of the world; she believed that if on Easter Sunday the candles didn't go out during the midnight service, there'd be a good buckwheat harvest, and if a person looked at a mushroom, it wouldn't grow any bigger; she believed the devil liked to be near water, and that every Jew carried a bloodstain on his chest; she was afraid of mice, snakes, frogs, sparrows, leeches, thunder, cold water, drafts of air, horses, goats, redheaded people, and black cats; she regarded crickets and dogs as unclean animals; she didn't eat veal, pigeon, crayfish, cheese, asparagus, artichokes, rabbit, or watermelon because a cut watermelon reminded her of the head of John the Baptist; and she couldn't mention oysters without shuddering. She loved to eat, but maintained strict fasts; she slept ten hours out of every twenty-four and didn't go to bed at all if Vasily Ivanovich had a headache; she'd never read a single book, except for *Alexis, or the Cottage in the Forest*,[5] and she wrote only one—at most two—letters a year; but she certainly knew how to run a household, dry produce, and make preserves, even though she never touched anything with her own hands and in general preferred to remain seated in one place. Arina Vlasevna was very kind and, in her own way, not at all stupid. She understood that there were some people on earth who were supposed to give orders and other, simple folk who were supposed to take orders, so she showed no aversion to servility or prostrations; but she always treated subordinates politely and kindly, never let a begger go away empty-handed, and never condemned anyone outright, although she was partial to a little gossip from time to time. In her youth she'd been very attractive, played the clavichord, and spoken a little French; but over the course of considerable wandering with her husband, whom she'd married against her will, she'd put on weight and forgotten both her music and her French. She loved and

3. Ancient name of the Russian state.
4. A folk remedy for various ailments consisting of thickened kvass (traditional Russian beverage) mixed with salt and brewed on the Thursday of Easter week.
5. A sentimental novel (1788) by the French writer Ducray-Duminil (1761–1819), which was translated into Russian three times and became very popular in the early nineteenth century.

feared her son incredibly; she left the running of the estate to Vasily
Ivanovich—and refused to interfere in any way: she used to groan, wave
her handkerchief, and raise her eyebrows higher and higher in horror
as soon as her husband began talking about the impending reforms and
his own machinations. She was apprehensive, constantly anticipating
some great misfortune, and used to cry whenever she thought about
anything sad . . . Such women are now becoming much harder to find.
God knows whether that's a good or a bad thing!

XXI

After getting out of bed, Arkady opened the window—the first thing
he saw was Vasily Ivanovich. Dressed in an Oriental robe fastened at
the waist with a very large handkerchief, the old man was digging en-
ergetically in his garden. He noticed his young guest; resting on his
shovel, he exclaimed, "Good health to you! Did you sleep well?"

"Splendidly," replied Arkady.

"Here I am, you see, just like Cincinnatus,[6] preparing a bed for some
late turnips. The time has come—thank the Lord!—when everyone
should provide his own sustenance with his own hands. There's no need
to rely on others; one must do one's own work. It seems Jean-Jacques
Rousseau[7] was right. Half an hour ago, my good sir, you'd have seen
me in a completely different situation. An old country woman was
complaining of the gripes—that's her language; we call it dysentery; I
. . . how can I best explain it? . . . I gave her a dose of opium; for another
woman, I extracted a tooth. I offered her some ether . . . but she refused.
All this I do *gratis—anamater*.[8] It's no wonder I do it: I'm a plebian,
after all, *homo novus*[9]—not from a well-established family like my better
half . . . Would you like to come out here in the shade and get a breath
of fresh air before morning tea?"

Arkady went out to join him.

"Welcome once again!" Vasily Ivanovich said, raising his hand in
military salute to the greasy skullcap covering his head. "I know you're
used to luxury and pleasure, but even great men of the world aren't
averse to spending a little time beneath a cottage roof."

"Good heavens," cried Arkady, "as if I were a great man of the world?
Nor am I used to luxury."

"Pardon me, pardon me," Vasily Ivanovich objected with a kindly
grimace. "Even though I've now been consigned to the archive, I've
been around a bit too—I can tell a bird by its flight. I'm also something

---

6. Lucius Cincinnatus (519?–348 B.C.), legendary Roman patrician and statesman who retired
   to his farm after defeating various enemies of the Roman state.
7. Swiss-French philosopher and political theorist (1712–78), who, among many other things,
   advocated the virtues of the simple life and physical labor.
8. *Gratis*: "free" (Latin). *En amateur*: "as an amateur" (French).
9. "New man" (Latin).

of a psychologist and physiognomist. I daresay, if I hadn't had that talent, I'd never have made it—I'd have been lost, an insignificant man like me. I can say without compliments: the friendship between you and my son makes me very happy. I've just seen him; it's his custom, as you probably know, to get up very early and explore the area. Allow me to ask, have you known my Evgeny for long?"

"Since last winter."

"I see. Allow me to ask—but, perhaps you'd care to sit down? Allow me to ask, as a father in all candor, what do you think of my Evgeny?"

"Your son is one of the most remarkable men I've ever met," Arkady replied spiritedly.

Vasily Ivanovich's eyes suddenly opened wide, his cheeks flushed slightly. The shovel slid from his hands.

"So, you expect . . ." he began.

"I'm convinced," Arkady said, interrupting him, "a great future awaits your son and he'll make your name famous. I've been certain of that since our first meeting."

"What . . . what was that?" Vasily Ivanovich could hardly speak. An ecstatic smile parted his broad lips and remained fixed there.

"Would you like to know how we met?"

"Yes . . . and in general . . ."

Arkady began to tell the story and talked about Bazarov with more energy and enthusiasm than he had that evening when he danced the mazurka with Odintsova.

Vasily Ivanovich listened with great attention, blew his nose, twisted his handkerchief in both hands, coughed, ruffled his hair—and, at long last, couldn't stand it: he leaned over to Arkady and kissed him on the shoulder.

"You've made me absolutely happy," he said, still smiling broadly. "I must tell you . . . I idolize my son; as for the old woman: you know how mothers are! But I never express my feelings in his presence because he doesn't like it. He objects to all emotional outbursts; many people condemn him for such severity of character and consider it a sign of arrogance or lack of feeling; but it's not appropriate to judge people like him by ordinary standards, isn't that right? Someone else in his place, for example, would've been a constant drag on his parents. In our case, would you believe it, from the day he was born he's never taken an extra copeck from us, so help me God!"

"He's an unselfish man, an honest man," Arkady observed.

"Unselfish, indeed. What's more, Arkady Nikolaich, not only do I idolize him, but I'm also proud of him. My greatest ambition is that one day the following words will appear in his biography: 'Son of a simple regimental doctor, but one who was able to recognize his son's talents early and spared no expense for his education . . .'" The old man's voice broke off.

Arkady squeezed his hand.

"What do you think?" Vasily Ivanovich asked after a brief silence. "He won't achieve the fame you expect for him in medicine, will he?"

"Of course it won't be medicine, but even in that field he'll prove to be one of our most important scholars."

"In what then, Arkady Nikolaich?"

"It's hard to say now, but he'll be famous."

"He'll be famous!" repeated the old man and sank into thought.

"Arina Vlasevna summons you to tea," said Anfisushka, walking past with an enormous dish of ripe raspberries.

Vasily Ivanovich gave a start.

"Will there be chilled cream with the raspberries?"

"Yes, sir."

"Make sure it's chilled! Don't stand on ceremony, Arkady Nikolaich, do have some. Why hasn't Evgeny come?"

"I'm here," Bazarov's voice rang out from Arkady's room.

Vasily Ivanovich turned around quickly.

"Aha! You wanted to see your friend. You're late, *amice*;[1] he and I've already had a nice long chat. Now it's time for tea: your mother's calling us. By the way, I have to speak with you."

"What about?"

"There's a peasant here suffering from icterus . . ."

"You mean jaundice?"

"Yes, chronic and very obstinate icterus. I've prescribed centaury and St. John's wort,[2] made him eat carrots, given him soda; but all these are *palliative* measures; he needs something more effective. Even though you make fun of medicine, I'm sure you can give me some useful advice. We'll talk about it later. Now let's go have tea."

Vasily Ivanovich jumped up briskly from the bench and began singing something from the opera *Robert le Diable*:[3]

> A law, a law, let's make a law,
> To live for hap . . . for hap . . . for happiness.

"What remarkable vigor!" Bazarov observed, moving away from the window.

It was midday. The sun was burning behind a thin layer of solid whitish clouds. Everything was silent, only the cocks crowed boisterously in the village, arousing in any listeners a strange sensation of drowsiness and ennui; somewhere high above the treetops could be heard the unceasing plaintive screech of a fledgling hawk. Arkady and Bazarov lay in the shade of a small haystack, having spread several armfuls of dry, rustling, though still green, fragrant hay.

---

1. "Old fellow" (Latin).
2. Two plants believed to have medicinal properties.
3. A very popular five-act opera, *Robert the Devil* (1831), by the dramatic composer Giacomo Meyerbeer (1791–1864).

"That aspen over there," Bazarov began, "reminds me of my child-hood. It's growing at the edge of a pit left from a brick shed; back then I was convinced that both the pit and the aspen possessed magical powers: I was never bored near them. At the time I didn't understand that I wasn't bored because I was still a child. Well, now I've grown up, and the magic doesn't work anymore."

"How much time did you spend here all together?" asked Arkady.

"A couple of years in a row; then we moved around. We led a life of wandering, trudging around towns for the most part."

"Has this house been here long?"

"Yes. My maternal grandfather built it."

"Who was he, that grandfather of yours?"

"The devil only knows. Some second-major or other; he served under Suvorov[4] and kept talking about a march across the Alps. He was probably lying."

"So that's why a portrait of Suvorov hangs in your drawing room. I love little houses like yours; they're so old and cozy, and they have a special smell."

"It's from lamp oil and sweet clover," said Bazarov, yawning. "As for the flies in these sweet little houses—ugh!"

"Tell me," began Arkady after a brief silence, "were your parents strict with you when you were a child?"

"You see what sort of parents I have. They're not strict."

"Do you love them, Evgeny?"

"I do, Arkady!"

"They love you very much!"

Bazarov was silent for a while.

"Do you know what I'm thinking?" he said at last, placing his hands behind his head.

"No, what?"

"I'm thinking: my parents have a pretty good life! At sixty my father manages to keep busy, talks about 'palliative' measures, sees patients, treats his peasants generously—in a word, has a fine time. And my mother's all right: her day's full of all sorts of activities, 'oohs' and 'ahs,' she's no time to think; while I . . ."

"While you?"

"While I think: here I lie under a haystack . . . The tiny space I occupy is so small compared to the rest of space, where I am not and where things have nothing to do with me; and the amount of time in which I get to live my life is so insignificant compared to eternity, where I've never been and won't ever be . . . Yet in this atom, this mathematical point blood circulates, a brain functions and desires something as well . . . How absurd! What nonsense!"

4. Count Alexander Suvorov (1729–1800), a famous Russian field marshal whose last achievement was a well-executed retreat across the Swiss Alps during the French Revolutionary Wars (1798–99).

"Let me say that what you're arguing can be applied to all people in general . . ."

"You're right," said Bazarov, interrupting him. "I was trying to say that they, that is, my parents, are occupied, and don't worry in the least about their own insignificance; they don't give a damn about it . . . While I . . . I feel only boredom and anger."

"Anger? Why anger?"

"Why? What do you mean, 'Why'? Have you forgotten?"

"I remember everything, but I still don't think you've any right to be angry. You're unhappy, I agree, but . . ."

"Hey! Well, Arkady Nikolaevich, I see you understand love like all our modern young men: 'Here chick, chick! Here, chick, chick!' But as soon as the chick starts to approach, you run like hell! I'm not like that. But enough of this. What can't be helped shouldn't even be talked about." He turned over on his side. "Look! Here's a heroic ant dragging away a half-dead fly. Go on, brother, pull! Don't pay any attention to her resistance; take advantage of the fact that as an animal you have the right not to feel any compassion, unlike us, self-destructive creatures that we are!"

"You shouldn't say that, Evgeny! When have you tried to destroy yourself?"

Bazarov raised his head. "That's the only thing I'm proud of. I haven't destroyed myself, and no woman's going to destroy me. Amen! Finished! You won't hear another word about it from me."

Both friends lay there for a while in silence.

"Yes," began Bazarov, "man's a strange being. When you look from the side or from a distance at the empty life our 'fathers' led, you think: what could be better? You eat, drink, and know you're acting in the most proper, judicious manner. But no; ennui overcomes you. You want to have contact with people, even if it's only to abuse them, you still want to have contact."

"You have to organize your life so that each moment is significant," Arkady declared thoughtfully.

"Look who's talking! The significant, even though false, perhaps, is sweet, though one can also become reconciled to the insignificant . . . but petty squabbles, that's the calamity."

"Petty squabbles don't exist for a man if he chooses not to acknowledge them."

"Hmmm . . . you've just uttered an *inverted commonplace*."

"What? What do you mean by that?"

"Here's what: to say, for example, 'enlightenment is useful' is a commonplace; but to say 'enlightenment is harmful' is an inverted commonplace. It seems more impressive, but in reality it's the same thing."

"Where does truth lie, on which side?"

"Where? I'll answer you like an echo, 'Where?' "

"You're in a melancholy mood today, Evgeny."

"Really? The sun must've gotten to me, and one shouldn't eat so many raspberries."

"In that case, it wouldn't be a bad idea to have a little snooze," Arkady observed.

"Perhaps; but don't look at me. Everyone's face looks stupid when they're asleep."

"Does it really matter what people think of you?"

"I don't know how to reply. A real man shouldn't care; a real man is someone you don't have to think about, but someone who should be obeyed or despised."

"That's strange! I don't despise anyone," said Arkady after some thought.

"Whereas I despise so many people. You're a tender soul, so wishy-washy, how could you despise anyone? . . . You're timid, and don't rely enough on yourself . . ."

"And you," Arkady said, interrupting him, "do you rely on yourself? Do you have such a high opinion of yourself?"

Bazarov was silent.

"When I meet a man who can hold his own next to me," he said with slow deliberation, "I'll change my opinion of myself. Despise! Why, just today, for example, as we were going past our bailiff Philip's cottage—the one that's so fine and white—you said, 'Russia will attain perfection when the poorest peasant has a house like that and each one of us should help bring that about . . .' Meanwhile, I've conceived a hatred for the poorest peasant—Philip or Sidor—those for whom I'm supposed to jump out of my skin and who won't even thank me for it . . . Besides, what the hell do I need his thanks for? So, he'll be living in a fine white hut while I'm pushing up burdock; well, then what?"

"Enough, Evgeny . . . listening to you today, one would have to agree willy-nilly with those who reproach us for not having any principles."

"You sound like your uncle. There aren't any general principles—you haven't even figured that out yet—there are only sensations. Everything depends on them."

"How so?"

"It just does. Take me, for example: I advocate a negative point of view—as a result of my sensations. I find it pleasant to negate, my brain is so organized—and that's that! Why do I like chemistry? Why do you like apples? As a result of our sensations. It's all the same thing. People will never get any further than that. Not everyone will tell you this, and I might not even tell you another time."

"What? Is honesty also a sensation?"

"Indeed it is."

"Evgeny!" began Arkady in a sad tone of voice.

"Yes? What is it? Don't you like that?" Bazarov cut in. "No, friend! Once you've decided to mow everything down—go ahead and don't spare yourself! . . . But we've philosophized enough. 'Nature induces the silence of sleep,' Pushkin said."

"He said nothing of the sort," Arkady replied.

"Well, even if he didn't, he could've and should've, as a poet. By the way, he must've served in the military."

"Pushkin was never a soldier."

"Really? But on every page he writes, 'To battle, to battle! For the honor of Russia!' "

"What sort of nonsense are you fabricating? That's slander, anyway."

"Slander? So what? What a word you've brought up to frighten me! Whatever slander you hurl at someone, you can always be sure he deserves twenty times worse."

"Let's go to sleep!" Arkady said in some annoyance.

"With pleasure," replied Bazarov.

But neither felt like sleeping. Some hostile feeling invaded the hearts of both young men. Five minutes later they opened their eyes and regarded each other in silence.

"Look," said Arkady suddenly, "a dry maple leaf's broken off and is falling to earth; its movements are like those of a butterfly in flight. Isn't it strange? What's saddest and dead resembles what's most joyous and alive."

"Oh, Arkady Nikolaich, my friend!" cried Bazarov. "One thing I ask of you: no fine talk."

"I talk the way I know how . . . Besides, that's despotism on your part. A thought entered my head: why shouldn't I express it?"

"Right; and why shouldn't I express my thought? I consider such fine talk indecent."

"What's decent then? Swearing?"

"Aha! I see you really do intend to follow in your uncle's footsteps. That idiot would be so pleased if he could hear you!"

"What did you call Pavel Petrovich?"

"I called him an idiot, just as he deserves."

"Why that's outrageous!" cried Arkady.

"Aha! That's family feeling showing itself," Bazarov said serenely. "My observation is that it's firmly rooted in people. A man's prepared to renounce everything, to part with all his prejudices; but to admit, for example, that his brother who steals handkerchiefs is a thief—that's way beyond his power. As a matter of fact, it's *my* brother, *mine*—even if he's not a genius—how could it be possible?"

"It wasn't family feeling at all, but a simple sense of justice," Arkady objected contentiously. "But since you don't understand that feeling, you lack that *sensation*, you can't make any judgments about it."

"In other words: Arkady Kirsanov is too exalted for my comprehension—I bow down and hold my tongue."

"Enough, please, Evgeny; we might end up really quarreling."

"Oh, Arkady! Do me a favor, let's have a real quarrel once and for all—to the bitter end, to the death."

"But if we do, we might wind up . . ."

"Fighting?" Bazarov cut him off. "So what? Here, in the hay, such idyllic surroundings, far from the world and other people's eyes—it wouldn't really matter. But you'd be no match for me. I'd grab you by the throat at once . . ."

Bazarov extended his long, tough fingers . . . Arkady turned around and prepared, as if in jest, to resist . . . But his friend's face appeared so malicious, his twisted grin and gleaming eyes contained such an earnest threat, that Arkady felt an instinctive fear . . .

"Ah! So this is where you've got to!" Vasily Ivanovich's voice rang out at that very moment, and the old army doctor appeared before the young men, dressed in a homemade linen jacket, wearing a homemade straw hat. "I've been looking all over for you . . . But you've chosen an excellent spot and you're engaged in a splendid pursuit. Lying on the 'earth,' looking up at the 'heavens' . . . You know, there's special significance in that."

"I look into the heavens only when I want to sneeze," muttered Bazarov and, turning to Arkady, added in a low voice, "Pity he interfered."

"Well, enough of that," Arkady whispered and squeezed his friend's hand surreptitiously. But no friendship can survive such confrontations for very long.

"I look at you, my young interlocutors," Vasily Ivanovich said meanwhile, shaking his head, resting his folded arms on a cleverly designed stick of his own making with a Turk's head for a handle, "I look at you and can't help admiring you. There's so much strength in you, youth in full bloom, ability, talent! You're simply—Castor and Pollux!"[5]

"So that's where he's got to—mythology!" Bazarov declared. "You can tell right away that in his own day he was a great Latinist! Don't I recall you once won a silver medal for a composition?"

"Dioscuri, Dioscuri!" repeated Vasily Ivanovich.

"That's enough, father, don't be so self-indulgent."

"Every once and a while it's allowed," muttered the old man. "Besides, I was looking for you, gentlemen, not to pay you any compliments; in the first place, I wanted to let you know we'll be eating soon; in the second place, I wanted to warn you, Evgeny . . . You're a clever lad, you understand people, and you understand women; therefore, you'll forgive them . . . Your mother requested a church service to celebrate your coming home. You mustn't think I'm asking you to be present at the service; it's already over; but Father Aleksei . . ."

"The cleric?"

---

5. Twin heroes and inseparable friends in Greek mythology, also called the Dioscuri; probably both sons of Zeus.

"Yes, the priest; he's going to . . . dine with us . . . I didn't expect it and advised against it . . . but that's how it turned out . . . he didn't understand me . . . Well, and Arina Vlasevna . . . Besides, he's very nice and reasonable."

"He won't eat my portion of dinner, will he?" Bazarov asked.

Vasily Ivanovich began laughing.

"For heaven's sake, what're you saying?"

"That's all I care about. I'm prepared to sit down at table with any man."

Vasily Ivanovich adjusted his hat.

"I knew beforehand," he said, "you're above any prejudice. Here I am, an old man, sixty-two years old, and I don't have any either. [Vasily Ivanovich didn't dare admit he'd also desired the church service . . . He was no less devout than his wife.] But Father Aleksei really wants to make your acquaintance. You'll like him, you'll see. He's not opposed to playing cards, and even . . . this is strictly *entre nous* . . . smokes a pipe."

"Is that so? After dinner we'll sit down to a game of cards and I'll clean him out."

"Ha, ha, ha! We'll see! I wouldn't be so sure about that!"

"Really? So you're harking back to the good old days?" Bazarov said with particular emphasis.

Vasily Ivanovich's bronze cheeks turned dark red. "You should be ashamed of yourself, Evgeny . . . That's all over and done with. Well, yes, I'm prepared to admit in front of this *gentleman* here that I had a certain passion in my youth—that's true; I certainly paid for it! But it's very hot. Allow me to sit down with you. I'm not disturbing you, am I?"

"Not in the least," replied Arkady.

Vasily Ivanovich lowered himself into the hay with a grunt.

"Your present berth reminds me, my dear sirs," he began, "of my military life in bivouacs, dressing stations, somewhere like this next to a haystack, and we were grateful for it." He sighed. "I've gone through a great deal, a very great deal in my time. For example, if you'll allow me, I'll tell you an interesting story about the plague in Bessarabia."[6]

"For which you received the St. Vladimir Cross?"[7] Bazarov broke in. "We've heard it, we've heard it . . . By the way, why aren't you wearing it?"

"I told you I have no prejudices," Vasily Ivanovich muttered (only the day before he'd removed the red ribbon from his jacket), and he set about relating the story of the plague. "Why, he's fallen fast asleep," he

---

6. Originally part of Roman Dacia, conquered by the princes of Moldavia in the fourteenth century and ceded to Russia in 1812.
7. Military decoration and order established by Catherine the Great in 1792 and named for the first Russian grand prince of Kiev.

whispered suddenly to Arkady, pointing to Evgeny and winking good-naturedly. "Evgeny! Wake up!" he added in a loud voice. "Let's go eat . . ."

Father Aleksei, a large, fine figure of a man with thick, carefully groomed hair and an embroidered belt around his violet-colored silk cassock, turned out to be a most clever and resourceful fellow. He was the first to extend his hand to Arkady and Bazarov, as if realizing in advance they had no desire to receive his blessing; in general he behaved in an unconstrained manner. He didn't belittle himself, nor did he offend others; incidentally, he enjoyed a chuckle over seminary Latin and rose to the defense of his bishop; he drank two glasses of wine, but refused a third; he accepted a cigar from Arkady, but didn't smoke it, saying he'd take it home with him. The only thing slightly unpleasant about him was that from time to time he'd slowly and carefully raise his hand to capture a fly on his own face and sometimes squash them there. He sat down at the green card table, an expression of moderate satisfaction on his face, and ended up winning two rubles fifty copecks in paper money from Bazarov: in Arina Vlasevna's house there was no notion whatever of reckoning in silver . . . [8] She sat next to her son as before (she didn't play cards), resting her cheek on her little fist as before, and stood up only to arrange for some new delicacy to be served. She was afraid of displaying any affection for Bazarov; he provided no encouragement and appreciated no displays. Besides, Vasily Ivanovich had urged her not to "disturb" him. "Young folks don't much like that," he explained to her. (It goes without saying what sort of dinner was served that day: Timofeich had galloped off at the crack of dawn in search of some special Circassian beef; the bailiff had set off in another direction to fetch turbot, ruff, and crayfish; for the mushrooms alone, the peasant women had received forty-two copecks in copper coins.) But Arina Vlasevna's gaze, directed constantly at Bazarov, expressed not only devotion and tenderness; it also reflected sorrow, combined with curiosity and fear, as well as a humble reproach.

Bazarov, however, was in no mood to analyze what precisely was reflected in his mother's gaze; he rarely addressed her, and when he did, it was only with a brief question. Once he asked for her hand to bring him "good luck"; she gently placed her soft little hand on his large, tough palm.

"Well," she asked after a little while, "did it help?"

"Made it worse," he replied with an offhand laugh.

"He takes far too many risks," Father Aleksei intoned, as if with sympathy, and stroked his fine beard.

"It's Napoleon's rule, good father, Napoleon's rule," Vasily Ivanovich put in and led with an ace.

---

8. A silver ruble was worth three and a half times a paper ruble.

"That's what got him sent to St. Helena,"[9] Father Aleksei replied and trumped the ace.

"Wouldn't you like some black currant drink, Enyushechka?" asked Arina Vlasevna.

Bazarov merely shrugged his shoulders.

"No!" he said to Arkady the next day. "I'm leaving tomorrow. It's boring here; I feel like working, but can't. I'll go back to your place in the country where I left all my things. At least there I can lock my door. Here my father keeps telling me, 'My study's at your service—no one'll bother you'; but he doesn't leave me alone for a moment. And it's awkward trying to keep him out. Then there's my mother. I can hear her sighing through the wall, but when I go out to see her—I have nothing to say to her."

"She'll be very upset," Arkady said, "and so will he."

"I'll return."

"When?"

"On my way back to Petersburg."

"I feel most sorry for your mother."

"Why? Has she been plying you with berries, or what?"

Arkady lowered his eyes.

"You don't know your own mother, Evgeny. She's not only a splendid woman, she's really very clever. This morning she chatted with me for half an hour, and it was very sensible and interesting."

"She was probably going on all about me."

"It wasn't only about you."

"You may be right; an outsider can see things more clearly. If a woman can keep up a conversation for half an hour, that's a good sign. But I'm still leaving."

"It won't be easy to break the news to them. They talk all the time about what we'll be doing two weeks from now."

"It won't be easy. I don't know what possessed me to tease my father today: he had one of his peasants on quitrent flogged the other day— that was the right thing to do; yes, yes, don't look at me with such horror! It was the right thing to do because the peasant's a thief and a terrible drunkard; but my father never expected I'd be apprised of the facts, as they say. He was very embarrassed; now it turns out I'll have to upset him again . . . Never mind! He'll survive."

Bazarov said, "Never mind!"—yet a whole day went by before he decided to tell Vasily Ivanovich of his intention. Finally, as he was saying good night to him in the study, he uttered with a forced yawn, "Oh, yes . . . I almost forgot to tell you . . . Have them send our horses to Fedot's tomorrow for the relay, will you?"

9. A British island in the Atlantic where Napoleon was exiled in 1815 and died in 1821.

Vasily Ivanovich was astounded.

"Is Mr. Kirsanov leaving us, then?"

"Yes, and I'm going with him."

Vasily Ivanovich recoiled from the blow.

"You're leaving?"

"Yes . . . I have to. Please arrange for the horses."

"All right," muttered the old man, "horses for the relay . . . all right . . . but . . . but . . . why?"

"I have to call in at his place for a little while. Then I'll come back here."

"Yes! For a little while . . . All right." Vasily Ivanovich took out his handkerchief and blew his nose, bending over almost to the ground. "Well, it . . . it'll all be done. But I thought you'd stay here . . . longer. Three days . . . It's, it's a little short after three years, a little short, Evgeny!"

"I tell you, I'll be back soon. I have to go."

"Have to . . . Well, then. Above all, one must do one's duty . . . So, you want the horses sent on? All right. Of course, Arina and I didn't expect this. She's just requested some flowers from our neighbor to decorate your room. [Vasily Ivanovich didn't even mention the fact that every morning at daybreak he stood, his bare feet in slippers, conferring with Timofeich, and, with trembling fingers, would take out one worn bank note after another, enjoining him to make various purchases, placing special emphasis on tasty delicacies and red wine, which, as far as he could tell, the young men really enjoyed.] The main thing is—freedom; that's my rule . . . you mustn't be hindered . . . you mustn't . . . ."

He suddenly fell silent and headed for the door.

"We'll see each other again soon, Father, really."

But without turning around, Vasily Ivanovich merely gestured in despair and left the room. Returning to his bedroom, he found his wife in bed and began praying in a whisper so as not to wake her. But she woke up anyway.

"Is that you, Vasily Ivanych?" she asked.

"Yes, Mother!"

"Are you coming from Enyusha? You know, I'm afraid he may not be comfortable sleeping on the sofa. I told Anfisushka to give him your old traveling mattress and some new pillows; I'd have given him our feather bed, but I seem to recall he doesn't like sleeping on anything too soft."

"Never mind, Mother, don't worry. He's fine. Lord, have mercy on us sinners," he continued his prayers in a low voice. Vasily Ivanovich felt sorry for his old wife; he didn't want to tell her that night what was in store for her.

Bazarov and Arkady left the next day. From early morning the entire house was plunged in gloom; Anfisushka kept dropping dishes; even Fedka was confused and ended up taking off his boots. Vasily Ivanovich fussed more than usual: he was obviously trying to put on a good show. He spoke in a loud voice and stamped his feet, but his face looked haggard and he kept avoiding his son's eyes. Arina Vlasevna wept quietly; she'd have broken down completely and lost all control of herself, if her husband hadn't spent two hours early that morning trying to dissuade her. When after repeated promises to return not later than in a month's time, Bazarov finally managed to tear himself away from the embraces that held him and climb into the coach; when the horses set off, the harness bells began to ring, and the wheels began to turn; when there was nothing left to see, the dust lifted, and Timofeich, stooped and tottering as he walked, crawled back to his room; when the old folks were left alone in their own little house, which now suddenly seemed shrunken and decrepit, Vasily Ivanovich, who for several moments continued bravely waving his handkerchief good-bye on the back porch, sank down on a chair, his head dropped to his chest. "He's forsaken us, forsaken us," he muttered, "forsaken us; he was bored here. Now I'm alone, completely alone!" he repeated several times, holding up his hand each time with his index finger erect. Then Arina Vlasevna went over to him and, leaning her gray head against his, said: "What's to be done, Vasya? A son's a piece cut off. He's like a falcon: he comes and goes whenever he likes; while you and I are like mushrooms growing in the hollow of a log: we sit side by side and never budge. Except that I'll always be here for you, as you will for me."

Vasily Ivanovich took his hands away from his face and embraced his wife, his helpmate, more firmly than he'd ever done in his youth; she comforted him in his grief.

XXII

In silence, only occasionally exchanging small talk, our friends arrived at Fedot's. Bazarov wasn't entirely satisfied with himself; Arkady was dissatisfied with him. In addition, he felt in his own heart that groundless grief familiar only to those very young. The coachman changed the horses and, climbing onto the box, asked, "Where to? Right or left?"

Arkady shuddered. The road to the right led into town, and from there toward home; the road to the left led to Odintsova's.

He glanced at Bazarov.

"Evgeny," he asked, "to the left?"

Bazarov turned away.

"What sort of stupid idea is that?" he muttered.

"I know it's stupid," replied Arkady. "But what does that matter? It wouldn't be the first time, would it?"

Bazarov pulled his cap down over his forehead.

"As you like," he said at last.

"To the left!" cried Arkady.

The coach headed in the direction of Nikolskoe. But, having decided to do something stupid, the friends maintained an even more stubborn silence than before and even seemed angry.

By the very way in which the butler met them on the steps of Odintsova's house, the friends realized they'd acted unwisely in yielding so suddenly to a passing whim. Obviously they hadn't been expected. They had to sit in the drawing room for rather a long time looking rather foolish. At long last Odintsova entered. She greeted them with her usual politeness, was surprised by their hasty return, and, as far as one could tell from her unhurried gestures and speech, was none too pleased by it. They hastened to explain that they'd merely called in along the way and would have to set off for town in about four hours. She confined herself to a slight exclamation, asked Arkady to convey her regards to his father, and sent for her auntie. The princess appeared looking very sleepy, which lent her wrinkled, old face an even more spiteful expression. Katya wasn't feeling very well and didn't emerge from her room. Arkady unexpectedly realized that he wanted to see Katya as much as he did Anna Sergeevna herself. The next four hours were spent in insignificant discussion of this and that; Anna Sergeevna both listened and talked without smiling. Only at the moment of their departure did any of her former affection seem to stir in her heart.

"I'm feeling rather depressed at the moment," she said, "but don't pay it any attention; come back again in a little while—I say this to both of you."

Bazarov and Arkady answered her with a silent bow, climbed back into their carriage, and, without stopping anywhere, headed home, to Marino, where they arrived safely the following evening. During the entire journey, neither one nor the other even mentioned Odintsova's name. Bazarov, in particular, hardly opened his mouth; he kept looking off to one side, away from the road, with a kind of embittered intensity.

In Marino everyone was very pleased to see them. The prolonged absence of his son had begun to worry Nikolai Petrovich; he gave a shout and began swinging his feet and bouncing on the sofa when Fenechka came running in with sparkling eyes to tell him of "the young gentlemen's" arrival; even Pavel Petrovich felt a certain pleasant agitation and smiled condescendingly as he shook hands with the returning travelers. Discussion and questions followed; Arkady spoke most of all, especially during supper, which lasted until long after midnight. Nikolai Petrovich ordered several bottles of porter, which had just been delivered from Moscow, and drank so much his cheeks turned red as raspberries and kept emitting not quite a childish, not quite a nervous laugh. The general sense of merriment was communicated to the servants as well. Dunyasha ran back and forth like a madwoman and kept slamming doors; meanwhile Peter, even at three o'clock in the morning, was still trying to strum a Cossack waltz on the guitar. The strings emitted a plaintive, pleasant sound in the still air, but, with the exception of a few brief initial grace notes, nothing resulted from the educated valet's efforts: nature had denied him musical talent, along with talent for anything else.

Meanwhile life at Marino hadn't been proceeding too smoothly; things were going badly for poor Nikolai Petrovich. His difficulties with the farm increased with every passing day—cheerless, senseless difficulties. Problems with the hired workers had become intolerable. Some demanded payment of their accounts or an increase; others left, even after receiving their wages in advance; horses fell ill; harnesses were worn out in no time at all; tasks were performed carelessly; the threshing machine ordered from Moscow turned out to be useless because of its enormous weight; another machine was ruined the very first time it was used; half the cattle shed burned down because a blind old woman, one of the house serfs, went out to fumigate her cow in windy weather carrying a burning ember . . . true, according to the testimony of the old woman, the difficulty arose from the fact that the master had decided to introduce some newfangled cheeses and dairy products. The bailiff grew lazy and even began gaining weight, as every Russian does when he comes upon "a bed of roses." To show his zeal, when he would catch sight of Nikolai Petrovich from a distance, he'd throw a stick at a passing piglet or threaten a half-naked urchin, but for the most part he just slept. The peasants on quitrent didn't make their payments on time and stole firewood; almost every night the watchman caught—and sometimes seized by force—peasants' horses grazing in the "farm" meadows. Nikolai Petrovich tried to establish monetary fines for any damages, but the matter usually ended when the horses were returned to their owners after a day or two of grazing on the master's land. To top it all, the peasants began quarreling among themselves: brothers demanded the redivision of their property because their wives couldn't coexist under the same roof; a fight would suddenly break out, everyone would jump to their feet, as if at a given signal, and rush to the office steps, often in a drunken state, with bruised faces, asking to see the master, demanding justice and reprisals; an uproar and clamor would ensue, the women's shrill shrieking mingling with the men's cursing. It was necessary to separate the feuding factions, shouting until one became hoarse, knowing full well it was impossible to arrive at a just solution. There weren't enough hands for the harvest: a neighboring landowner with a most benign countenance had agreed to supply him with reapers for two rubles an acre, and then cheated him in a most unabashed way; his own peasant women demanded exorbitant wages, while the grain went to seed; they were behind schedule with the mowing and the Board of Guardians[1] was

---

1. Organ of local government concerned with issues of trusteeship, foundling hospitals, and credit operations, including the mortgaging of estates.

threatening and demanding immediate payment in full of all interest due . . .

"I've no strength left!" Nikolai Petrovich exclaimed in despair more than once. "I can't fight with them myself, my principles won't allow me to summon the local police, and one can't accomplish anything without the fear of punishment!"

"*Du calme, du calme,*"[2] Pavel Petrovich would reply to this, while he himself would hum, frown, and tug at his mustache.

Bazarov kept himself away from all these "squabbles"; besides, as a guest, it wasn't his place to interfere in other people's affairs. The day after their arrival in Marino he set to work on his frogs, infusoria,[3] and chemical compounds, spending all his time on them. Arkady, on the other hand, considered it his duty, if not to help his father, then at least to display some willingness to help. He listened to him patiently and once even offered some suggestions, not so much to have them followed, but rather to show interest. Managing the estate didn't arouse any revulsion in him: he even used to dream about agricultural activity with pleasure, but at the present time other thoughts were swarming in his head. To his own astonishment, Arkady constantly thought about Nikolskoe; previously he'd merely have shrugged his shoulders if anyone had told him he could be bored under the same roof with Bazarov, and whose roof at that—his father's! But he really was bored and yearned to get away. He tried taking long walks to the point of exhaustion, but that didn't help. While chatting with his father on one occasion, he learned that Nikolai Petrovich had in his possession several rather interesting letters written some time ago to his late wife by Odintsova's mother; Arkady wouldn't leave him alone until he produced those letters. Nikolai Petrovich was forced to rummage through twenty boxes and trunks to find them. After obtaining these half-decayed documents, Arkady seemed to calm down, as if he now had a goal. "I say this to both of you," he whispered over and over to himself. "That's what she herself said. I'll go, I'll go, damn it all!" But he recalled their last visit, the chilly reception, his previous awkwardness, and was overcome by timidity. The "what the hell" attitude of youth, a secret desire to try his luck, put his own powers to the test, without anyone's protection, finally won out. Scarcely ten days had passed since his return to Marino when, on the pretext of studying how the Sunday schools[4] were functioning, he galloped off to town and from there to Nikolskoe. Constantly urging the driver on, he proceeded like a young officer advancing into battle: he was afraid and cheerful, breathless with impatience. "The main thing's not to think," he repeated to himself. The driver happened to be something of a daredevil; he stopped in front of every tavern and

2. "Be calm" (French).
3. Microscopic organisms found in decayed organic matter and stagnant water.
4. Established to further adult literacy first in Petersburg and Kiev in 1859, then in other cities and towns.

asked, "One for the road?" Or "What about one for the road?"—and, after consuming *one for the road*, he didn't spare the horses. There, at last, the high roof of the familiar house . . . "What am I doing?" suddenly flashed through Arkady's mind. "But I can't turn back now!" The troika of horses rushed on ahead, the driver whooping and whistling at them. Now the little bridge thundered beneath their hooves and wheels, then the alley of trimmed pine trees drew closer and closer . . . A girl's pink dress flashed against the dark green, a young face peeked out from beneath the light fringe of a parasol . . . He recognized Katya and she, him. Arkady had the driver stop the galloping horses; he leapt out of the carriage and went toward her. "It's you!" she said, gradually blushing all over. "Let's go see my sister; she's out in the garden; she'll be very glad to see you."

Katya led Arkady into the garden. The meeting with her struck him as a particularly happy omen; he was delighted to see her, as if she were family. Everything seemed to be working out splendidly: no butler, no formal announcement. At a turn in the path he caught sight of Anna Sergeevna. She stood with her back to him. Hearing his footsteps, she turned around slowly.

Arkady began to feel embarrassed again, but the first words she uttered quickly put him at ease. "Hello, you fugitive!" she said in an even, affectionate tone of voice and moved to greet him, smiling and squinting from the sun and wind. "Where did you find him, Katya?"

"Anna Sergeevna," he began, "I've brought you something you never expected . . ."

"You've brought yourself," she said. "That's best of all."

XXIII

After seeing Arkady off with sarcastic expressions of regret and letting him know that he was not in the least deceived about the real purpose of his journey, Bazarov eventually went off on his own: he was possessed by a passion for work. He no longer argued with Pavel Petrovich, all the more so because the latter assumed an excessively aristocratic demeanor in his presence and expressed his opinions more with sounds than words. On only one occasion was Pavel Petrovich about to enter the fray against the *nihilist* concerning the controversial question of noblemen's rights in the Baltic provinces,[5] but he suddenly stopped, and declared with cold politeness, "However, we can't really understand each other; at least I lack the honor of understanding you."

"Certainly not!" exclaimed Bazarov. "Man's in a position to understand everything—how the ether vibrates as well as what transpires on the sun; but he's in no position to understand how another person can blow his nose differently from the way he blows his own."

---

5. German landowners living in these provinces (Lithuania, Latvia, and Estonia) opposed the emancipation of the serfs.

"What? Is that supposed to be clever?" asked Pavel Petrovich and stalked out.

However, he sometimes asked permission to be present at Bazarov's experiments, and once even brought his sweet-smelling face, washed with the finest of soaps, close to the microscope to see how transparent infusoria swallow green specks of dust and carefully chew them using some very efficient little devices in their throat. It was Nikolai Petrovich who, much more frequently than his brother, visited Bazarov; he'd have come every day to "study," as he used to say, if the business of managing his estate hadn't kept him away. He didn't get in the young scientist's way: he sat somewhere off in a corner of the room watching carefully, from time to time allowing himself to ask a discreet question. During dinners and suppers he'd attempt to direct the conversation to physics, geology, or chemistry, since all other subjects, even those pertaining to agriculture, not to mention politics, could lead to mutual dissatisfaction, if not to direct confrontation. Nikolai Petrovich surmised that his brother's loathing for Bazarov hadn't diminished in the least. An insignificant episode, one among many, confirmed this assumption. Cholera began to make an appearance here and there in the neighborhood and even "carried off" two people from Marino itself. One night Pavel Petrovich endured a rather severe attack. He suffered until morning, but refused to call for Bazarov's assistance; when he saw him the next day, in reply to his question "Why wasn't I sent for?"—he replied, still looking very pale, but already cleanly shaved and immaculately brushed, "Don't I recall your declaring that you don't believe in medicine?" So the days passed. Bazarov worked stubbornly and glumly . . . Meanwhile in Nikolai Petrovich's house there was one creature to whom if he could not exactly open his heart, he was always glad to chat . . . That creature was Fenechka.

He used to meet her most often in the early mornings, in the garden or courtyard; he never went to her room, and only once did she come to his door to ask whether or not she should bathe Mitya. Not only did she trust him and have no fear of him, she actually felt freer around him and even behaved more naturally with him than with Nikolai Petrovich. It's hard to say why this was so, perhaps because she sensed Bazarov's lack of any aristocratic vestiges, any air of superiority that both attracts and repels. In her eyes he was both an excellent doctor and a simple man. Unembarrassed by his presence, she'd attend to her baby; once, when she suddenly felt dizzy and got a headache, she'd even accepted a spoonful of medicine from his hand. In Nikolai Petrovich's presence she seemed to avoid Bazarov; she did that not out of cunning, but out of a sense of decency. She was more afraid of Pavel Petrovich than ever; some time ago he'd begun following her and would appear unexpectedly, as if out of nowhere, behind her back, wearing his English suit, standing there with his immobile, watchful face, his hands in his pockets. "It gives me the chills," Fenechka complained once to Dunyasha; the latter sighed in reply and thought about another "unfeeling" man. Bazarov, without even suspecting it, had become the *cruel tyrant* of her heart.

Fenechka liked Bazarov; but he liked her, too. Even his face would change when he talked with her: it took on a cheerful, almost gentle expression, and a playful attentiveness was combined with his usual casual attitude. Fenechka grew more attractive with every passing day. There comes a time in the life of young women when they suddenly begin to unfold and blossom like summer roses; such a time had come for Fenechka. Everything contributed to it, even the intense July heat, then at its most extreme. Dressed in a light white dress, she herself appeared lighter and whiter: she didn't tan in the sun, but the heat, from which she couldn't protect herself, would turn her cheeks and ears a light pink, suffuse her whole body with gentle indolence, and be reflected in the dreamy languor of her pretty little eyes. She could hardly do any work; her hands would slip down into her lap. She could scarcely walk and constantly sighed and complained with comic helplessness.

"You ought to go swimming more often," Nikolai Petrovich said to her.

He'd built a large bathing place, covered with a canopy, at one pond that hadn't dried up completely.

"Oh, Nikolai Petrovich! You die from the heat getting there and die again on the way back. And there's no shade in the garden."

"It's true, there's no shade," Nikolai Petrovich replied, wiping his brow.

Once, at about seven o'clock in the morning, as Bazarov was returning from an outing, he came upon Fenechka in a lilac arbor that had long since flowered, but was still thick and green. She was sitting on a bench, wearing a white kerchief on her head as usual; next to her lay a large heap of red and white roses still wet from the dew. He greeted her.

"Ah! Evgeny Vasilich!" she said, raising the edge of her kerchief a little so she could look at him, and in so doing bared her arm to the elbow.

"What are you doing here?" asked Bazarov, sitting down next to her. "Are you making a bouquet?"

"Yes, for the breakfast table. Nikolai Petrovich likes it."

"But it's still a long time until breakfast. What a pile of flowers!"

"I've gathered them now because it'll soon be too hot and I won't be able to go out. This is the only time I can breathe. I've grown weak from all this heat. I'm even afraid I might be ill."

"What an imagination! Let me check your pulse." Bazarov took her hand, looked for a vein that was beating evenly, but didn't even start counting. "You'll live a hundred years," he said, letting go of her hand.

"Oh, God forbid!" she cried.

"Why? Don't you want to live a long time?"

"A hundred years! I have a grandmother who was eighty-five—what a martyr she was! Dark, deaf, hunched over, coughing all the time; she was only a burden to herself. What sort of life is that?"

"So it's better to be young?"

"Of course."

"Why is it better? Tell me!"

"Why? Why, when you're young, you can do everything—come, and go, and fetch, and you don't have to ask anyone . . . What could be better?"

"It doesn't matter to me whether I'm young or old."

"You say it doesn't matter? You really can't mean that."

"Judge for yourself, Fedosya Nikolaevna. What good's my youth to me? I live alone, all on my own . . ."

"That depends on you."

"It doesn't all depend on me! Someone should take pity on me."

Fenechka glanced sidelong at Bazarov but didn't say anything.

"What book do you have there?" she asked after a little while.

"This one? It's a scientific book, very difficult."

"You're always studying. Isn't it boring? You must know everything already."

"Obviously not everything. Try to read a bit of it."

"I won't understand a thing. Is it in Russian?" Fenechka asked, taking the heavily bound volume into her hands. "It's so thick!"

"It's in Russian."

"I still won't understand a thing."

"I don't care if you understand it. I want to watch you read. When you do, the tip of your nose wiggles very sweetly."

Fenechka, who was trying to decipher in a low voice the article "On Creosote" she'd opened up to, started laughing and put the book aside . . . It slipped from the bench onto the ground.

"I also like it when you laugh," Bazarov said.

"Enough of that!"

"I like it when you talk. It's like a babbling brook."

Fenechka turned her head away. "Oh, you!" she said, sorting through the flowers with her fingers. "Why should you listen to me? You've talked with such clever women."

"Ah, Fedosya Nikolaevna! Believe me, all the clever women in the world aren't worth your little elbow."

"Well, whatever will you think of next?" whispered Fenechka, clasping her hands.

Bazarov picked up the book from the ground.

"It's a medical book; why did you throw it down?"

"Medical?" repeated Fenechka and turned to him. "Do you know what? Since you gave me those drops, remember? Mitya sleeps so soundly! I don't know how to thank you; you're really very kind."

"As a matter of fact, doctors have to be paid," Bazarov remarked with a smile. "Doctors are mercenary, you know."

Fenechka raised her eyes to look at Bazarov, eyes that seemed even darker from the whitish reflection on the upper part of her face. She didn't know whether he was joking or not.

"If you like, with pleasure . . . I'll have to ask Nikolai Petrovich about . . ."

"You think I want money?" Bazarov interrupted her. "No, I don't want any money from you."

"What, then?" asked Fenechka.

"What?" repeated Bazarov. "Guess."

"I'm not very good at guessing."

"Then I'll tell you; I want . . . one of those roses."

Fenechka started laughing again and even clapped her hands, so amusing did Bazarov's request seem to her. She laughed and at the same time felt flattered. Bazarov stared at her intently.

"Please, if you like," she said at last. Bending down to the bench, she began sorting through her roses. "What color do you prefer, red or white?"

"Red, and not too big."

She straightened up.

"Here, take it," she said, but immediately pulled back her outstretched hand and, biting her lip, glanced at the entrance to the arbor, then pricked up her ears.

"What is it?" asked Bazarov. "Nikolai Petrovich?"

"No . . . he went out to the fields . . . and I'm not afraid of him . . . but Pavel Petrovich . . . I thought that . . ."

"What?"

"I thought I saw *him* there. No . . . it's no one. Here, take it." Fenechka gave Bazarov the rose.

"Why're you afraid of Pavel Petrovich?"

"He always frightens me. It's not what he says, but the way he looks at me. Besides, you don't like him either. Remember how you used to argue with him all the time? I don't even know what your quarrels were about, but I saw how you twisted him around your little finger . . ."

Fenechka demonstrated with her own hands how, in her opinion, Bazarov twisted Pavel Petrovich around his little finger.

Bazarov smiled.

"And if he started to gain the upper hand," he asked, "would you stand up for me?"

"How could I stand up for you? No one can gain the upper hand over you."

"You think? I know one hand that could knock me over with a finger, if it wanted to."

"Whose hand is that?"

"You really don't know? Smell how sweet this rose is, the one you just gave me."

Fenechka stretched out her little neck and brought her face close to the flower . . . The kerchief slipped from her head onto her shoulders, revealing a mass of soft, dark, shining, slightly disheveled hair.

"Wait a moment, I want to smell it with you," Bazarov said. Leaning over he planted a kiss firmly on her parted lips.

She shuddered, pushed him away with both her hands against his chest, but she pushed so weakly that he was able to renew and prolong his kiss.

A dry cough was heard behind the lilacs. Fenechka instantly retreated to the other end of the bench. Pavel Petrovich appeared, made a slight bow, and said with malicious despondence, "So you're here," and then withdrew. Fenechka immediately gathered all her roses and left the arbor. "That was wrong, Evgeny Vasilevich," she whispered as she went out. Her voice contained a note of genuine reproach.

Bazarov recalled another recent scene and felt both guilty and contemptuously annoyed. But he shook his head at once, ironically congratulating himself on his "formal admission into the ranks of womanizing Céladons"[6] and then returned to his own room.

Meanwhile Pavel Petrovich left the garden; walking slowly, he made his way to the woods. He remained there for rather a long time; when he came back to breakfast, Nikolai Petrovich inquired solicitously after his health because his face looked so dark.

"You know, I sometimes suffer from an excess of bile," Pavel Petrovich replied serenely.

XXIV

Two hours later he knocked at Bazarov's door.

"I must apologize for disturbing you during your scientific work," he began, sitting down on the chair near the window and resting both hands on his beautiful walking stick with an ivory handle (he usually took walks without a stick). "But I'm compelled to ask you to spare me five minutes of your time . . . no more."

"All my time is at your disposal," replied Bazarov, whose face rapidly changed expression as soon as Pavel Petrovich had crossed his threshold.

"Five minutes is all I need. I've come to put a question to you."

"A question? What about?"

"Be so good as to hear me out. At the beginning of your stay here in my brother's house, when I still afforded myself the pleasure of con-

6. Céladon is the womanizing hero of *L'Astrée* (pub. 1607–10) by the French pastoral novelist Honoré d'Urfé (1567–1625).

versing with you, I had the occasion to hear your opinions on many matters; but, as far as I can recall, neither between us nor in my presence was the subject of a duel ever discussed, that is, dueling in general. Allow me to inquire what opinion you hold on that subject."

Bazarov, who'd stood up to meet Pavel Petrovich, sat back down on the edge of the table and crossed his arms.

"Here's my opinion," he said. "From a theoretical standpoint, dueling is ridiculous; but, from a practical standpoint, well, that's a different matter."

"That is, you mean to say, if I've understood you correctly, no matter what your theoretical view of dueling, in practice you wouldn't allow yourself to be insulted without demanding satisfaction."

"You've divined my meaning entirely."

"Very good, sir. I'm very glad to hear you say that. Your words have removed any uncertainty . . ."

"Any indecision, you mean."

"It's all the same, sir; I express myself so I'll be understood; I'm no . . . seminary rat. Your words relieve me of a certain unpleasant obligation. I've decided to fight a duel with you."

Bazarov opened his eyes very wide.

"With me?"

"With you, absolutely."

"What on earth for?"

"I could explain the reason to you," Pavel Petrovich replied. "But I prefer to keep silent on that score. To my way of thinking, you're superfluous here; I can't stand you, I despise you, and if that's not enough . . ."

Pavel Petrovich's eyes were gleaming . . . Bazarov's eyes were also flashing.

"Very well, sir," he said. "Further explanations are unnecessary. You've taken it into your head to test your chivalric spirit on me. I could deny you that pleasure, but—so be it!"

"I'm sincerely grateful to you," replied Pavel Petrovich, "and now I hope you'll accept my challenge without forcing me to resort to violent measures."

"That is, leaving aside all allegory, without resorting to your walking stick?" Bazarov observed coolly. "That's entirely correct. There's absolutely no need for you to insult me. Nor would it be altogether safe for you to do so. You can remain a gentleman . . . I also accept your challenge as a gentleman."

"Splendid," replied Pavel Petrovich, placing the stick in the corner. "Now let's exchange a few words about the conditions of our duel; first I'd like to know if you consider it necessary to resort to the formality of a small quarrel to serve as a pretext for my challenge?"

"No, it's better to dispense with such formalities."

"That's what I think, too. I assume it would also be inappropriate to delve into the real reasons for our confrontation. We can't stand each other. What more is needed?"

"What more?" Bazarov repeated ironically.

"Concerning the actual conditions of our duel, since there won't be any seconds—after all, where would we find them?"

"Precisely, where would we?"

"Then I have the honor of proposing the following: we'll fight early tomorrow morning, let's say at six o'clock, beyond the grove, with pistols, at a distance of ten paces . . ."

"Ten paces? That's fine; we can despise each other at that distance."

"We could set it at eight paces," observed Pavel Petrovich.

"We could, why not?"

"We'll each fire twice; and, just in case, each of us will have a short note in his pocket blaming himself entirely for his own demise."

"I don't entirely agree with that," said Bazarov. "It sounds a bit like a French novel, somewhat unlikely."

"Perhaps. Still, you do agree it would be unpleasant to arouse any suspicion of murder?"

"I agree. But there's another way to avoid that grim outcome. We won't have seconds, but there could be a witness present."

"Who would that be, may I ask?"

"Why, Peter."

"What Peter?"

"Your brother's valet. He's a man who's attained the very summit of contemporary education and would fulfill the role with all the *comilfo*[7] required in such circumstances."

"You must be joking, my dear sir."

"Not at all. After considering my proposal, you'll see it's replete with common sense and simplicity. You can't hide a pig in a poke; I'll take it upon myself to prepare Peter in an appropriate manner and bring him along to the site of our bloody battle."

"You continue to jest," Pavel Petrovich said, getting up from his chair. "But after the generous acquiescence you've demonstrated, I've no right to complain . . . So, everything's been settled . . . By the way, you don't have any pistols, do you?"

"Where would I get pistols, Pavel Petrovich? I'm not a warrior."

"In that case, I can offer you my own. You may be sure I haven't fired them in the last five years."

"That's very comforting news."

Pavel Petrovich took his walking stick.

"Then, my good sir, all that remains is for me to thank you and allow you to return to your work. I have the honor of taking my leave."

7. *Comme il faut*: "appropriateness" (French).

"Until our next pleasant meeting, my dear sir," said Bazarov, seeing his guest out.

Pavel Petrovich left; Bazarov remained standing in front of the door and suddenly exclaimed: "Damn it all! So elegant and so stupid! What a farce we've just acted! That's how trained dogs dance on their hind legs. But it was impossible to refuse; he'd have thrashed me, and then . . . [Bazarov grew pale at the very thought of it, all his pride suddenly rearing up.] Then I'd have had to strangle him like a little kitten." He returned to his microscope, but his heart was pounding; the serenity required for scientific observation had disappeared. "He must've seen us today," he thought. "But can he really be intervening on his brother's behalf? What's so important about a kiss? There must be more to it. Bah! Could he be in love with her himself? Of course, he is; it's as clear as day. What a mess, just think! . . . Bad!" he concluded finally. "It's bad from whatever side you look at it. In the first place, I'll have to risk getting shot and I'll have to leave; then there's Arkady . . . and gentle old Nikolai Petrovich. It's bad, very bad."

That day was particularly quiet and uneventful. Fenechka was no-where to be seen; she stayed in her little room, like a mouse in its hole. Nikolai Petrovich had a worried look. He was informed that some rust had appeared on his wheat, the crop on which he'd placed such great hope. Pavel Petrovich oppressed everyone, even Prokofich, with his frigid courtesy. Bazarov began writing a letter to his father, but tore it up and threw it under the table. "If I die," he thought, "they'll find out; but I won't die. No, I'll stick around for a while yet." He told Peter to report to him the next day at dawn for some important business; Peter thought he planned to take him along to Petersburg. Bazarov went to bed late and was tormented by disordered dreams all night . . . Odintsova whirled in front of him; she was his mother and was being followed by a little kitten who had black whiskers, and this kitten was Fenechka; Pavel Petrovich appeared to him as a large forest with which he'd still have to fight a duel. Peter woke him at four o'clock; he got dressed at once and left with him.

The morning was lovely, the air, fresh; small, dappled clouds stood like fleecy lambs in a clear, pale blue sky; light dew scattered on leaves and grass glistened like silver on spider webs; the damp, dark earth seemed to retain traces of the rosy dawn; the sky was filled with the songs of larks. Bazarov arrived at the grove, sat down in the shade at the edge, and only then explained to Peter what was expected of him. The educated valet was scared to death; Bazarov calmed him with the assurance that all he had to do was stand at a distance and watch. He wouldn't have to accept any responsibility. "Meanwhile," he added, "just think how important your role will be!" Peter wrung his hands in despair and hung his head; turning green, he leaned against a birch tree.

The road from Marino circled the little grove; it was covered with a light layer of dust, undisturbed since the day before by wheels or feet. Bazarov glanced down the road carelessly, tore off and chewed some blades of grass, and kept repeating to himself, "What stupidity!" The morning chill caused him to shudder once or twice . . . Peter regarded him gloomily, but Bazarov merely grinned: he was no coward.

The sound of horses' hooves rang out along the road . . . A peasant appeared from behind some trees. He was driving two horses harnessed together; going past Bazarov, he gave him a strange look without raising his cap, which, apparently, troubled Peter, striking him as a bad omen. "Looks like he got up early, too," thought Bazarov, "but at least he's going to work, while here we . . ."

"I think he's coming," Peter whispered all of a sudden.

Bazarov raised his head and saw Pavel Petrovich. Dressed in a light checked jacket with trousers as white as snow, he strode quickly along the road; under his arm he carried a box wrapped in green cloth.

"Excuse me, it seems I've made you wait," he said, nodding first to Bazarov, then to Peter, whom at this moment he treated a bit like a second. "I didn't want to wake my valet."

"Never mind, sir," replied Bazarov. "We just got here ourselves."

"Ah! All the better!" Pavel Petrovich said, glancing around. "No one in sight, no one to interfere . . . Shall we begin?"

"Indeed."

"I assume you don't require any further explanation?"

"Correct."

"Would you care to load?" asked Pavel Petrovich, removing the pistols from the box.

"No; you load while I measure off the distance. I have longer legs," added Bazarov with a grin. "One, two, three . . ."

"Evgeny Vasilich," muttered Peter with difficulty (shaking as if in a fever). "If you'll permit me, I'll move away."

"Four . . . five . . . Go on, brother, go on; you can even stand behind the tree and cover your ears, but don't close your eyes; and if anyone falls, come help him up. Six . . . seven . . . eight . . ." Bazarov stopped. "Enough?" he asked, turning to Pavel Petrovich, "or shall I add a few more?"

"As you wish," he replied, inserting a second bullet.

"Well, let's add a few more paces." Bazarov drew a line on the ground with the toe of his boot. "Here's the barrier. By the way: how many paces from the barrier will each of us stand? That's an important question as well. There was no discussion of this yesterday."

"I suggest ten," replied Pavel Petrovich, handing Bazarov both pistols. "Be so good as to choose."

"I will. You'll agree, Pavel Petrovich, our duel is so unusual as to be ridiculous? One need only look at the face of our second."

"You seek to make light of everything," replied Pavel Petrovich. "I don't deny the strange nature of our duel, but I consider it my duty to warn you that I intend to fight seriously. *A bon entendeur, salut!*"[8]

"Oh! I don't doubt we're determined to annihilate each other; but why not laugh and combine *utile* with *dulci*?[9] So, you speak to me in French, I reply in Latin."

"I intend to fight seriously," repeated Pavel Petrovich and went to take up his position. Bazarov, on his side, counted ten paces from the barrier and stopped.

"Ready?" asked Pavel Petrovich.

"Absolutely."

"We can begin."

Bazarov moved forward slowly, while Pavel Petrovich advanced toward him, his left hand in his pocket, the other gradually raising the barrel of the pistol . . . "He's aiming straight for my nose," thought Bazarov, "and he's squinting hard, the scoundrel! This is a most unpleasant sensation. I'll stare at his watch chain . . ." Something whizzed sharply past Bazarov's ear, and, at the same moment a shot rang out. "I heard it; that means I'm all right" flashed quickly through his mind. He took another step and without aiming squeezed the trigger.

Pavel Petrovich shuddered slightly and grabbed his thigh. A stream of blood trickled down his white trousers.

Bazarov tossed his pistol away and approached his opponent.

"Are you wounded?" he asked.

"You had the right to summon me to the barrier," Pavel Petrovich said. "The wound's not serious. According to our conditions, each of us still has one shot left."

"Well, forgive me, that can wait for another time," replied Bazarov, grabbing Pavel Petrovich, who'd begun to turn pale. "Now I'm no longer a duelist, but a doctor. First I must examine your wound. Peter! Come here. Peter! Where have you got to?"

"It's nothing at all . . . I don't need any assistance," Pavel Petrovich said haltingly," and . . . we must . . . once more . . ." He tried to give his mustache a tug, but his hand grew weak, his eyes rolled up, and he lost consciousness.

"What have we got here? A faint! What next?" Bazarov cried unwittingly, as he lowered Pavel Petrovich onto the grass. "Let's have a look!" He took out a handkerchief, wiped away the blood, and felt around the wound . . . "The bone's intact," he muttered through his teeth. "The bullet entered one muscle but not too far; the *vastus externus* has been hit. He'll be up and dancing in three weeks! . . . But fainting! Oh, these high-strung people are too much! Just look at his delicate skin!"

"Is he dead, sir?" Peter's quavering voice croaked from behind.

Bazarov looked around.

8. "Let he who has ears listen" (French).
9. "Sweet" and "useful" (Latin), from the famous treatise on poetic form *Ars Poetica* by Horace (65–8 B.C.).

"Go get some water, friend, as fast as you can; he'll outlive us both."

But the enlightened servant seemed not to understand these words and didn't budge. Pavel Petrovich opened his eyes slowly. "He's dying!" whispered Peter and began crossing himself.

"You're right . . . What a stupid face!" remarked the wounded gentleman with a forced smile.

"Get some water right away, you devil!" shouted Bazarov.

"There's no need . . . It was a momentary *vertige*[1] . . . Help me sit up . . . that's fine . . . This scratch only needs to be wrapped, and I'll make it home on foot, or else they can send the droshky[2] for me. Our duel, if you agree, need not be continued. You behaved honorably . . . today, note I said 'today.' "

"There's no need to dwell on the past," replied Bazarov. "As for the future, there's no point in worrying your head about that either, because I plan to leave here today. Now let me bind your leg; your wound isn't serious, but it's always better to stop the bleeding. First we must bring this creature back to his senses."

Bazarov shook Peter by the collar and sent him off for the droshky.

"Be sure not to scare my brother," Pavel Petrovich said to him. "Don't even think of telling him what's happened."

Peter ran off; while he went to fetch the droshky, the two opponents sat on the ground in silence. Pavel Petrovich tried not to look at Bazarov; he still didn't want to be reconciled with him; he was ashamed of his own arrogance and failure, ashamed of the whole business, even though he felt it couldn't have turned out better. "At least he won't be hanging around here any longer," he comforted himself. "Thank heaven for that." The silence persisted, painful and awkward. Both of them felt uncomfortable. Each was aware that the other understood him. Friends find that experience pleasant, but for enemies, it's extremely unpleasant, especially when they find it impossible either to reach any understanding or to go their separate ways.

"Did I tie the bandage too tight around your leg?" Bazarov asked finally.

"No, it's all right, it's fine," replied Pavel Petrovich. After a moment he added: "There's no fooling my brother. We'll have to tell him we quarreled over politics."

"Fine," said Bazarov. "You can tell him I insulted all Anglomaniacs."

"Splendid. What do you suppose that fellow's thinking about us now?" continued Pavel Petrovich, pointing to the same peasant who, a few minutes before the duel, had been driving his harnessed horses past Bazarov; now, going down the road, he "kowtowed" and doffed his cap at the sight of the "masters."

"Who knows?" replied Bazarov. "Most likely he's not thinking any-

1. "Dizzy spell" (French).
2. A low, open four-wheeled carriage in which passengers sit astride a narrow bench connecting the front and rear axles.

thing at all. The Russian peasant's just like the mysterious stranger that Mrs. Radcliffe[3] used to go on about at such length. Who can understand him? He doesn't even understand himself."

"Ah! So that's what you think!" Pavel Petrovich began and suddenly cried: "Look what that idiot Peter's gone and done! My brother's galloping toward us!"

Bazarov turned and saw the pale face of Nikolai Petrovich in the droshky. He jumped down before it had even stopped and rushed toward his brother.

"What's all this about?" he asked in an agitated voice. "Evgeny Vasilich, tell me, what's going on?"

"Nothing," replied Pavel Petrovich, "you've been disturbed for no reason. Mr. Bazarov and I had a little quarrel, and I've had to pay a small price for it."

"What was the cause of it, for God's sake?"

"How shall I put it? Mr. Bazarov referred disrespectfully to Sir Robert Peel.[4] I hasten to add, I'm completely to blame for everything, while Mr. Bazarov's behaved himself in an exemplary way. I challenged him."

"Good heavens, you're bleeding."

"Did you think I had water in my veins? But this bloodletting may even be good for me. Isn't that right, Doctor? Help me get into the droshky and don't give way to melancholy. I'll feel fine tomorrow. That's it; splendid. Drive on, coachman."

Nikolai Petrovich followed the droshky; Bazarov was going to remain behind . . .

"I must ask you to take care of my brother," Nikolai Petrovich said to him, "until another doctor can be summoned from town."

Bazarov nodded his head in silence.

An hour later Pavel Petrovich was already lying in bed with a proper bandage tied skillfully around his leg. The whole household was in a state of agitation; Fenechka didn't feel at all well. Nikolai Petrovich wrung his hands surreptitiously, while Pavel Petrovich laughed and made jokes, especially with Bazarov; he put on a fine white linen shirt, a fashionable morning jacket, and a fez; he didn't allow the curtains to be drawn and complained amusingly about the need to refrain from eating.

But toward evening he grew feverish and his head started to ache. The doctor arrived from town. (Nikolai Petrovich refused to listen to his brother, and Bazarov himself requested it. Bazarov spent the whole day in his own room, feeling bitter and angry, dropping in to see the patient for very brief visits; he happened to meet Fenechka a few times, but she scurried away from him in terror.) The new doctor prescribed cooling

3. Anne Radcliffe (1764–1823), a very popular writer of Gothic tales of mystery and intrigue.
4. English conservative statesman and prime minister (1788–1850) noted for his powerful oratory and persuasive character.

drinks, meanwhile confirming Bazarov's diagnosis that there was no danger of any kind. Nikolai Petrovich told him that his brother had accidentally wounded himself, to which the doctor replied, "Hmmm." But, when twenty-five rubles in silver were suddenly placed in the doctor's hand, he said: "You don't say! That sort of thing happens quite frequently, you know."

No one in the house got undressed or went to bed. Nikolai Petrovich kept tiptoeing in to look at his brother and left on tiptoe as well; Pavel would doze, moan a little, say to him, "*Couchez-vous*,"[5] and then ask for something to drink. Once Nikolai Petrovich had Fenechka bring him a glass of lemonade; Pavel Petrovich stared at her intently and emptied the glass. Toward morning the fever worsened a bit and he became slightly delirious. At first Pavel Petrovich uttered disconnected words; then he suddenly opened his eyes and, seeing his brother next to his bed, bending over him solicitously, he asked, "Nikolai, don't you think Fenechka has something in common with Nellie?"

"With what Nellie, Pasha?"

"How can you ask that? With Princess R.[6] Especially the upper part of her face. *C'est de la même famille.*"[7]

Nikolai Petrovich made no reply, but inwardly was amazed at the persistence of former passions in a man. "Just see when that's come to the surface," he thought.

"Ah, how I love that silly creature!" Pavel Petrovich moaned, sadly clasping his hands behind his head. "I won't let any insolent fellow touch her . . ." he muttered several moments later.

Nikolai Petrovich merely sighed; he didn't even suspect to whom these words might pertain.

Bazarov came in to see him around eight o'clock the next morning. He'd already managed to pack his belongings and free his frogs, insects, and birds.

"You've come to say good-bye to me?" Nikolai Petrovich asked, getting up to greet him.

"Exactly, sir."

"I understand and approve entirely. My poor brother's at fault, of course: he's been punished for it. He said he put you in an impossible position, leaving you no choice. I believe you found it impossible to avoid this duel, which . . . which, to a certain extent, can be explained by the persistent antagonism that exists between your respective views. [Nikolai Petrovich got a bit lost in his own words.] My brother's a man of the old school, hot-tempered and stubborn . . . Thank God it ended the way it did. I've taken all necessary precautions to prevent the news from spreading."

5. "Go to bed" (French).
6. See above, pp. 22–26.
7. "It's of the same stock" (French).

"I'll leave you my address in case of any consequences," Bazarov said in an offhanded manner.

"I trust there won't be any, Evgeny Vasilich . . . I'm very sorry your stay in my house had such . . . an ending. It's all the more upsetting that Arkady . . ."

"I'll most likely be seeing him," replied Bazarov; every sort of "explanation" and "declaration" always aroused impatience in him. "In case I don't, I ask that you give him my regards and beg him to accept my regrets."

When he learned of Bazarov's departure, Pavel Petrovich wished to see him and shake his hand. Even then Bazarov remained as cold as ice; he realized that Pavel Petrovich simply wanted to appear magnanimous. He didn't manage to say good-bye to Fenechka: he merely exchanged glances with her through the window. Her face looked sad to him. "Done for, no doubt!" he said to himself . . . "Well, she'll survive somehow!" On the other hand, Peter was so overcome he wept on his shoulder until Bazarov stifled his emotions by asking, "Do your eyes always drip water?" Dunyasha had to take refuge in the grove to hide her dismay. The party responsible for all this grief climbed into the cart, lit a cigar, and after some four versts, when, at a bend in the road, the Kirsanov estate, stretching in a long line with its new manor house, came into view for the last time, he merely spat, muttered: "Damned aristocrats!" and wrapped himself up in his overcoat.

Pavel Petrovich soon recovered, but had to stay in bed for almost a week. He endured his *captivity*, as he described it, rather well, except that he fussed a great deal over his toilette and insisted that everything be scented with eau de cologne. Nikolai Petrovich used to read to him from journals, Fenechka waited on him as before, bringing him bouillon, lemonade, soft-boiled eggs, and tea; but a secret terror would seize her each time she had to enter his room. Pavel Petrovich's unexpected action had frightened everyone in the house, her most of all; only Prokofich was undisturbed and described how in his day gentlemen used to fight duels, "but it was only noble gentlemen who fought between themselves, while upstarts like that one they'd have flogged in the stable for his insolence."

Fenechka's conscience hardly bothered her, but from time to time she was tormented by the real cause of the quarrel; besides, Pavel Petrovich would look at her in such a strange way . . . even when her back was turned toward him she still felt him staring at her. She grew thin from constant inner agitation and, as so often happens, became even more attractive.

Once—it was morning—Pavel Petrovich was feeling better and had been moved from his bed to the sofa; after inquiring about his health, Nikolai Petrovich set off for the barn. Fenechka brought him a cup of tea and, after placing it on the little table, was just about to leave. Pavel Petrovich detained her.

"Where are you off to, Fedosya Nikolaevna?" he began. "Do you really have things to do?"

"No, sir . . . yes, sir . . . I must go pour the tea."

"Dunyasha will do it if you're not there; sit here for a while with a sick man. Besides, I want to have a little chat with you."

Fenechka sat down in silence on the edge of the armchair.

"Listen," said Pavel Petrovich, tugging at his mustache. "I've been wanting to ask you something for a long time: why are you so frightened of me?"

"Me, sir?"

"Yes, you. You never look at me; it's as if your conscience wasn't clear."

Fenechka blushed, but glanced up at Pavel Petrovich. He seemed a bit strange and her heart began quivering softly.

"Your conscience is clear, isn't it?" he asked her.

"Why shouldn't it be?" she whispered.

"Any number of reasons! Besides, whom could you have wronged? Me? Unlikely. Other people here in the house? That's also hard to believe. My brother? But you love him, don't you?"

"I do."

"With all your heart and soul?"

"I love Nikolai Petrovich with all my heart."

"Really? Look at me, Fenechka [it was the first time he called her that . . .]. You know, it's a great sin to lie!"

"I'm not lying, Pavel Petrovich. If I didn't love Nikolai Petrovich there'd be nothing left for me to live for!"

"And you wouldn't trade him for anyone else?"

"Who would I trade him for?"

"Any number of people! Why, even for the gentleman who just left here."

Fenechka stood up.

"Good Lord, Pavel Petrovich, why are you tormenting me? What have I done to you? How can you say such a thing? . . ."

"Fenechka," said Pavel Petrovich in a somber voice, "I saw . . ."

"What did you see, sir?"

"There . . . in the arbor."

Fenechka turned red to her ears and the roots of her hair.

"How was I to blame for that?" she uttered with difficulty.

Pavel Petrovich raised himself up a little.

"You weren't to blame? No? Not at all?"

"Nikolai Petrovich is the only one in the world I love and ever will love!" Fenechka said with unexpected force, while sobs rose in her throat. "As to what you saw, I'll declare on Judgment Day that I'm not to blame and wasn't, and it'd be better for me to die right here and now than be suspected of doing such a thing to my benefactor Nikolai Petrovich . . ."

But at this point her voice failed her; at the same time she realized that Pavel Petrovich had seized her and was squeezing her hand . . . She looked at him and froze. He was even paler than before; his eyes were gleaming and, what was even more astonishing, a single, large tear was running down his cheek.

"Fenechka!" he said in a very strange whisper. "Love him, love my brother! He's such a good, kind man! Don't betray him for anyone in the world, don't listen to anyone else! Think what could be more terrible than not loving and not being loved! Never forsake my poor brother Nikolai!"

Fenechka was so astounded that her eyes dried and her terror disappeared. But imagine her surprise when Pavel Petrovich, Pavel Petrovich himself, brought her hand toward his lips and leaned over, without kissing it, merely emitting convulsive sighs from time to time . . .

"Good Lord!" she thought, "is he having some sort of attack? . . ."

At that very moment his whole desolate life was trembling inside him.

The staircase creaked under quick footsteps . . . He pushed her away and let his head drop back on the pillow. The door flung open—and a happy, fresh, ruddy Nikolai Petrovich appeared. Mitya, just as fresh and ruddy as his father, dressed only in a little shirt, was bouncing up and down on his father's chest, catching hold of the big buttons on his country coat with his bare little feet.

Fenechka simply threw herself at him, wound her arms around him and her son, and rested her head on his shoulder. Nikolai Petrovich was surprised: Fenechka, bashful and modest, never displayed any affection in the presence of a third party.

"What's the matter?" he asked. He glanced at his brother and handed Mitya to Fenechka. "You aren't feeling worse, are you?" he inquired, going up to Pavel Petrovich.

The latter buried his face in his cambric handkerchief.

"No . . . it's . . . nothing . . . On the contrary, I feel much better."

"You were in too great a hurry to move to the sofa. Where're you going?" added Nikolai Petrovich, turning to Fenechka; but she'd already slammed the door behind her. "I came to show you my little bogatyr;[8] he missed seeing his uncle. Why did she take him away? What's the matter with you? Something's happened in here, hasn't it?"

"Brother!" Pavel Petrovich announced solemnly.

Nikolai Petrovich shuddered. He felt terrified, but didn't understand why.

"Brother," Pavel Petrovich repeated. "Promise me you'll carry out one request of mine."

"What is it? Tell me."

"It's very important; in my opinion all the happiness of your life

---

8. A hero of legendary strength in Russian folklore.

depends on it. All along I've been thinking about what I want to say to you . . . Brother, fulfill your obligation, the obligation of an honest, generous man; end temptation and the bad example you're setting, you, the best of men."

"What do you mean, Pavel?"

"Marry Fenechka . . . She loves you; she's the mother of your son."

Nikolai Petrovich took a step back and flung his arms open wide.

"Is it you saying this, Pavel? You, whom I always considered the most implacable foe of such marriages? Is it you saying this? Surely you must know it was solely out of respect for you that I didn't fulfill what you justly describe as my obligation."

"You were wrong to respect me in this instance," Pavel Petrovich replied with a mournful smile. "I'm beginning to think that Bazarov was right when he accused me of aristocratism. No, dear brother, we've spent enough time putting on airs and worrying about what other people think: we've already become old and tranquil folk; it's time for us to put aside all vanity. Let's do our duty, precisely as you say, and let's see if we can achieve happiness in the bargain."

Nikolai Petrovich rushed to embrace his brother.

"You've opened my eyes once and for all!" he cried. "It's not for nothing I've always said you were the kindest, smartest man in the whole world; now I see you're as reasonable as you are magnanimous."

"Easy, easy," Pavel Petrovich said, interrupting him. "Don't hurt the leg of your reasonable brother, who, at age fifty, fought a duel like a young lieutenant. And so, it's all settled: Fenechka will be my . . . *belle-soeur.*"[9]

"My dear Pavel! But what will Arkady say?"

"Arkady? He'll be delighted, of course! Marriage isn't one of his principles; on the other hand, his sense of equality will be gratified. And, in fact, what do class distinctions matter *au dix-neuvième siècle?*"[1]

"Ah, Pavel, Pavel! Let me kiss you again. Don't worry, I'll be careful."

The brothers embraced.

"What do you think, shouldn't you tell her what you intend to do right away?" asked Pavel Petrovich.

"What's the rush?" Nikolai Petrovich replied. "You didn't mention it to her, did you?"

"Mention it? Me? *Quelle idée!*"[2]

"Well, that's splendid. First of all, you must get well. This won't run away from us; we must think about it, consider it . . ."

"But you've decided?"

"Of course I've decided, and I thank you from the bottom of my heart. I'll leave you now; you must get some rest. Any sort of excitement

9. "Sister-in-law" (French).
1. "In the nineteenth century" (French).
2. "What an idea!" (French).

can be harmful . . . We'll talk more about it. Go to sleep, my dear;
God grant you good health."

"Why does he feel so grateful to me?" wondered Pavel Petrovich when
left alone. "As if it didn't all depend on him! As soon as he gets married,
I'll go somewhere far away, to Dresden or Florence and live there until
I pass on."

Pavel Petrovich wiped his forehead with eau de cologne and closed
his eyes. Lit by the bright daylight, his handsome, emaciated head resting
on the white pillow looked like the head of a dead man . . . In effect,
he was a dead man.

XXV

In the garden at Nikolskoe, Katya and Arkady were sitting on a turf
seat in the shade of a tall ash tree; on the ground next to them lay Fifi,
her long body forming that graceful curve sportsmen refer to as "a hare's
lie." Both Arkady and Katya were silent; he held in his hands a half-
open book, while she picked a few remaining crumbs of white bread
from a basket and tossed them to a small family of sparrows that, with
their characteristic timorous impudence, were hopping about and chirping at her feet. A faint breeze, rustling in the leaves of the ash, moved
pale gold spots of light slowly back and forth across the dark path and
Fifi's yellow back; Arkady and Katya were enveloped in deep shade; only
occasionally did a bright streak gleam in her hair. They were both silent;
but it was precisely the way they were silent, the way they sat there side
by side, that made their trusting intimacy so apparent: each one seemed
not to be thinking about the other, while secretly rejoicing in the other's
proximity. Their faces had changed since last we saw them: Arkady
appeared calmer, Katya, livelier and bolder.

"Don't you think," Arkady began, "that the *ash* tree[3] is very aptly
named in Russian? No other tree is as light and translucent against the
sky as it is."

Katya raised her eyes and said, "Yes," and Arkady thought: "She never
reproaches me for using fine phrases."

"I don't like Heine,"[4] Katya said, indicating with her eyes the book
Arkady was holding, "when he laughs or cries; I like him when he's
pensive and sad."

"I like him when he laughs," remarked Arkady.

"Remnants of your satirical inclination showing through . . . ["Remnants!" thought Arkady. "If Bazarov could only hear that!"] Wait a bit,
we'll remake you."

"Who'll remake me? You?"

---

3. The Russian word for the ash tree is *yasen'*, while the adjective *yasnyi* means "clear, bright."
4. Heinrich Heine (1797–1856), a German romantic poet and strong supporter of the ideals of
the French Revolution.

"Who? My sister; Porfiry Platonovich, with whom you no longer quarrel; and Auntie, whom you escorted to church a few days ago."

"I couldn't refuse! And as far as Anna Sergeevna's concerned, you recall, she agreed with Bazarov about many things."

"My sister was under his influence at the time, just like you."

"Just like me! Have you decided that I've already freed myself from his influence?"

Katya was silent.

"I know," Arkady continued, "you never liked him."

"I can't pass judgment on him."

"You know something, Katerina Sergeevna? Every time I hear that, I don't believe it . . . There's no one about whom each of us can't pass judgment! It's merely an excuse."

"Well, then I'll say he . . . it's not exactly that I don't like him, but I feel he's totally different from me, and I'm different from him . . . and you're different from him, too."

"Why's that?"

"How can I explain it to you? . . . He's a predator, while you and I are domesticated."

"Am I domesticated?"

Katya nodded her head.

Arkady scratched behind his ear.

"Listen, Katerina Sergeevna: that's really an insult."

"Do you really want to be a predator?"

"No, not a predator, but strong and energetic."

"That doesn't come from wishing . . . Your friend didn't want to be like that, yet he has it in him."

"Hmmm! So you assume he exercised great influence on Anna Sergeevna?"

"Yes. But no one can keep the upper hand with her for very long," Katya added in a low voice.

"Why do you think that?"

"She's very proud . . . That's not what I wanted to say . . . she's very eager to maintain her own independence."

"Who isn't?" asked Arkady, while the question, "What use is it?" flashed through his head. "What use is it?" also flashed through Katya's head. When young people are together frequently and intimately, they constantly hit upon one and the same idea.

Arkady smiled; drawing slightly closer to Katya, he said in a whisper, "Admit it, you're just a little bit afraid of *her*."

"Of whom?"

"*Her*," Arkady repeated meaningfully.

"What about you?" Katya asked in turn.

"Me, too; notice I said *too*."

Katya threatened him with her finger.

"That surprises me," she began. "My sister's never been so favorably disposed toward you as she is now, much more so than on your first visit here."

"Is that so?"

"You haven't noticed? Doesn't it make you happy?"

Arkady became thoughtful.

"What have I done to deserve Anna Sergeevna's goodwill? Was it perhaps that I came bearing letters from your mother?"

"For that and for some other reasons I won't list."

"Why not?"

"I just won't."

"Oh! I know why: you're very stubborn."

"That's right."

"And observant."

Katya gave Arkady a sidelong glance.

"Does that make you angry, perhaps? What're you thinking about?"

"I'm wondering where you acquired those powers of observation you genuinely possess. You're so timid and distrustful, so removed from everyone . . ."

"I've lived alone for a long time: that forces you to become reflective. But am I really so removed from everyone?"

Arkady cast a grateful glance at Katya.

"That's all well and good," he continued, "but people in your position, that is, with your income, rarely have that gift; it's as hard for the truth to reach them, as it is for it to reach the tsar."

"But I'm not rich."

Arkady was amazed and didn't understand Katya immediately. "Why, of course," the thought suddenly occurred to him, "the estate belongs entirely to her sister!" That idea was not altogether unpleasant to him.

"You said that so well."

"What?"

"You said it well: simply, without embarrassment, without posturing. By the way, I imagine there must be something special, a particular kind of vanity in the feeling of a person who knows and says he's poor."

"I've never experienced anything of that sort, thanks to my sister; I mentioned my income simply because it seemed appropriate at the time."

"I see; but you must admit, you too possess a bit of that vanity we were just talking about."

"For instance?"

"For instance, you—forgive my question—you wouldn't marry a wealthy man, would you?"

"If I loved him very much . . . No, I think even then I wouldn't do it."

"Ah! You see!" cried Arkady. After waiting a little while, he added, "Why wouldn't you?"

"Because even our folk songs warn about unequal matches."

"Perhaps you want to dominate or . . ."

"Oh, no! Why? On the contrary, I'm ready to submit, but inequality is difficult to accept. However, to respect oneself and submit—that I understand, that's happiness. But a subservient existence . . . No, I've had enough of that."

"Enough of that," Arkady repeated after Katya. "Yes, yes," he continued, "it's not for nothing you're related to Anna Sergeevna; you're just as independent as she is, but you're more discreet. I'm sure you wouldn't ever be the first to express your feelings, no matter how strong or sacred they were . . ."

"How else could it be?"

"You're just as clever as she is; and you have just as much character as she does, if not more . . ."

"Don't compare me to my sister, please," Katya interrupted him hurriedly. "It's not at all to my advantage. You seem to have forgotten my sister is both beautiful and clever, and . . . you in particular, Arkady Nikolaevich, shouldn't say such things, especially with such a serious expression."

"Why me in particular? And why do you think I'm joking?"

"Of course, you're joking."

"You think so? What if I'm convinced about what I'm saying? What if I feel I've yet to express myself forcefully enough?"

"I don't understand you."

"Really? Well, now I see I've overestimated your powers of observation."

"How?"

Arkady made no reply and turned away, while Katya looked in her basket for a few more crumbs and began tossing them to the sparrows; but the swing of her hand was too strong, and the birds flew away before they could peck at the food.

"Katerina Sergeevna!" Arkady began suddenly. "It's probably all the same to you, but you should know that not only wouldn't I trade you for your sister, I wouldn't trade you for anyone else in the world."

He stood up and quickly walked away, as if frightened by the words that had just escaped his lips.

Katya dropped both hands and the basket into her lap; she lowered her head, her eyes following Arkady for a long time. Gradually a crimson flush covered her cheeks; but her lips didn't form a smile and her dark eyes expressed confusion and some other, still unnamed feeling.

"Are you alone?" Anna Sergeevna's voice rang out near her. "I thought you came out into the garden with Arkady?"

Katya slowly raised her eyes to her sister (elegantly, even exquisitely dressed, she was standing on the path and scratching Fifi's ears with the tip of her closed parasol), and said slowly, "I'm alone."

"I see that," her sister replied with a laugh. "Has he gone back to his room?"

"Yes."

"Were you reading together?"

"Yes."

Anna Sergeevna took hold of Katya's chin and raised her face.

"You didn't quarrel, I hope?"

"No," said Katya, gently removing her sister's hand.

"How solemnly you reply! I thought I'd find him here and propose he take a walk with me. He's always asking me. They've brought you some shoes from town; go try them on. Yesterday I noticed your old ones had worn out. In general you don't pay enough attention to such things, and you have such nice little feet! And your hands are so pretty . . . though a bit large, so you must make the most of your little feet. But you're certainly no coquette."

Anna Sergeevna continued farther down the path, her beautiful dress rustling lightly. Katya stood up from the bench; picking up her Heine, she also walked away—but not to try on the shoes.

"Charming little feet," she thought, slowly and lightly climbing the stone steps of the terrace baked by the sun. "Charming little feet, you say . . . Well, soon he'll be lying at these feet, won't he?"

But she immediately felt ashamed and quickly ran up the stairs.

Arkady was walking along the corridor toward his own room; the butler caught up with him and announced that Mr. Bazarov was sitting there waiting for him.

"Evgeny!" muttered Arkady, almost in fear. "Has he been here long?"

"He's just arrived and asked that he not be announced to Anna Sergeevna, but be shown right up to your room."

"Has something bad happened at home?" Arkady wondered, and hurriedly ran up the stairs and opened the door at once. Bazarov's appearance reassured him immediately, although a more experienced eye might have discerned in the still energetic, but haggard figure of his unexpected guest signs of internal agitation. With a dusty coat over his shoulders, a cap on his head, he was perched on the windowsill; he didn't stand even when Arkady flung himself on his neck with noisy exclamations.

"What a surprise! How on earth did you get here?" he said, bustling about the room like a man who imagines himself delighted and wishes to show that he is. "Is everything all right at home? Everyone's well, I hope."

"Everything's fine at home, though not everyone's well," Bazarov replied. "But stop your jabbering; have them bring me some kvass,[5] sit

5. A traditional Russian beverage, slightly alcoholic, usually made from flour or dark rye bread soaked in water and malt.

down, and listen to what I have to say in a few, but I hope rather telling, phrases."

Arkady quieted down and Bazarov told him about his duel with Pavel Petrovich. Arkady was very surprised, even saddened; but he didn't think it necessary to say that; he merely asked whether his uncle's wound was serious or not. The wound was very interesting, indeed, but not from any medical point of view. He was forced to smile, even though he felt sick at heart and somehow ashamed. Bazarov seemed to understand him.

"Yes, friend," he said, "that's what it means to live with feudal types. You become one yourself and take part in chivalric tournaments. Well, sir, I've decided to head home 'to the fathers,' "[6] Bazarov concluded, "and along the way I stopped by here . . . to tell you all this, I would've said, if I didn't believe a useless lie was stupid. No, I stopped by here —the devil knows why. You see, it's sometimes useful for a man to take himself by the scruff of the neck and pull himself up like a radish from a row in the vegetable garden; I did that several days ago . . . I wanted to have one more look at what I was leaving behind, at the row in which I'd been planted."

"I hope these words don't refer to me," Arkady objected with some annoyance. "I hope you're not planning to leave *me* behind."

Bazarov stared at him intently, almost piercingly.

"Would that really upset you so much? It seems to me it's *you* who've left me behind. You're so fresh and pure . . . Your affair with Anna Sergeevna must be proceeding well."

"What affair with Anna Sergeevna?"

"Wasn't it because of her you came here from town, my little fledgling? By the way, how are the Sunday schools[7] getting on? Aren't you in love with her? Or have you already decided to be discreet about it?"

"Evgeny, you know I've always been honest with you; I can assure you, I can swear to you, you're mistaken."

"Hmmm! A new word," Bazarov observed in a low voice. "But you've got no reason to get excited; it doesn't matter to me. A romantic would say, 'I feel our paths are beginning to diverge'; while I merely say, we're fed up with each other."

"Evgeny . . ."

"My dear boy, it's no disaster. The world's full of things to get fed up with! Now I think it's time for us to say farewell. Since my arrival, I've felt really rotten, as if I'd been reading Gogol's letter to the wife of the governor of Kaluga.[8] Incidentally, I told them not to unhitch my horses."

"Good heavens, that's impossible!"

"Why so?"

6. A sarcastic and ominous reference to *"ad patres"*; see above, p. 91, n. 1.
7. See above, p. 109, n. 4.
8. A letter by the Russian writer Nikolai Gogol (1809–52) to A. O. Smirnova originally included in his conservative and sententious work *Selected Passages from Correspondence with Friends* (1847), but forbidden by the censor and not published until 1857.

"I'm not even thinking about myself: it'd be the height of rudeness to Anna Sergeevna, who'd certainly want to see you."

"Well, you're wrong about that."

"On the contrary, I'm sure I'm right," Arkady retorted. "And why're you pretending? It it's come to that, didn't you really stop here to see her?"

"That may be, but you're still wrong."

Arkady was right. Anna Sergeevna did want to see Bazarov and sent him an invitation through the butler. Bazarov changed his clothes before he went to see her: as it turned out, he'd packed a change of outfit so he could get to it easily.

Odintsova didn't receive him in the room where he'd abruptly confessed his love for her, but in the drawing room. She politely extended the tips of her fingers, but her face expressed unintended tension.

"Anna Sergeevna," Bazarov hastened to say, "first of all, let me set your mind at ease. Before you stands a mortal who's long since come to his senses and hopes that others have also forgotten his indiscretions. I'm going away for a long time; as you'll agree, I'm no tender creature, but I'd prefer not to carry away with me the thought that you'll remember me with repugnance."

Anna Sergeevna sighed deeply like a person who's just climbed to the top of a hill, and her face was enlivened with a smile. She extended her hand to Bazarov once again and responded to his handshake.

"Let's let bygones by bygones," she said, "all the more so since, in all honesty, I was at fault then, if not for flirting, then for something else. In a word: let's be friends just as we were before. That was only a dream, wasn't it? And who remembers dreams?"

"Who remembers them? Besides, love is . . . such a spurious feeling."

"Really? I'm so glad to hear that."

Thus Anna Sergeevna expressed herself, and thus Bazarov expressed himself; they both thought they were telling the truth. Was the truth, the whole truth, contained in their words? They didn't know, and the author knows even less. But a conversation ensued between them as if they believed one another completely.

Anna Sergeevna asked, among other things, what he'd been doing at the Kirsanovs. He was just about to tell her about his duel with Pavel Petrovich, but hesitated at the thought that she might think he was trying to appear interesting; he told her he'd spent all his time there working.

"And I," said Anna Sergeevna, "I was depressed at first, God knows why, and even thought about going abroad, just imagine! . . . But then it passed; your friend Arkady arrived and once again I returned to my old routine, resumed my usual role."

"What role is that, if I may ask?"

"The role of aunt, guardian, mother, whatever you want to call it. Incidentally, you know that formerly I never really appreciated your close friendship with Arkady Nikolaevich; I considered him rather insignificant. But now I've come to know him better and am convinced he's clever . . . The main thing is, he's young, so young . . . not like you and me, Evgeny Vasilich."

"Is he still so timid in your presence?" Bazarov asked.

"Was he ever?" Anna Sergeevna began, but after pausing a little, added: "Now he's more confident and talks to me. Before he used to avoid me. But I didn't seek out his company either. He's become good friends with Katya."

Bazarov was annoyed. "A woman can't help dissembling," he thought.

"You say he was avoiding you," he said with a cold grin, "but surely it's probably no secret to you that he was in love with you?"

"What? He, too?" burst forth from Anna Sergeevna's lips.

"He, too," repeated Bazarov with a humble bow. "Did you really not know that? Have I told you something new?"

Anna Sergeevna lowered her eyes.

"You're mistaken, Evgeny Vasilich."

"I don't think so. But perhaps I shouldn't have mentioned it." He added to himself, "And as for you, no more dissembling from now on."

"Why not mention it? But I suggest that here again you're attributing too much importance to a passing fancy. I'm beginning to suspect you're inclined to exaggerate."

"Let's not talk about it any more, Anna Sergeevna."

"Why not?" she replied, but then directed the conversation in a different direction. She still felt awkward with Bazarov, even though she'd told him, and she herself believed, that everything had been forgotten. Exchanging the simplest words with him, even joking, she experienced a slight sense of apprehension. Just as people on a steamship at sea chat and laugh in a carefree manner, as though they were on dry land, but if only the slightest interruption occurs, the least indication of something out of the ordinary, each and every face immediately assumes an expression of special alarm, testifying to the constant awareness of constant danger.

Anna Sergeevna's conversation with Bazarov didn't last very long. She became distracted, replied in an absentminded manner, and finally suggested they move into the main hall, where they found the princess and Katya. "Where's Arkady Nikolaevich?" the hostess inquired; after learning that he'd not been seen for more than an hour, she sent for him. He was not to be found right away: he'd made his way to the very depths of the garden and, resting his chin on clasped hands, sat there, lost in thought. They were deep and important, these thoughts of his, but not sad. He knew that Anna Sergeevna was alone with Bazarov, but felt none of his previous jealousy; on the contrary, his face was brightening slowly; he seemed to be surprised at something, delighted by it, and had made up his mind about it.

XXVI

The late Odintsov didn't care for innovations, but he tolerated "a certain play of ennobled taste"; consequently, in his garden, between the greenhouse and the pond, he built himself a structure resembling a Greek portico made of Russian bricks. In the rear blind wall of this portico or gallery, there were six niches for statues, which Odintsov had planned to order from abroad. These were supposed to represent: Solitude, Silence, Meditation, Melancholy, Modesty, and Sensitivity. Only one of them, the goddess of Silence, with her finger on her lips, had actually been delivered and set in place; but that same day some boys from the estate had broken the statue's nose, and even though a local plasterer had managed to provide her with a new one, "twice as good as the previous nose," Odintsov had ordered her removed. The statue turned up in a corner of the threshing barn, where it stood for many years, arousing superstitious horror among the peasant women. The front part of the portico had long since become overgrown with thick bushes; only the capitals of the columns could be seen above the abundant greenery. Inside the portico it was cool, even at midday. Anna Sergeevna didn't like visiting the place ever since she'd seen a grass snake there; but Katya came often to sit on a large stone bench under one of the niches. Surrounded by fresh scents and shade, she used to read, work, or surrender herself to absolute silence, a feeling probably familiar to everyone, the charm of which consists in a scarcely conscious, quiet attentiveness to the broad wave of life constantly flowing in and around us.

The day after Bazarov's arrival, Katya was sitting on her favorite bench and Arkady was once again sitting next to her. He'd asked her to accompany him to the portico.

There was about an hour left before breakfast; the dewy morning had already been replaced by the hot day. Arkady's face retained its expression of the previous day; Katya had a worried look. Her sister, right after tea, had summoned her to the study and, after some preliminary compliments, which always frightened Katya a bit, advised her to be more careful in her behavior with Arkady and particularly to avoid private conversations with him, which had apparently been noticed by Auntie and others in the household. In addition, Anna Sergeevna hadn't been in a very good mood the previous evening; even Katya felt some consternation, as if she were to blame for something. In acceding to Arkady's request, she told herself it would be the last time.

"Katerina Sergeevna," he began in a somewhat bashful, free-and-easy manner. "Since I've had the good fortune to reside in the same house with you, we've discussed many things, but there's still one very important . . . question . . . for me at least, which I haven't touched on. Yesterday you noted that I've been remade during my time here," he added, both catching and avoiding the inquisitive glance Katya was directing at him. "As a matter of fact, I have changed a great deal; you yourself know that better than anyone else—you, to whom I essentially owe this change."

"I? . . . To me? . . ." replied Katya.

"I'm no longer the haughty little boy I was when I came here," continued Arkady. "I've not reached the age of twenty-three for nothing; I still wish to be useful as I did before, to devote all my strength to the truth; but I'm no longer searching for ideals where I did previously; they're appearing to me . . . much closer at hand. Up to now I didn't understand myself; I set myself tasks beyond my powers . . . My eyes have recently been opened thanks to one feeling . . . I'm not expressing myself altogether clearly, but I hope you'll understand me."

Katya said nothing in reply, but stopped looking at Arkady.

"I suppose," he began again, but in a more excited tone of voice, while a chaffinch in the birch foliage above him burst into carefree song, "I suppose it's the obligation of every honest man to be entirely candid with those . . . those people who . . . in a word, those he's closest to; therefore I . . . I intend . . ."

But here Arkady's eloquence failed him; he lost his train of thought, stumbled, and was forced to fall silent for a moment; Katya still didn't raise her eyes. She seemed not to understand where all this was leading and kept waiting for something more.

"I foresee that I may surprise you," Arkady began, after mustering his strength again, "all the more so since this feeling relates in a certain way . . . in a certain way—mind you—to you. Yesterday, you may recall, you reproached me for a lack of seriousness," continued Arkady, looking like a man who's entered a swamp and feels as if he's sinking deeper and deeper with every step, but who still goes on in the hope he might soon get to the end of it. "This same reproach is often directed at . . . falls upon . . . young men, even when they no longer deserve it; and if I had more self-confidence . . . ["Help me, please help me!" Arkady thought in desperation, but Katya still wouldn't turn her head.] If I could hope for . . ."

"If only I could be sure of what you're saying," Anna Sergeevna's clear voice rang out at that very moment.

Arkady immediately fell silent and Katya grew pale. A little path ran right past the bushes that concealed the portico. Anna Sergeevna was walking along it, accompanied by Bazarov. Katya and Arkady couldn't see them, but heard their every word, the rustle of her dress, their breathing. They took several steps and stopped right in front of the portico, as if deliberately.

"Don't you see?" Anna Sergeevna continued. "You and I were mistaken; we're not all that young anymore, especially me; we've lived our lives, we're tired out; we're both—why pretend it's not so?—clever peo-

ple: at first we interested each other, our curiosity was aroused . . . but
then . . ."

"Then it fizzled," Bazarov inserted.

"You know that wasn't the cause of our separation. But whatever
happened, the main thing was we didn't need each other; there was too
much—how can I put it?—too much alike in us. We didn't understand
that at first. On the other hand, Arkady . . ."

"Do you need him?" asked Bazarov.

"Enough of that, Evgeny Vasilich. You say he's not indifferent to
me, and it's always seemed to me that he liked me. I know I could pass
for his aunt; but I don't want to hide from you the fact that I've begun
thinking about him more often. There's a kind of charm in that young,
fresh feeling . . ."

"The word *fascination* is more applicable in such circumstances,"
Bazarov said, interrupting her; a note of seething vexation could be
heard in his calm but hollow voice. "Arkady was very secretive with me
yesterday and didn't say anything about you or your sister . . . That's a
serious symptom."

"He's just like a brother to Katya," Anna Sergeevna said, "and I like
that about him, although perhaps I shouldn't permit such intimacy
between them."

"Are you saying that as . . . a sister?" Bazarov said, dragging out his
words.

"Naturally . . . But why are we standing here? Let's move on. This
is a strange conversation for us to have, isn't it? I'd never have expected
I'd be able to talk to you like this. You know I'm afraid of you . . . yet
at the same time I trust you because you're really a very kind person."

"In the first place, I'm not kind at all; in the second, I've lost all
importance for you, and you tell me I'm a kind person . . . That's just
like placing a wreath of flowers on a corpse's head."

"Evgeny Vasilich, we don't have the power to . . ." Anna Sergeevna
started to say, but the wind came up, rustled the leaves, and carried her
voice away.

"But you're free to . . ." Bazarov said after a short pause.

It was impossible to make out any other words; the footsteps died away
and everything became quiet.

Arkady turned to Katya. She was sitting in the same position, but her
head was hanging even lower.

"Katerina Sergeevna," he began, his voice trembling, his hands
clasped tightly together. "I love you irrevocably, forever and ever; I love
no one else but you. I wanted to tell you, find out your opinion, and
ask for your hand, because I'm not a wealthy man and feel I'm ready
to make any sacrifice . . . You're not answering? You don't believe me?
You don't think I'm serious? Just consider these last few days! Surely
you must be convinced by now that everything—understand what I

say—everything else has long since disappeared without trace. Look at me, say one word . . . I love . . . I love you . . . please believe me!"

Katya gave Arkady a bright and serious look and, after a long pause for thought, with scarcely a smile, said, "Yes."

Arkady jumped up from the bench.

"Yes! Katerina Sergeevna, you said, 'Yes'! What does that mean? That I love you, that you believe me? . . . Or . . . or . . . I dare not go on . . ."

"Yes," Katya repeated, and this time he understood her. He took hold of her lovely large hands; sighing with ecstasy, he pressed them to his heart. He was hardly able to stand and merely repeated, "Katya, Katya . . ." while she wept innocently, laughing softly at her own tears. He who's never seen such tears in the eyes of a beloved has yet to experience the degree to which, totally consumed by gratitude and shame, a man can be happy on earth.

The next day, early in the morning, Anna Sergeevna summoned Bazarov to her study and with forced laughter showed him a folded piece of writing paper. It was a letter from Arkady: he was asking for her sister's hand in marriage.

Bazarov read through the letter quickly and made an effort not to display the malicious feeling welling up immediately inside him.

"So that's how it is," he said. "And it seems that as recently as yesterday, you supposed he loved Katya like a brother. What do you intend to do now?"

"What do *you* advise me to do?" Anna Sergeevna asked, continuing to laugh.

"Well, I suppose," replied Bazarov also with a laugh, even though he didn't feel at all cheerful and didn't want to laugh any more than she did, "I suppose you should give the young couple your blessing. The match is a fine one in all respects; Kirsanov has a considerable income, he's his father's only son, and the father's a good fellow who won't object."

Odintsova paced around the room. Her color alternated between pink and pale.

"You think so?" she asked. "Well then? I don't see any obstacles . . . I'm happy for Katya . . . and for Arkady Nikolaich. Naturally I'll wait for his father's reply. I'll send word to him myself. But it turns out I was right yesterday when I said we were both too old . . . How is it I didn't foresee this? That surprises me!"

Anna Sergeevna began laughing once again and immediately turned away.

"Young people today have become awfully sly," Bazarov observed and also started laughing. "Good-bye," he said after a brief pause. "I hope this matter's concluded in the best possible way; I'll enjoy it from afar."

Odintsova quickly turned to face him.

"Are you really leaving? Why shouldn't you stay *now*? Do stay . . . it's nice talking to you . . . like walking along the edge of an abyss. At first you're timid, but then you feel more courageous. Do stay."

"Thanks for the offer, Anna Sergeevna, and for the flattering opinion of my conversational skills. But I find I've already spent too much time in spheres alien to my nature. Flying fish can survive in the air only for a short while; soon they've got to flop down into the water. Allow me to return to my own element."

Odintsova looked at Bazarov. A bitter smile was tugging at his pale face. "This man used to love me!" she thought; she felt sorry for him and extended her hand with sympathy.

But he understood her, too.

"No!" he said, taking a step back. "I may be a poor man, but up to now I've never accepted charity. Good-bye, madame; I wish you good health."

"I'm sure we'll be seeing each other again," Anna Sergeevna said with an unintentional movement.

"Anything can happen!" replied Bazarov; he bowed and left.

"So, you've decided to make a nest for yourself?" he said to Arkady that same day, squatting as he packed his suitcase. "Well, it's a fine thing to do. But there was no reason to be so underhanded about it. I expected things to take a completely different direction. Perhaps you yourself were taken aback by it?"

"I really didn't expect anything like this when we separated," replied Arkady. "But why are you being so underhanded now when you say, 'It's a fine thing you do'—as if I didn't know your views on marriage?"

"Hey, my dear friend!" Bazarov said. "The things you say! You see what I'm doing: it turns out there's empty space in my suitcase and I'm stuffing hay into it. That's just how it is in the suitcase of our lives; it doesn't matter what you stuff in, as long as there's no empty space. Please, don't be offended: you probably recall my former opinion of Katerina Sergeevna. Other young ladies pass for being clever merely because they can sigh cleverly; but your young lady can stand up for herself, so much so she'll have you under her thumb—well, that's as it should be." He slammed the top of the case shut and stood up from the floor. "Now I say once again in farewell . . . because there's no reason to deceive ourselves: we're saying good-bye forever, and you know that too . . . You've behaved sensibly; you're not made for our bitter, tart, lonely existence. There's no arrogance in you, no malice; there's only youthful audacity and youthful fervor; that's not commensurate to our task. You aristocrats can never get any further than noble submission or noble indignation, and all that's nonsense. You, for instance, you won't fight—yet you think you're a fine fellow—but we want to fight.

What of it? The dust we raise will blind your eyes, our mud will splatter you, but you haven't reached our level; you admire yourself unconsciously, take pleasure in abusing yourself; but we find all this boring —give us someone else! We've got to smash someone else! You're a fine fellow, but you're still a soft, liberal gentleman—*eh vollatoo*,[9] as my father would say."

"Are you saying good-bye forever, Evgeny?" asked Arkady sadly. "Have you nothing else to say to me?"

Bazarov scratched the back of his head.

"I do, Arkady, I do have something else to say to you, but I won't say it because it's romanticism—that is, getting sugary. You just go and get married as soon as you can; fix up your nest and have lots and lots of children. They'll be smart enough to be born at a better time than you and me. Hey! I see the horses are ready. It's time! I've said good-bye to everyone . . . Well, then, shall we embrace?"

Arkady threw himself on the neck of his former mentor and friend, and tears literally gushed from his eyes.

"That's what it means to be young!" Bazarov said serenely. "But I'm relying on Katerina Sergeevna. Just wait and see how she'll comfort you!"

"Farewell, brother!" he said to Arkady, after climbing into the cart; pointing to a pair of jackdaws sitting side by side on the stable roof, he added, "There you are! Study that example!"

"What does that mean?" asked Arkady.

"What? Are you really that weak in natural history or have you forgotten that the jackdaw's the most respectable family bird? Let that be an example to you! . . . Farewell, signor!"

Bazarov was telling the truth. While talking with Katya that evening, Arkady forgot all about his mentor. He'd already begun to submit to her; Katya felt this and wasn't at all surprised. The next day he was supposed to leave for Marino to see Nikolai Petrovich. Anna Sergeevna didn't want to get in the young couple's way, and it was only out of a sense of propriety that she didn't leave them alone for too long. She magnanimously kept the princess away from them; the old woman had been reduced to a fit of tears by news of the impending marriage. At first Anna Sergeevna was afraid that the sight of their happiness might be too difficult for her to bear; but it turned out to be the complete opposite: it not only failed to oppress her, but even interested her, mellowed her at long last. Anna Sergeevna was both gladdened and saddened by this fact. "Apparently Bazarov was right," she thought, "it was curiosity, mere curiosity, love of serenity, and egoism . . ."

"Children!" she said aloud to herself. "Tell me, is love an imaginary feeling?"

---

9. *Et voilà tout*: "and that's all" (French).

But neither Katya nor Arkady even understood her. They avoided her; the conversation they'd overheard accidentally wouldn't leave their minds. But Anna Sergeevna soon calmed them down; that wasn't too hard for her to do: she herself calmed down.

XXVII

Bazarov's old parents were all the more delighted with their son's sudden arrival since it was so unexpected. Arina Vlasevna was so flustered and scurried around the house so much that Vasily Ivanovich compared her to a "partridge": the cropped tail of her short jacket actually did make her look a bit like a bird. Meanwhile he himself mumbled and chewed the amber mouthpiece of his pipe; clutching his neck with his fingers, he twisted his head as if checking to see that it was attached properly and suddenly opened his broad mouth and laughed without ever emitting a sound.

"I've come to stay with you for six whole weeks, old man," Bazarov said to him. "I want to work, so please don't disturb me."

"You'll even forget what I look like, that's how much I'll disturb you!" replied Vasily Ivanovich.

He kept his promise. After installing his son in his study again, not only did he keep himself hidden away, but he also kept his wife from making any unnecessary demonstrations of affection. "You and I, my dear woman," he said to her, "pestered Enyusha too much on his first visit here: now we have to be smarter." Arina Vlasevna agreed with her husband, but gained very little from it because she saw her son only at the table and was absolutely afraid to talk to him. "Enyushenka!" she'd start to say, and before he'd even time to turn around, she was already fingering the laces of her handbag and would mutter: "Never mind, it's nothing, I was only . . ." Then she'd go off to find Vasily Ivanovich and, resting her cheek on her hand, would say to him, "My dear, how can I find out what Enyusha would like for dinner today, cabbage soup or borsch?"[1] "Why didn't you ask him yourself?" "I'd be pestering him!" But Bazarov soon stopped locking himself in: the fever to work had *deserted* him and been replaced by dreary boredom and vague restlessness. A strange lethargy could be detected in all his movements; even his step, usually forceful and decisively bold, was different. He stopped taking walks alone and began seeking company; he took tea in the living room, wandered around the garden with Vasily Ivanovich, and smoked his pipe with him "in peace and quiet"; he even inquired once about Father Aleksei. At first Vasily Ivanovich was overjoyed by this change, but his joy was short-lived. "Enyusha's breaking my heart," he complained to his wife in secret. "It's not that he's dissatisfied or angry; that wouldn't mean a thing. He's embittered and gloomy—that's what's so terrible. He's always silent—it'd be better if he'd berate us; he's growing

---

1. Traditional Russian soup made with beets, cabbage, and potatoes, among other ingredients.

thin and his color is poor." "Good Lord!" whispered the old woman, "I'd like to put an amulet around his neck, but he wouldn't let me." Several times Vasily Ivanovich tried in a most careful manner to question Bazarov about his work, his health, Arkady . . . But Bazarov replied unwillingly and carelessly; once, noticing that his father's conversation seemed to be slowly leading up to something, he said to him in annoyance: "Why are you always tiptoeing around me? That's even worse than what you were doing before." "Well, well, well, I didn't mean anything!" poor Vasily Ivanovich hastened to reply. His political allusions were just as unproductive. Once, having mentioned progress in connection with the impending emancipation of the serfs, he hoped to arouse his son's sympathy: "Yesterday I was coming past the fence and overheard our local peasant lads: instead of singing a folk song, they were bawling out some romance:[2] 'The true time has come, my heart is full of love . . .' That's progress for you."

Sometimes Bazarov would set off for the village and, in his usual mocking manner, enter into conversation with some peasant. "Well, brother," he'd say to him, "expound your views on life to me: after all, they say you have all the strength, the future of Russia is yours, the new epoch in history will begin with you—you'll give us real language and laws." The peasant would either say nothing at all or utter a few phrases such as, "Well, we're like . . . also, because, that is . . . it's how it is, about, the bounds." "Tell me what the peasant *mir*[3] is all about?" Bazarov would ask, interrupting him. "Is it the same *mir* that rests on three fishes?"

"It's the earth that rests on three fishes, sir," the peasant would explain reassuringly, in a patriarchal-magnanimous singsong voice, "but against ours, that is, the *mir*, as everyone knows, it's the landowner's will; because you're our fathers. And the stricter the master, the better for the peasant."

On one occasion, after listening to this kind of thing, Bazarov shrugged his shoulders contemptuously and turned away, while the peasant returned to his house.

"What was he wanting?" asked another peasant, middle-aged and sullen, from a distance, standing on the threshold of his hut, who'd overheard the conversation with Bazarov. "Was it the arrears, or what?"

"Not the arrears, my friend!" the first peasant replied, and his voice no longer had any trace of that patriarchal singsong quality; on the contrary, it contained a note of offhand severity. "He was just blabbing, felt like wagging his tongue. He's a gentleman, you know; you think he understands anything?"

"How could he?" replied the other peasant. Shoving back their caps

2. The spread of nineteenth-century "popular culture" among the people threatened to replace authentic folk culture.
3. The Russian village commune—see above, p. 42, n. 5; the word also means "world" and thus gives rise to the confusion Bazarov exploits. The peasant assures him that it's the world, not the commune, that rests on three fishes (as Russian folk tradition had it).

and tugging their belts, they both began talking about their own needs
and wants. Alas! Bazarov, who'd shrugged his shoulders contemptuously,
who thought he knew how to talk to peasants (so he'd boasted in that
argument with Pavel Petrovich), that same self-confident Bazarov didn't
even suspect that in their eyes he was still something of a laughing-
stock . . .

However, he finally found something to do. Once in his presence
Vasily Ivanovich was bandaging a peasant's wounded leg, but the old
man's hands were trembling and he was unable to deal with the strips
of cloth; his son helped him and from that time on began assisting him
in his practice, even though he never stopped making fun of the treat-
ments he advocated and of his father, who'd immediately administer
them. But Bazarov's ridicule didn't upset Vasily Ivanovich in the least;
it even comforted him. Holding his greasy dressing gown across his
stomach with two fingers and smoking his pipe, he listened to Bazarov
with pleasure; the more malicious his son's quips, the more good-
naturedly did he laugh, displaying every last one of his blackened teeth.
He even quoted these sometimes stupid or meaningless remarks; for
example, in the course of several days, for no good reason, he'd keep
repeating, "Well, that's the last straw!" merely because his son, after
hearing that he was going off to a morning liturgy, had used that expression. "Thank heavens! He's no longer so depressed!" he whispered to
his spouse. "You should've seen how he abused me today!" On the
other hand, the fact that he had such an assistant made him ecstatic
and filled him with pride. "Yes, yes," he'd say to some peasant woman
in a man's coat and horn-shaped headdress,[4] as he handed her a bottle
of Goulard's extract[5] or a jar of white ointment, "my dear, you should
thank God every minute of the day that my son's visiting us: now you're
being treated with the most scientific, most up-to-date methods, do you
understand that? Even Napoleon, emperor of the French, doesn't have
a better doctor." But the peasant woman, who'd come to complain that
she felt "hoisted by the gripes" (the meaning of which words, however,
even she was unable to explain), merely bowed and reached into her
bosom, where she'd stashed four eggs wrapped in the end of a towel.[6]

Bazarov once even pulled a tooth for a passing peddler selling cloth;
even though the tooth was really quite ordinary, Vasily Ivanovich pre-
served it as a rare specimen. Showing it to Father Aleksei, he constantly
repeated, "Just look at those roots! What strength that Evgeny has! The
peddler almost jumped up straight in the air . . . I think if it's been an
oak tree instead of a tooth, he'd have pulled that out, too!"

"Most praiseworthy!" said Father Aleksei at last, not knowing what
to reply or how to escape the rapturous old man.

---

4. The *kichka* was the headdress worn by married peasant women.
5. A remedy (*Aqua vegetomineralis Goulardi*) named for the French physician Thomas Goulard
   (1720–90), who invented it.
6. I.e., as a payment for the doctor's services.

On one occasion a peasant from the neighboring village brought his brother, who was sick with typhus, to see Vasily Ivanovich. Lying face-down on a straw litter, the unfortunate man was dying; dark spots already covered his body and he'd long since lost consciousness. Vasily Ivanovich expressed his regret that no one had thought of seeking medical assistance sooner and declared that there was no hope of saving him. In fact the peasant was unable even to get his brother back home: he died in the cart along the way.

Some three days later Bazarov entered his father's room and asked if he had any strong caustic.

"I do; what for?"

"I have to . . . cauterize a cut."

"Whose?"

"Mine."

"What do you mean, yours? How so? What cut? Where?"

"Right here on my finger. Today I went to the village—you know, the one from which they brought that man with typhus. For some reason they wanted to have an autopsy performed, and I hadn't done one in a long time."

"Well?"

"Well, I asked the local doctor if I could; and, well, I cut myself."

Vasily Ivanovich suddenly turned completely pale; without saying a word, he rushed to the cupboard and returned at once with a piece of strong caustic in his hands. Bazarov wanted to take it and leave.

"For God's sake," said Vasily Ivanovich, "let me do that myself."

Bazarov grinned.

"Never miss a chance to practice your trade!"

"Please don't joke. Show me your finger. The cut's not too big. Is this painful?"

"Press harder; don't be afraid."

Vasily Ivanovich finished.

"What do you think, Evgeny, wouldn't it be better to burn it with a hot iron?"

"That should've been done sooner; now, as a matter of fact, even the caustic's of no use. If I'm infected, it's already too late."

"What do you mean . . . too late?" Vasily Ivanovich could hardly utter the words.

"I'll say it is! It's already more than four hours since it happened."

Vasily Ivanovich cauterized the cut a little longer.

"Didn't the local doctor have any caustic?"

"No."

"My God, how can that be? A doctor—and he doesn't have such an essential thing!"

"You should've seen his lancets," said Bazarov and left the room.

Throughout that evening and during the course of the whole next day, Vasily Ivanovich resorted to any possible pretext for entering his son's room; although he never mentioned the wound and even tried talking about peripheral matters, he still stared so intently into his son's eyes and scrutinized him so anxiously that Bazarov lost all patience and threatened to leave. Vasily Ivanovich gave him his word not to disturb him, all the more so since Arina Vlasevna, from whom he'd naturally concealed everything, had begun to pester him, wanting to know why he couldn't sleep and what was wrong with him. He held out for a few days, although his son's appearance, which he continued to monitor on the sly, wasn't much to his liking . . . but on the third day at dinner he couldn't endure it. Bazarov sat there looking down at his plate, not touching any of his food.

"Why aren't you eating, Evgeny?" he asked, his face assuming a most casual expression. "The food's well prepared, isn't it?"

"I don't feel like it, so I'm not eating."

"Don't you have any appetite? What about your head?" he added in a timid voice. "Does it ache?"

"Yes. Why shouldn't it ache?"

Arina Vlasevna sat up straight and pricked up her ears.

"Please don't be angry, Evgeny," continued Vasily Ivanovich, "won't you let me check your pulse?"

Bazarov stood up.

"Without even checking my pulse, I can tell you I have a fever."

"And shivers?"

"And shivers. I'm going to lie down; you send me some lime flower tea. I must've caught a cold."

"That's why I heard you coughing last night," said Arina Vlasevna.

"I caught a cold," repeated Bazarov and moved away.

Arina Vlasevna set about preparing the tea from lime flowers, while Vasily Ivanovich went into the next room and tore his hair in silence.

Bazarov didn't get up at all that day and spent the whole night in a heavy, semiconscious torpor. Around one o'clock in the morning, he made an effort to open his eyes and saw before him in the lamplight his father's pale face and ordered him to go away; he obeyed, but immediately crept back in on tiptoe and, half-hidden by the cupboard doors, stared relentlessly at his son. Arina Vlasevna didn't go to bed either; leaving the door to the study slightly open, she kept going in to see "how Enyusha was breathing" and to have a look at Vasily Ivanovich. All she could see was his motionless, hunched-over back, but even that afforded her some relief. In the morning Bazarov tried to get up; his head started spinning and his nose began bleeding; he lay down again. Vasily Ivanovich attended him in silence; Arina Vlasevna came in to ask him how he was feeling. He replied, "Better," and turned toward the wall. Vasily Ivanovich motioned his wife away with both hands; she bit her lip to keep from crying and left the room. Everything in the house suddenly seemed to grow darker; everyone's face fell and a strange silence prevailed; a boisterous rooster was carried away from the yard to the village, unable to understand for the longest time why he was so mistreated. Bazarov continued lying there, facing the wall. Vasily Ivanovich put several questions to him, but these queries exhausted Bazarov, and the old man fell silent in his armchair, only occasionally cracking his knuckles. He went out into the garden for a few moments, stood there like a statue as if overwhelmed by some inexplicable consternation (a look of consternation never left his face the whole time), and returned to his son once again, trying to avoid his wife's inquiries. At last she grabbed him by the hand and feverishly, almost threateningly, demanded, "What's wrong with him?" Then he came to his senses and forced himself to smile at her in reply; but, to his own horror, instead of a smile, he emitted a strange laugh. That morning he sent for a doctor. He thought it necessary to inform his son so he wouldn't get angry.

Bazarov suddenly turned around on the sofa, stared at his father slowly and intently, and asked for something to drink.

Vasily Ivanovich gave him some water and managed to feel his forehead. It was burning with fever.

"Old man," began Bazarov in a hoarse and deliberate voice, "things don't look very good. I'm infected and in a few days you'll be burying me."

"Evgeny!" he whispered, "what're you saying? Good Lord! You've caught a cold . . ."

"Enough of that!" Evgeny said, interrupting him without hurrying. "A doctor isn't allowed to talk like that. You know I've got all the symptoms of infection."

"What symptoms . . . of infection, Evgeny? . . . Mercy!"

"Then what's this?" Bazarov said, and raising the sleeve of his shirt, he showed his father the ominous red blotches appearing on his arm.

Vasily Ivanovich shuddered and froze with fear.

"Let's assume," he said at last, "let's assume . . . if . . . even if it's some kind of . . . infection . . ."

"*Pyaemia,*"[7] his son prompted him.

"Well, yes . . . something like . . . an epidemic . . ."

"*Pyaemia,*" Bazarov repeated sternly and distinctly. "Or have you already forgotten your textbooks?"

"Well, yes, yes, whatever you say . . . Still, we're going to cure you!"

"Not on your life! But that's not the point. I never expected to die so soon; to tell you the truth, it's a most unpleasant circumstance. You and Mother must now make the most of your strong faith; here's a chance to put it to the test." He drank down a little more water. "I want to ask you one thing . . . while my head's still working. You know

7. An infection caused by the presence of pus-producing microorganisms in the bloodstream.

tomorrow or the day after my brain will tender its resignation. Even now I'm not too sure I'm expressing myself clearly. When I was lying there before, I seemed to see red dogs running all around me and you pointing at me as if I were a woodcock. Just like I was drunk. Can you understand me well?"

"Good heavens, Evgeny, you're speaking just as you should."

"All the better; you told me you sent for a doctor . . . You did that to comfort yourself . . . now comfort me: send someone to fetch . . ."

"Arkady Nikolaevich?" the old man interrupted.

"Who's Arkady Nikolaevich?" asked Bazarov, as if lost in thought. "Oh, yes! That fledgling! No, don't bother him; he's become a jackdaw. Don't be surprised, it's not delirium just yet. Send someone to fetch Odintsova, Anna Sergeevna; she's a landowner who lives nearby . . . Do you know her? [Vasily Ivanovich nodded his head.] Tell her that Evgeny Bazarov sends his greetings and wants her to know he's dying. Will you do that?"

"Yes, I will . . . But is it really possible you're going to die, Evgeny? . . . Judge for yourself! Where will justice be found afterward?"

"I don't know; but send someone to fetch her."

"I will right away, and I'll write to her myself."

"No, why? Tell her I send greetings, nothing else's needed. Now I'm going to return to my dogs. It's odd! I want to focus on death, but nothing comes of it. I see some sort of spot . . . and nothing else."

He turned back clumsily to the wall; Vasily Ivanovich left the study and when he reached his wife's bedroom, threw himself down on his knees in front of the icons.

"Pray, Arina, pray!" he moaned. "Our son's dying."

The doctor, the same country doctor who lacked the caustic, arrived and after examining the patient, advised them to continue waiting it out and then added a few words about the possibility of recovery.

"Have you ever seen people in my condition *not* set off for the Elysian fields?"[8] asked Bazarov; suddenly grabbing the leg of a heavy table that stood next to the sofa, he shook it and pushed it away. "Strength," he said, "what strength I still possess, yet I have to die! . . . At least an old man has time to get used to the idea of leaving life behind. It renounces you, and that's all there is to it! Who's weeping over there?" he added, after a little while. "Mother? Poor dear! Who'll she feed her wonderful borsch to now? And you, Vasily Ivanovich, are you sniveling, too? Well, if Christianity doesn't help you, be a philosopher, a stoic, or something! You boasted you were a philosopher, didn't you?"

"What kind of philosopher am I?" wailed Vasily Ivanovich, tears streaming down his cheeks.

Bazarov grew worse with every passing hour; his illness took a rapid

---

8. In Greek mythology, the happy otherworld for heroes favored by the gods.

course, as is usually the case with surgical poisonings. He hadn't yet lost his memory and could still understand what people were saying to him; he was still fighting. "I don't want to become delirious," he whispered, clenching his fists, "what nonsense that is!" Then he'd say, "Well, eight take away ten, what's left?" Vasily Ivanovich went around like a man possessed, suggesting first one remedy then another; the only thing he actually did was cover his son's legs. "Wrap him up in cold sheets . . . give him an emetic . . . mustard plasters on the stomach . . . bleeding," he kept saying anxiously. The doctor, whom he implored to stay, would nod his head in agreement, give the patient lemonade to drink, and asked first for a pipe for himself, then for something "fortifying and warming," that is, vodka. Arina Vlasevna sat on a small low stool near the door and from time to time went out to say a prayer; a few days ago a small mirror from her dressing table slipped out of her hands and broke, something she'd always considered a bad omen. Even Anfisushka couldn't say anything to her. Timofeich had set off to fetch Odintsova.

The night wasn't a very good one for Bazarov . . . He was cruelly tormented by fever. Toward morning he felt a bit better. He asked Arina Vlasevna to comb his hair, kissed her hand, and drank a few mouthfuls of tea. Vasily Ivanovich cheered up a little.

"Thank God!" he declared. "The crisis has come . . . the crisis has gone."

"Just imagine!" muttered Bazarov. "What a word can mean! He finds one and says it, 'crisis,' and now he feels relieved. It's an astonishing thing how a man can still believe in words. For instance, if you call him a fool, but don't give him a beating, he gets depressed; if you call him a clever fellow, but don't give him any money, he feels terrific."

This short speech of Bazarov, reminiscent of his previous "sallies," evoked great tenderness in Vasily Ivanovich.

"Bravo! Well said, very well said!" he exclaimed, pretending to applaud.

Bazarov smiled wanly.

"So then, what do you think?" he asked. "Has the crisis come or gone?"

"You're better, that's what I see, that makes me happy," replied Vasily Ivanovich.

"Well, splendid; it's always good to be happy. Did you remember to send someone for her?"

"Of course I did."

This change for the better didn't last long. The illness resumed its attacks. Vasily Ivanovich sat next to Bazarov. Some kind of unusual anguish seemed to be tormenting the old man. Several times he was about to say something—but couldn't.

"Evgeny!" he said at last. "My son, my dear, kind son!"

This special form of address had an impact on Bazarov . . . He turned his head a little; obviously trying to free himself from the burden of oppressive oblivion, he uttered, "What is it, Father?"

"Evgeny," continued Vasily Ivanovich, going down on his knees in front of Bazarov, even though his son hadn't opened his eyes and couldn't see him. "Evgeny, you're better now; God willing, you'll recover; but make use of this time, console your mother and me, do your duty as a Christian! It's terrible for me to have to say this to you; but it's even more terrible to . . . it's forever, Evgeny . . . just think what that would be like . . ."

The old man's voice broke off; but on his son's face, even though he continued lying there with his eyes closed, he could see a strange look.

"I won't refuse, if it would provide you some consolation," he said at last. "But I think there's no need to hurry. You yourself say I'm better."

"Better, Evgeny, better; but who knows, it's all in God's hands, while doing your duty . . ."

"No, I want to wait a bit," Bazarov said, interrupting him. "I agree that the crisis has come. And if we're wrong, so what? They administer the sacrament to people who've lost consciousness, don't they?"

"Evgeny, for heaven's sake . . ."

"I'll wait. Now I want to sleep. Don't bother me."

He turned his head back to its previous position.

The old man got up and then sat down in the armchair; grabbing hold of his chin, he began gnawing on his own fingers . . .

The sound of carriage springs, particularly noticeable in the depths of the countryside, suddenly reached his ears. The light wheels came closer and closer; now he could even hear horses snorting . . . Vasily Ivanovich jumped up and rushed to the small window. A twin-seated carriage drawn by four horses was entering the courtyard of his little house. Without even stopping to consider what all this might mean, in a burst of nonsensical joy, he ran out onto the steps . . . A footman in livery opened the carriage door; a lady wearing a black veil and black mantilla was emerging . . .

"I'm Odintsova," she said. "Is Evgeny Vasilevich still alive? Are you his father? I've brought a doctor with me."

"Benefactress!" cried Vasily Ivanovich; grabbing her hand, he pressed it feverishly to his lips, while the doctor who accompanied Anna Sergeevna, a small man with a German face, wearing glasses, climbed out of the carriage in a deliberate manner. "He's still alive, my Evgeny's still alive, and now he'll be saved! Wife! Wife! . . . An angel's been sent to us from heaven . . ."

"Good Lord, what is it?" muttered the old woman as she came running from the living room. Without understanding anything, right there in the hall, she threw herself at Anna Sergeevna's feet and began kissing her dress like a madwoman.

"What's this? What're you doing?" Anna Sergeevna objected; but Arina Vlasevna didn't hear her, and Vasily Ivanovich merely repeated: "Angel! Angel!"

"*Wo ist der Kranke?* Where is the patient?" the doctor said at last, not without a certain indignation.

Vasily Ivanovich came to his senses. "Here, here, please come with me, *werthester Gerr Kollega,*"[9] he added, recalling a phrase from memory.

"Eh!" replied the doctor, smiling sourly.

Vasily Ivanovich led him into the study.

"It's a doctor from Anna Sergeevna Odintsova," he said, bending over to his son's ear. "And she's come as well."

Bazarov suddenly opened his eyes. "What did you say?"

"I said Anna Sergeevna Odintsova's here and has brought a gentleman with her, a doctor."

Bazarov looked around the room.

"She's here . . . I want to see her."

"You'll see her, Evgeny; but first we must have a little chat with the doctor. I'll tell him the history of your illness since Sidor Sidorych has gone [that was the name of the local doctor], and we'll have a short consultation."

Bazarov looked at the German. "Well, confer quickly, but not in Latin; after all, I know the meaning of '*jam moritur.*' "[1]

"*Der Herr scheint des Deutschen mächtig zu sein,*"[2] began this latest follower of Aesculapius,[3] addressing Vasily Ivanovich.

"*Ikh . . . gabe . . .*[4] We'd better speak Russian," said the old man.

"*Ach,* so! Zat iss how it iss . . . Pleeze . . ."

And the consultation began.

Half an hour later Anna Sergeevna entered the study accompanied by Vasily Ivanovich. The doctor managed to whisper to her that there was no point in even thinking about the patient's recovery.

She glanced at Bazarov . . . and stopped at the door, so astounded was she by the sight of the inflamed and at the same time deathly countenance, its dim eyes directed at her. She was simply seized by a cold, enervating terror; the thought that she wouldn't have felt like that if she'd really loved him momentarily flashed through her mind.

"Thank you," he said with effort, "I didn't expect this. It's a good deed. So, we meet again, as you promised."

"Anna Sergeevna was so kind . . ." Vasily Ivanovich began.

"Leave us, Father. You'll allow it, Anna Sergeevna, won't you? It seems that now . . ."

---

9. *Würdigster Herr Kollege:* "most worthy colleague" (German).
1. "He's already dying" (Latin).
2. "Apparently the gentleman has a good command of German" (German).
3. Legendary Greek physician and god of medicine.
4. *Ich habe:* "I have" (German).

With a nod of his head, he indicated his outstretched, enfeebled body. Vasily Ivanovich left the room.

"Well, thank you," Bazarov repeated. "It's a regal gesture. They say that tsars also visit the dying."

"Evgeny Vasilich, I hope that . . ."

"Hey, Anna Sergeevna, let's speak the truth. It's all over for me. I've fallen beneath the wheel. It now seems there was no reason at all to think about the future. Death's an old story, but new for each person. Up to this point I haven't been afraid . . . unconsciousness will come and then, that's that! [He waved his hand weakly.] Well, what do I have to tell you? . . . I did love you! It didn't mean anything then and it means even less now. Love's just a form, and my own form's going to pieces already. I'd rather say how lovely you are! And now you stand here looking so beautiful . . ."

Anna Sergeevna gave an involuntary shudder.

"Never mind, don't be alarmed . . . sit down . . . Don't come near me: my illness is contagious."

Anna Sergeevna crossed the room quickly and sat down on an armchair next to the sofa where Bazarov was lying.

"Oh, magnanimous one!" he whispered. "Oh, how near, how young, fresh, pure . . . in this nasty room! . . . Well, farewell! Live a long life, that's best of all, enjoy it while there's still time. You see what an ugly spectacle I am: a worm half-crushed, but still writhing. I used to think: I'll do so much, I won't die, not me! There're tasks to perform, and, after all, I'm a giant! Now the giant's only task is to die in a decent manner, even though no one really cares about that either . . . All the same, I'm not going to start wagging my tail."

Bazarov fell silent and began reaching for his glass. Anna Sergeevna gave him a drink without removing her glove, drawing her breath apprehensively.

"You'll forget me," he began again. "The dead make no companions for the living. My father'll tell you what a great man Russia's losing . . . That's nonsense, but don't try to argue with the old man. Don't deny the child anything that comforts him . . . you know what I mean. And be kind to my mother. After all, you won't find people like them anywhere in the world, even if you search by daylight with a candle . . . I'm needed by Russia . . . No, obviously I'm not needed. Who is needed? The shoemaker's needed, the tailor's needed, the butcher . . . sells meat . . . the butcher . . . wait a minute, I'm getting all confused . . . There's a forest here . . ."

Bazarov put his hand on his forehead.

Anna Sergeevna bent over to him.

"Evgeny Vasilich, I'm here . . ."

He took her hand at once and lifted himself up.

"Farewell," he said with unexpected strength, his eyes gleaming with their last light. "Farewell . . . Listen . . . you know, I didn't kiss you then . . . Blow on the dying lamp and let it go out . . ."

She pressed her lips to his forehead.

"That's enough!" he said, sinking back into his pillow. "Now . . . darkness . . ."

Anna Sergeevna left quietly.

"Well?" asked Vasily Ivanovich in a whisper.

"He's asleep," she replied, barely audible.

Bazarov wasn't fated to awaken again. Toward evening he sank into complete unconsciousness and died the next day. Father Aleksei performed religious rites over him. When they were administering extreme unction, just as the holy oil touched his breast, one of his eyes opened and, at the sight of the priest in his vestments, the smoking censer, the candle in front of the icon, something resembling a shudder of horror seemed to pass momentarily across his deathly countenance. When he finally drew his last breath and the sound of universal lamentation filled the house, Vasily Ivanovich was overcome with sudden frenzy. "I said I'd rebel," he cried hoarsely, his face inflamed and contorted, brandishing his fist in the air as if threatening someone, "and I do rebel, I do!" But Arina Vlasevna, all in tears, put her arms around his neck and they both dropped to their knees. "That's how it was," Anfisushka used to relate afterward in the servants' quarters, "side by side, their little heads drooping, just like lambs at midday . . ."

But the heat of midday passes, evening comes, then night, and the return to a quiet refuge where sweet sleep awaits all who are tired and tormented . . .

XXVIII

Six months passed. White winter had arrived with its cruel stillness of cloudless frosts, thick, squeaky snow, pink hoarfrost on trees, pale emerald green sky, caps of smoke above chimneys, clouds of steam from doors opened hurriedly, people's fresh faces nipped by the cold, and the brisk trot of shivering horses. The January day was already nearing its end; evening cold was tightening its grip on the motionless air, and the bloodred sunset was quickly fading. Lights burned in the windows of the house at Marino; Prokofich, in a black frockcoat and white gloves, was setting the table for seven with special solemnity. A week before in the small parish church, two weddings had taken place, quietly and almost without witnesses: Arkady to Katya and Nikolai to Fenechka; on this very day, Nikolai Petrovich was giving a farewell dinner for his brother, who was leaving to go to Moscow on business. Anna Sergeevna had also repaired there right after the wedding, having gifted the young couple handsomely.

At precisely three o'clock everyone gathered at the table. Mitya was seated there as well; he'd already been provided with a nanny who wore a brocade peasant headdress. Pavel Petrovich took his place between Katya and Fenechka; the "husbands" were seated next to their wives. Our friends had changed of late; they all seemed to have grown stronger and better looking. Only Pavel Petrovich was thinner, which, however, lent his expressive features even more elegance and made him look even more like a *grand seigneur* . . . Fenechka had also changed. In a new silk dress, with a broad velvet band in her hair, a gold chain around her neck, she sat in respectful stillness, respectful of herself and her surroundings, and smiling as if she wanted to say, "You must forgive me, I'm not to blame." And she wasn't the only one—all the others were also smiling and seemed to be asking forgiveness; everyone was feeling a little awkward, a little melancholy, and, in reality, very happy. Each one attended to the other's needs with amusing solicitude, as if everyone had agreed to play a role in some good-natured comedy. Katya was the calmest of all: she looked around confidently; it was apparent that Nikolai Petrovich had already managed to fall dotingly in love with her. Before the end of dinner, he stood up; glass in hand, he turned to Pavel Petrovich.

"You're leaving us . . . dear brother, you're leaving us," he began. "Of course, not for long; but I can't help expressing what I . . . what we . . . how much I . . . how much we . . . The trouble is, I really don't know how to make speeches! Arkady, you say something."

"No, Papa, I haven't prepared anything."

"As if I've made extensive preparations! Brother, let me simply embrace you and wish you all the best; come back to us as soon as you can!"

Pavel Petrovich exchanged kisses with everyone, including even little Mitya, of course; what's more, in Fenechka's case, he kissed her hand, which she didn't know how to offer properly; drinking a second glass, he said with a deep sigh, "Be happy, my friends! Farewell!" This last word uttered in English went almost unnoticed, but everyone was touched.

"To the memory of Bazarov," Katya whispered into her husband's ear, clinking glasses with him. Arkady squeezed her hand firmly in reply, but decided not to propose that toast aloud.

That would seem to be the end. But perhaps some of our readers would like to know what each of our characters is doing now, at this very moment.[5] We're prepared to satisfy their curiosity.

Odintsova recently married, not for love, but out of conviction, one of Russia's future statesmen, a very clever man, a lawyer, with good practical sense, a strong will, and a remarkable talent with words—still young, kind, and cold as ice. They live together in great harmony, and

5. I.e., *after* the emancipation of the serfs, which occurred in February 1861.

perhaps will live long enough to find happiness . . . perhaps even love. Princess Kh. passed away, forgotten the day she died. The Kirsanovs, father and son, have settled at Marino. Their affairs have begun to improve. Arkady has become a zealous proprietor and the "farm" is already bringing in a fairly substantial income. Nikolai Petrovich has become an arbitrator[6] and works at it with all his might; he's constantly traveling throughout the district; he delivers long speeches (being of the opinion that peasants must be "made to understand," that is, driven to exhaustion by frequent repetition of one and the same thing); but, to tell the truth, he fails to satisfy fully either the educated nobles who talk with *chic* or melancholy about the *mancipation* (pronouncing the French nasal *an*) or the uneducated nobles, who swear unceremoniously at that "damned *muncipation.*" He's seen as far too generous by both sides. Katerina Sergeevna gave birth to a son, Kolya, while Mitya's already running around and talking spiritedly. After her husband and child, Fenechka, Fedosya Nikolaevna, adores no one as much as her daughter-in-law, and whenever Katya sits down at the piano, she's happy to spend the whole day there with her. We must also say a word or two about Peter. He's become perfectly numb from stupidity and self-importance and now pronounces every "e" as "u"—but he also married and received a considerable dowry with his bride, the daughter of the town vegetable-gardener, who turned down offers from two fine suitors because neither of them owned a watch, whereas Peter owned not only a watch but also a pair of patent leather boots.

In Dresden, on the Brühl Terrace, between two and four in the afternoon, the most fashionable time for strolling, you can meet a man aged about fifty, already quite gray, seeming to suffer from gout, but still handsome, elegantly dressed, with the special air conferred only on those who've spent considerable time mixing with high society. This is Pavel Petrovich. He left Moscow to go abroad to improve his health and took up residence in Dresden, where he associates mostly with the English and with visiting Russians. With the English he behaves simply, almost modestly, but not without dignity; they find him a bit of a bore, but respect him for being "a perfect gentleman," as they say. With Russians he's more casual, gives vent to his spleen, makes fun of himself and them; but this is all accomplished in a very nice, easy, decent manner. He holds Slavophile views: it's well known that in high society this is considered *très distingué.*[7] He doesn't read anything in Russian, but keeps a silver ashtray in the shape of a peasant's bast sandal[8] on his writing desk. He's much sought after by our tourists. Matvei Ilich Kolyazin, finding himself a member of the "temporary opposition,"[9] gra-

---

6. After the emancipation, an official appointed to serve as mediator between landowners and peasants.
7. "Very distinguished" (French).
8. Shoes or sandals woven from bast (tree) fibers were worn by peasants.
9. A group of reactionaries opposed to the reforms carried out by Alexander II.

ciously paid him a visit on his way to take the waters in Bohemia; meanwhile, the locals, with whom he has very little to do, practically grovel before him. No one can obtain a ticket to the court chapel, the theater, etc., as quickly and easily as *der Herr Baron von Kirsanoff*. He still does as much good as he can and continues to make something of an impression: it's not for nothing he was once a social lion. But life's become a burden for him . . . more than he suspects . . . One need only catch a glimpse of him in the Russian church, where, leaning against the wall on one side, he sinks deep into thought and remains motionless for some time, his teeth clenched in bitterness, then suddenly comes to his senses and begins crossing himself almost imperceptibly . . .

Kukshina also wound up living abroad. She's now in Heidelberg, studying not natural science, but architecture, where, in her own words, she's discovered some new laws. As before she still hobnobs with students, especially young Russians studying physics and chemistry, with whom Heidelberg's filled to the brim, and who, astonishing their naive German professors at first with their sober view of things, subsequently astonish those same professors with their total inactivity and absolute idleness. With two or three chemistry students who can't distinguish oxygen from nitrogen, but who're filled with self-importance and a penchant for negation, and with the great Elisevich,[1] too, Sitnikov, who's also preparing himself for greatness, wanders around Petersburg and, according to his own assurances, is carrying on Bazarov's "work." They say he was given a beating not too long ago, but wasn't kept down for long: in an obscure little article, hidden in an obscure little journal, he implied that the fellow who beat him was a coward. He calls this irony. His father orders him about as before, and his wife considers him a perfect fool . . . and a man of letters.

There's a little village graveyard in one remote corner of Russia. Like almost all our graveyards, it's a sorry sight: ditches surrounding it have long since been overgrown; gray wooden crosses have fallen over and lie rotting beneath their once-painted little roofs; headstones have been displaced as if someone had pushed them aside from below; two or three pitiful trees barely provide any shade; some sheep graze unchecked around the graves . . . Among them there's one grave untouched by people, untrampled by animals: only birds perch on it and sing in the heat. An iron railing surrounds it; two young pine trees have been planted there, one on each side: Evgeny Bazarov lies buried in this grave. Two feeble old people come frequently from the nearby village to visit it— a man and his wife. They walk with a heavy step, supporting each other; when they approach the railing, they fall on their knees and remain there for a long time, weeping bitterly, gazing attentively at the headstone

1. See above, p. 52, n. 6.

under which their son lies buried: they exchange a few words, brush the dust off the stone, move a branch of the pine tree, and pray once again; they can't forsake this place where they seem to feel closer to their son, to their memories of him . . . Can it really be that their prayers and tears are futile? Can it really be that love, sacred, devoted love is not all-powerful? Oh, no! However passionate, sinful, rebellious the heart buried in this grave, the flowers growing on it look out at us serenely with their innocent eyes: they tell us not only of that eternal peace, that great peace of "indifferent" nature; they tell us also of eternal reconciliation and life everlasting . . .